DARK AWAKENING

ECHOES OF DESTINY

THE CHILDREN OF THE GODS
BOOK EIGHTY-EIGHT

I. T. LUCAS

Dark Awakening: Echoes of Destiny **is a work of fiction**! Names, characters, places, and incidents are products of the author's imagination or are used fictitiously and are not to be construed as real. Any similarity to actual persons, organizations, and/or events is purely coincidental.

Published by Evening Star Press, LLC.

EveningStarPress.com

ISBN: 978-1-962067-56-0

CONTENTS

1

THE SABOTEUR

The whiz of the automatic shutters going up jarred the saboteur awake, and as she looked out the window, she cursed under her breath.

The sky was brightening, the first hints of dawn creeping over the horizon, and the village would be stirring soon.

If she were wise, she would abandon her mission and postpone it to the following night, but she was more driven than wise, and patience was not coded into her genetics. If she didn't complete the task when she'd set out to do so, she would be jittery and irritated until it was done, and that would draw unwanted attention, which could blow her cover.

Besides, even if she did get caught, she could handle whoever witnessed her transgression by forcing them to keep quiet.

Well, it depended on who caught her. Some were more difficult to influence than others.

It would be better to make sure that she didn't get caught.

Slipping out of the house through the sliding door in her bedroom, she swung her backpack over her shoulders and walked out of the backyard through the flimsy gate. Then, she was ducking inside the carefully manicured shrubbery to avoid the cameras posted along the walkways and finding the narrow paths between plants.

She'd mapped out the locations of all the hidden cameras scattered throughout the village and knew them by heart. Each step was calculated, avoiding the cameras' lines of sight and any branches that might snap underfoot. The dew-dampened grass muffled her footsteps, a small mercy in the quiet of early morning.

Her target was a trash incinerator. In the past, they had simply been located in block enclosures between the houses, making them easy targets, but that had recently changed. Now they presented a bigger challenge thanks to William's crew installing surveillance cameras inside the enclosures.

Not that the damn cameras were a serious deterrent for her.

A smirk played on the saboteur's lips as she recalled the hours spent scouring the internet for ways to fool the cameras. She had tested the method she'd learned from a video, and it worked without a hitch.

Perhaps once she'd gotten free of this bastion of virtue-signaling immortals, she would use the method for something more impactful than damaging trash incinerators and electrical automatic blackout shutters.

After all, she would have to find ways to support herself and her band of followers.

Provided that she had followers.

Hopefully, once they learned of her abilities, they would realize how valuable she was to their plans and make her their leader. She could force them, but she didn't want to use her talent on her own people. She wanted them to follow her because they valued her and not because she gave them no choice.

As she made her way to the incinerator she'd marked as her target the day before, the cool morning air nipped at her skin, and the fact that it had even registered was a testament to how spoiled she'd become. Compared to the winters of her childhood, this place was paradise, but the good weather and comfortable living came with a cost that she and some of the others were not willing to pay.

Ducking behind the east wall of the enclosure, the saboteur pulled out a small mirror from her pocket. A mix of excitement and fear coursing through her veins, she cleaned the surface, making sure there were no blemishes on the smooth surface, and angled it carefully so it reflected the camera's view at itself, creating a loop of empty space.

It wasn't perfect, but she only needed it to work for a few seconds. No one would notice anything now, but once the sabotage was discovered, she had no doubt that the Guardians would go over every moment of the camera feed.

The trick had taken hours of practice to perfect, each failure only fueling her determination to succeed.

With swift, practiced movements, she accessed the incinerator's control panel. Her fingers worked quickly, severing some wires and crossing others. The satisfying spark of destruction brought a fleeting sense of accomplishment. For a moment, she allowed herself to admire her handiwork, imagining the chaos it would cause later in the day.

It was a small act of rebellion, but it sent a clear message that not everything in this perfectly constructed world was under their control.

Just as the saboteur was about to slip away, the sound of a door opening nearby froze her in place. She was crouching, half hidden by the bushes, but her hiding place was far from ideal, and she had to stay perfectly still, or the two immortal females who were stepping out the door would hear her.

They were dressed in gym clothes, and she prayed to the Mother of All Life that they intended to jog in the opposite direction. If they were headed to the gym, she was in deep shit. They would walk right by her, and there was a good chance they would see her.

The manicured greenery did not offer enough cover.

Why did the Kra-ell crew assigned to landscaping duty have to be so thorough? They had been sentenced to community service, not awarded a contract with a bonus for a job well done. There was no reason for them to put so much effort into their punishment.

True, those males were alive thanks to the clan's intervention, but then none of them would be here if the clan hadn't decided to 'liberate' them.

Pressed against the ground, she could feel the damp earth seeping through her clothes, and a twig dug painfully into her side, but she didn't dare move to adjust her position. The discomfort was nothing compared to the fear of discovery.

"What a beautiful morning for a run," one of the immortals said as she stretched her calves on the porch of her house.

"Absolutely perfect," said the other. "Though I'm surprised to see you up this early. You came home after two in the morning. Couldn't sleep?"

The saboteur held her breath, willing them to start their run and leave, but to her dismay, the women seemed in no hurry to begin their jog.

"Oh, you know how it is," the first woman said with a laugh. "I had a very energizing night with Hivak."

The other one laughed. "There is nothing like a shot of venom to get you going in the morning."

The saboteur grimaced. Was the Mother punishing her?

It was bad enough that the dampness from the ground was seeping into her bones, that her muscles were screaming in protest at the awkward position, and that an annoying itch had begun to form on her nose, which she had to use every ounce of willpower not to reach up and scratch, she also had to listen to the immortals talking about sex.

Ugh, just go on your run already!

As the two idiots kept blabbering, the sky grew lighter, and the saboteur's anxiety spiked. Soon, more villagers would wake up, making her escape even more difficult or impossible.

Despite the cool morning air, a bead of sweat trickled down her forehead. She could handle one or two witnesses, but not more than that, and if she were caught it would mean the end of everything she had worked for.

Just when she thought she couldn't bear it any longer, the women finally stopped gossiping and started jogging away from her.

The saboteur remained still for several more agonizing moments, ensuring they were far off and no one else was coming her way before allowing herself to move.

Releasing a shaky breath, she extracted herself from the bushes, wincing at the scratch of branches against her skin. Her clothes were damp and dirty, evidence of her close call that she wouldn't be able to hide if confronted.

She had to make it home without anyone seeing her.

As she slunk toward her house, using the same hidden paths between the greenery, the village was beginning to wake in earnest, the distant sound of voices carrying on the morning air. She quickened her pace, knowing that each passing second increased her risk of being seen.

As she reached the sliding door to her bedroom and pulled it open, the relief made her weak at the knees.

Safe in the privacy of her room, she allowed herself a small smile of satisfaction. Another blow had been struck, another message sent. And the immortals were still none the wiser.

It was exhilarating.

She peeled off her damp clothes, hiding them at the bottom of her laundry basket, and stepped into the shower. Letting the warm water wash away the evidence of her morning activities, she was already planning her next strike.

She had to be more careful, though, more precise.

The stakes were too high to allow for errors.

2

ELL-ROM

Ell-rom lay awake in bed, his eyes fixed on Jasmine's peaceful sleeping form and his body still humming with the afterglow of their love-making. The bedside lamp cast a warm light over her features, highlighting the gentle curve of her cheek, the sweep of her lashes against her skin, and her slightly parted lips. She looked so relaxed, so at ease in his arms.

It was the venom's effect, and he had done that for her, giving her this euphoric trip to another realm.

Ell-rom felt foolish for being so proud of himself for finally achieving something that any immortal male could do, let alone a half-god, half-Kra-ell male like him.

Not that there was any other like him or like his sister.

He and Morelle were each one of a kind. There were no other hybrids like them in the entire galaxy. They were the product of a forbidden relationship between the son of the king of the gods and the daughter of the Kra-ell queen.

It was an impressive pedigree, but it needed to remain hidden. If their grandfather ever discovered that he and Morelle had survived the crash, he would annihilate Earth just to get rid of them.

The thought wiped the satisfied smile off his face.

Did the Eternal King know about his death-ray mental ability?

Was that why he feared them so much?

The title Death Ray had been coined by Jasmine, and although it was apt, Ell-rom did not like it. He didn't want the ability to kill with a thought.

Was that cowardly on his part?

Probably.

Some people deserved to be eliminated, and he shouldn't let his former training as a priest make him soft.

Ell-rom chuckled softly. Why was he thinking about death rays and vermin that needed eliminating when he was holding the woman he loved more than life itself, having just shared with her the most profound connection of his life?

Jasmine had been his anchor from the moment he had awakened from stasis, confused and frightened, in a world he didn't understand, and she hadn't left his side ever since.

Closing his eyes, he let the memories wash over him.

He remembered the disorientation of those first few days, the struggle to make sense of a world that seemed alien and overwhelming. The fear that had gripped him when he'd realized that he didn't remember who he was or where he had come from.

But throughout this time of confusion, there had been Jasmine. Her gentle presence had been like a beacon in the darkness of his mental state. From the moment he first saw her face, peering down at him as he emerged from stasis, something in him had immediately recognized her as vital to his existence.

His lips curved into a soft smile as he recalled their first real conversation, the way Jasmine had patiently explained things to him. She had been his anchor in a sea of uncertainty, a constant source of comfort and strength as he fought to regain some semblance of self-identity while adjusting to life on Earth.

Things had been going so well when the dream about his deadly thought-projecting ability had rattled what little foundation he'd managed to set, but again, Jasmine had been there, offering support without judgment, helping him to see his power not as a curse but as a part of himself to be understood, controlled, and used for the greater good.

He recounted his victories—the progress he had made in his physical recovery, facing his aversion to blood, learning to shroud. Small as those victories might be, each was a milestone, a step towards reclaiming his autonomy and becoming the male he wanted to be for Jasmine, for Annani, and for Morelle.

He had a family now, a whole clan of blood relatives who seemed to welcome him and his twin sister with open arms.

As he thought of Morelle, Ell-rom's chest constricted. She was still in a coma, still struggling to break through the barrier of consciousness and emerge to join him at their final destination after the journey that had begun over seven thousand years ago.

Well, the keep was just one small step before they arrived at the hidden village where Annani and her clan lived.

Tracing patterns on Jasmine's bare shoulder, he contemplated the future that stretched before them. There were still so many unknowns, like the search for Khiann, Annani's long-lost love, the full extent of his own abilities, and the challenges of integrating into this new world.

Ell-rom was ready.

He felt stronger now and more optimistic about the future because he was loved, and he had just sealed his and Jasmine's connection with a venom bite.

The memory sent a shiver of pleasure through him.

He brushed a strand of hair from Jasmine's face, his touch feather-light to avoid waking her. The trust she had shown in him and her unwavering belief in his goodness, even when he doubted himself, humbled him.

His gaze drifted to the window, where the first hints of dawn were beginning to lighten the sky. He marveled at the sight, at the simple beauty of a new day beginning. Every sunrise was still a wonder to him, a reminder of the life he had been given a second chance to live.

3

KIAN

Kian stared at the ceiling, sleep eluding him despite the early hour. The numbers of the digital clock on his nightstand glowed in the dark, mocking him with their slow progression.

5:37 a.m.

He sighed, his mind too heavy with disturbing thoughts to go back to sleep.

The large assembly he had called for this evening loomed over him like a dark cloud. He dreaded what he needed to do, and he was angry at the saboteurs who had forced his hand.

Was this their intention all along? To sow discord in the village by stirring things up?

Unable to keep lying still, he quietly slipped out of bed, careful not to disturb Syssi. He padded to the bathroom, the cool tiles a welcome contrast to the warmth of the bed he'd left behind. As he splashed water on his face, he caught his reflection in the mirror and did not like what he saw.

No wonder people thought he was intimidating. He looked like a killer for hire when he was angry.

When he returned to the bedroom, he found Syssi awake.

She looked at him with concern and a hint of accusation. "Why are you up already?"

A long time ago, he had promised her never to get up before her because she hated to wake up alone, and unless there was an emergency, Kian did his best to make good on his promise.

He ran a hand through his hair. "I woke up and couldn't fall back asleep."

Syssi sat up, the blanket pooling around her waist. "Intruding thoughts?"

He sank onto the edge of the bed, the mattress dipping under his weight. "This evening, I need to inform the adult residents of the village that they're all going to be interrogated, and so will the teenagers. Children ten years old and up will be questioned too, using the same compulsion as the adults to ensure that we get truthful answers." He shook his head. "I feel like a banana republic dictator."

Syssi took his hand. "You are not a dictator, and the village is not a banana republic. Let's talk over cappuccinos." She threw the blanket off, reached for her robe, and pushed her feet into her slippers.

He hated to drag her out of bed so early, but he needed her calming influence and sage advice. In matters of emotional intelligence and diplomacy, no one was better than his wife.

As Syssi walked over to her coffee station by the bar, Kian settled onto the couch. Listening to the familiar sounds of Syssi preparing their cappuccinos, he already felt calmer than when he had woken up.

The aroma of freshly brewed coffee soon filled the air, a familiar comfort, and then Syssi returned, two steaming cups in hand.

"You are not a dictator." She settled beside him on the couch and handed him his cup. "You discussed this with the council, and all the members agreed that questioning everyone was necessary."

Kian took a sip of his coffee, savoring the rich flavor. "I didn't put it to a vote."

"But no one objected." Syssi tucked her legs underneath her. "Perhaps I should help you to write a speech. We could work on making your delivery more...how should I say it…mellow?" Her eyes twinkled with amusement. "Something that will sound a little more diplomatic than your usual style."

"Don't make me sound too mellow." He took another sip before putting the cup down. "Leaders need to be decisive and unapologetic, or they're perceived as weak, and what follows is usually a disaster because without respect, there is no compliance, and without compliance, lawlessness rules."

Syssi nodded sagely. "When the cat's away, the mice will play."

A chuckle escaped Kian despite his somber mood. "That's not the right idiom for the occasion."

Syssi shrugged. "It's the best I can come up with at five in the morning."

"Fair enough." He wrapped an arm around her shoulders. "I need to prepare a speech that will sound resolute but won't alienate the community."

Syssi pulled her phone out of her robe pocket and activated the speech-to-text feature.

"I stand before you today with a heavy heart and a solemn duty," she started and glanced at him. "Recent events have forced me to take actions that I wish were unnecessary, but which I believe are crucial for the safety and stability of our community."

Kian shook his head. "Too wordy. That's not how I talk."

"Yeah, you are right." Syssi erased what she'd dictated and activated the speech-to-text feature again. "Recent acts of sabotage are threatening our security and unity. After consulting with the council, I've decided on a necessary but difficult course of action. Every village resident—immortal, Kra-ell, and human—will be questioned."

Kian nodded. "That's good, and it sounds like me, but it's not really diplomatic, is it?"

Syssi rolled her eyes. "Do you want me to go back to the first version?"

"Can't you come up with something in the middle?"

"I can try."

It took another hour for them to agree on a speech they were both happy with.

"I'm texting it to you." Syssi typed on the screen of her phone.

"Thank you." He leaned forward and picked up his cup.

There wasn't much left, and it was cold, but it was still good.

"Do you want me to make you another one?" Syssi asked.

"Yeah." He sighed. "I need it."

She looked at him with a raised brow. "You still sound troubled. Are you still unhappy with the speech we've come up with?"

"It's not that." He gave her a sad smile. "There is more on my mind than the assembly tonight. I'm also worried about the search for Khiann. I don't want to disappoint my mother, and I don't have much faith in Jasmine's tarot reading. They predicted the prince when he was meant for her, but I doubt they will do that to predict someone else's prince."

"What about the ruins? If we find them, we will have a good starting point for Jasmine's scrying efforts. I don't think that part of her talent is limited to things pertaining only to her own love life."

Kian didn't think so either but locating the ruins wouldn't be easy. Hell, it might be impossible.

"Did you sketch another picture of what you saw in your vision?"

Kian preferred using the sketch to search for archeological findings in obscure texts to having Syssi summon another vision so soon after her last one.

Syssi nodded. "I'm still refining the details. Have you talked with Kalugal? If anyone knows where to look for mentions of obscure archeological finds, it would be him."

"I haven't. But I will."

A crackling noise came through the baby monitor, halting their discussion, and then the unmistakable demanding voice of their daughter, "Mama!"

Kian and Syssi exchanged surprised glances.

Allegra loved to sleep, and she hated being woken up. It was very unusual for her to be up so early.

Syssi smiled. "She must have sensed we were awake and wanted to join the party." She pushed to her feet and offered him a hand up. "Come, let's greet her together. Our baby girl loves it when Mommy and Daddy come to her room in the morning."

Allegra was standing in her crib when they entered, her eyes alit with joy. "Mama! Dada!"

She knew how to say Mommy and Daddy, but most of the time, she still stuck to the earlier Mama and Dada.

Kian didn't mind. In fact, he preferred it.

Scooping Allegra up, he pressed a kiss to her cheek. "Good morning, my little princess."

"Dada," she said, reaching out to pat his face. "Mama."

Syssi leaned in, kissing Allegra's other chubby cheek. "Did you have good dreams, sweetheart?"

As their daughter winced and wiggled in Kian's arms, Syssi smiled. "Do you need to go potty?"

Kian thought it was too early to start potty training their baby, but Syssi was convinced that Allegra was ready.

"Potty! Book!"

Kian stifled a chuckle. "I'll get the book."

As Syssi set Allegra down on her potty, Kian picked out one of the cardboard books and handed it to her. "Is this one good?"

Allegra shifted, making herself more comfortable before reaching for the book.

Was there a cuter sight than that?

As their daughter started 'reading,' the first true rays of sunlight streamed through the nursery's window, painting the room in warm hues.

They waited patiently until Allegra was done and headed to the kitchen with her.

"Are you in the mood for pancakes, sweetie?" Syssi asked.

Allegra's eyes lit with excitement, and she clapped her hands. "Cakes!"

Kian smiled. It was so easy to love and please a small child, but would it still be so easy when she got older and needed more than a hug and a tasty treat to be happy?

4

JASMINE

Jasmine drifted slowly back to consciousness, her mind still filled with the remnants of vivid, ethereal dreams. She had been flying, soaring over landscapes both familiar and fantastical, her body weightless and free. Translucent beings had waved at her as she passed, their forms shimmering like sunlight on water.

The memory of it lingered, a gossamer veil between sleep and wakefulness.

As reality began to seep back in, Jasmine became aware of the warmth surrounding her, the solid presence of Ell-rom's body against hers. She opened her eyes to find him gazing at her, his expression so full of love and tenderness that it made her heart swell like a balloon.

"Hey," she murmured, her voice still husky with sleep.

"Hey, yourself," Ell-rom replied with a smile tugging at his lips. His hand came up to cup her cheek. "How are you feeling?"

Jasmine took a moment to assess herself. Her body felt languid, pleasantly heavy, and there was a lingering buzz of euphoria coursing through her veins. The spot where Ell-rom had bitten her tingled, a phantom reminder of the profound connection they had shared.

"Amazing," she said, a slow smile spreading across her face. "Incredible."

She was no stranger to the euphoric high that the venom induced, but somehow, it had been even better with Ell-rom. She wondered whether this was because his venom was more potent than Edgar's or because of the profound love they shared.

His answering smile was radiant. "It was," he agreed, pulling her closer.

As Jasmine snuggled into his embrace, she thought how surreal it was for her to be in the arms of an alien prince.

She'd rescued him, but fate, or the Mother of All Life, wanted her to find him and save him. The goddess had guided her all along.

Perhaps later, when she dragged herself out of bed, she should offer her thanks to the goddess for the great boon she had bestowed on her.

Ell-rom was still a work in progress, but he had made great strides.

Jasmine's lips curved into a soft smile as she recalled the early days of his recovery. The patience it had taken to explain even the simplest concepts, the joy of seeing the world anew through his eyes. It had been challenging but also incredibly rewarding. With each passing day, she had found herself falling deeper in love with this extraordinary being who viewed the world with wonder and curiosity.

Her thoughts drifted to the obstacles they still had to face, like Ell-rom's struggle with his deadly ability, which was still a source of fear and anxiety for both of them.

And then there was the matter of her own latent abilities. The discovery that she possessed paranormal talents had been shocking at first, but now it filled her with a sense of purpose. Her scrying abilities, her connection to the tarot, those gifts that had once seemed like mere curiosities now held the potential to change lives and reunite long-lost loved ones.

As Jasmine's thoughts turned to the search for Khiann, the weight of Annani's hope was daunting. She didn't want to think about that as she lay in Ell-rom's arms, basking in the afterglow of their lovemaking.

She lifted her head, meeting Ell-rom's gaze, and the love she saw there, the adoration, filled her with a warmth and a sense of well-being so sweet that it was intoxicating.

"What are you thinking about?" Ell-rom feathered his fingers over her exposed skin.

It tickled, and she giggled, leaning in to press a soft kiss to his lips. "How lucky I am to have found you."

"I'm the lucky one," he murmured.

"We are both lucky." She kissed him again. "This is such an incredible feeling."

"The love?"

"Yes, but it's more than that." She frowned as she tried to put the feeling into words. "I'm not alone anymore. It's no longer just Jasmine or Jaz, as my human friends call me. It's Jasmine and Ell-rom. We are a package deal."

"What's a package deal?"

"It means that you don't get one without the other. We are a pair."

"I like it." He smoothed his hand down her back, cupping her bottom. "I never want to be alone again."

It occurred to her then that he hadn't been. Before entering stasis, Ell-rom had always had Morelle by his side. Twins shared a special connection, and once Morelle was awake, Jasmine would have to share Ell-rom with her.

The burst of jealousy shamed her.

Ell-rom and Morelle had grown up inseparable. She couldn't expect him to distance himself from his sister just because his mate was greedy and wanted him all to herself.

Hopefully, Morelle was as wonderful as her brother, so it wouldn't be a problem. Surely, she would want what was best for Ell-rom and would realize how important Jasmine was to him.

The bond they shared went beyond the physical, beyond even the emotional. It was a connection of souls, a merging of beings that transcended the boundaries of species and time.

The euphoria of his venom was still humming through her veins, a physical reminder of their joining.

In this perfect moment, Jasmine was content to simply be, to feel the steady beat of Ell-rom's heart against her cheek, to breathe in his familiar scent, and to revel in the love that surrounded them like a tangible force.

But the sun was up, and the world outside their room began to stir. It was time to get out of bed.

"Ready to face the day, my love?" she asked.

He shook his head. "I want to stay right here with you in my arms."

She smiled. "I guess we could stay in bed a little longer."

5

ROB

Rob sat at the kitchen table with his laptop open and the cursor blinking steadily on a half-finished line of code. The late morning sun streamed through the window, warming his face, but his heart was still cold, still bleeding silently as pain turned into anger and then to indifference.

As promised, Toven had returned his devices after the council meeting, along with a new clan phone. They'd all been fitted with new security measures, but Toven had claimed not to know what those measures were.

Despite owning the most technologically advanced company in the world, the guy was not particularly tech-savvy. Toven was one more proof that the real geniuses were not the creators of revolutionary new products but those who saw the potential to monetize their inventions.

Rob had a much better idea about what had been done to his devices. To start with, they would show his location to be somewhere else, and all his communications would be monitored. Any proprietary work he did would no longer be private, but he didn't mind. Given the technological marvels he had witnessed just entering this hidden oasis, he had no doubt that the clan had no need of what he was doing for his company.

It was truly a wondrous new world he was discovering, and he could just imagine how difficult it must have been for Margo to keep this a secret from him. Not that she had a choice. His sister was under the same compulsion he was to keep the immortals and their existence among humans a secret.

He couldn't blame her for that, but she could have told him her suspicions about Lynda.

Would he have believed her, though?

Perhaps not right away.

He would have most likely accused her of disliking Lynda and wanting to put a wedge between them, but perhaps he would have paid more attention to the way his fiancée had acted.

Whatever.

It was water under the bridge now, and he should let it go.

He should focus on the mind-boggling concept of his own potential for immortality. It was as if someone had suddenly rewritten the rules of his existence. Everything he'd planned, every goal he'd set for his life, suddenly seemed small and insignificant in the face of eternity.

Rob ran a hand through his hair. He needed a new plan, but where to even begin when contemplating immortal life?

Lifting his head, he glanced at Mia.

His sister's best friend sat on a lounger, facing the sliding doors of the living room and the greenery outside, totally absorbed in sketching on her tablet. She was working on illustrations for a new book, not because she needed to work for money, but because she loved creating. Her face was composed, her posture relaxed, and she looked like she didn't have a care in the world.

Rob wanted to be like Mia, to find something he loved to do, something he was passionate about, and to be absorbed in creative work.

Toven was a writer, too, but he was less serious about his creative side than Mia. He had a business to run, and he was a council member.

Still, if anyone could give Rob advice about eternal life, it would be his gracious host, the god who had lived for over seven thousand years.

Mind-boggling didn't even begin to describe it, and even more so that Mia was Toven's mate and that the love between them was so palpable it electrified the air around them.

Rob's heart squeezed with envy.

He wanted that kind of love.

Neither Mia nor Toven would ever even look at another, let alone betray each other's trust.

Unbidden, Rob's mind drifted to Lusha.

She was seeing someone, and he would never court her, doing to another what had been done to him, but he could enjoy her company as a friend. Talking to her had been refreshing and easy. He didn't need to hide anything from her, and besides, Lusha was the only person he had befriended in the village so far.

That needed to change. He had to start socializing, get to know some immortal males, and choose his inducer. It would have been easy if Toven offered to do that, but he hadn't, and Rob didn't want to ask.

With a sigh, he closed his laptop, got to his feet, and walked into the living room.

Mia looked up from her tablet and smiled. "Everything okay, Rob?"

"I'm restless," he admitted. "How am I supposed to choose an inducer?"

Mia pursed her lips. "Toven can talk to Kian, and they can find you someone, but it would be better if you find your inducer yourself." She put her tablet on the side table adjacent to her lounger. "They make a big deal out of the induction ceremony, and you will need to pledge to stay best friends with your inducer for life, so it should be someone you like and trust."

For some reason, learning that the induction involved a ceremony and, therefore, witnesses eased Rob's mind. "I would like that, of course. But how am I supposed to get to know males in the village?"

"The gym might be a good place to meet people," Mia said. "But if you are not into fitness, you can try Atzil's bar. It's only open three nights a week, though. Friday, Saturday, and Sunday."

Rob was an introvert, and striking up a conversation with a stranger was not high up on his list of favorite things to do, especially when the stranger was not a woman, but if he had to choose a location to do that, he would choose a gym rather than a bar.

"Where is the gym located?"

"In the underground structure, but today might not be a good day unless you go right now."

"Why?"

"A whole village assembly is scheduled for this evening, and attendance is mandatory."

He frowned. "What's going on?"

Mia shrugged as if it wasn't a big deal, but the calm she'd enjoyed while sketching was replaced with tension. "There's been some trouble in the village. Minor thefts, sabotage of garbage incinerators, automatic shutters, and other nonessential equipment. The assembly was called to inform everyone that each resident of the village will be interrogated."

"That sounds a bit extreme for small infringements. It's not like anyone's house was robbed or someone was murdered."

"Fates forbid." Mia put a hand over her chest. "The problem is that things like that never happened in the village until the Kra-ell arrived, and everyone suspects them, but Kian doesn't want them to feel singled out, so he's interrogating everyone."

"The Kra-ell?" Rob asked. "What are they? A different immortal clan?"

"No, they are a different species of beings originating from the same planet as the gods." Mia launched into an explanation about the Kra-ell, who they were, how they had gotten to Earth, and how they had ended up living with the immortals in their village.

Rob listened, fascinated and even more overwhelmed by this new facet of the hidden world he'd stumbled into. "What do they look like? Can I tell them apart from humans and immortals?"

"The purebloods look quite different than humans and immortals, but some of the hybrids are almost indistinguishable unless you know what to look for. If you want to see Kra-ell, you might stop by the playground. The Kra-ell tend to have more children than the immortals, so there is a good chance to spot some mothers with young children there. There is also Aliya at the café. She's a hybrid, but she leans more toward her Kra-ell side. She looks more like the purebloods."

Rob remembered seeing two beautiful brunettes behind the counter, but he hadn't interacted with either of them. He had only talked with Marina, the blue-haired human who worked there.

"I didn't notice anything different about the ladies working in the café, but I'll pay more attention this time."

"Do you need me to show you the way?" Mia offered.

Rob smiled. "I can manage on my own, and if I get lost, I'm sure someone will point me in the right direction."

6

ELL-ROM

"You did great," Jasmine said as they entered the lobby. "You are not even short of breath."

Shortness of breath had not been an issue. Ell-rom's leg and back muscles were.

He couldn't wait to sit down and have something to drink, but he was adamant about making it to the penthouse without voicing a single complaint.

The morning walk outside had been Julian's idea, and the medic had entrusted Jasmine to supervise Ell-rom and make sure he rested every so often. It had been lovely to experience the world outside and note all the things he had missed on his first walk.

As they entered the penthouse, Ell-rom was surprised to see two unfamiliar people sitting on the couch in the living room.

A tall, lean man with light hair and intelligent eyes sat

next to a petite brunette whose smile seemed to light up the room.

Jasmine's face broke into a grin of recognition. "Shai! What a pleasant surprise." She turned to Ell-rom. "Ell-rom, this is Shai, Kian's assistant."

Shai rose to his feet and extended his hand. "It's a pleasure to finally meet you, Ell-rom. We've all heard so much about you."

Ell-rom returned the handshake, noting that Shai's grip was firm and confident. "The pleasure is mine," he said, the greeting still feeling slightly foreign on his tongue.

He was sure that the Kra-ell used a different form of greeting or none at all. It was one more question he intended to pose to Jade once he secured an audience with her.

The petite brunette stood as well, her eyes sparkling with barely contained excitement. "I'm Geraldine," she said, her voice as bubbly as her demeanor. "I'm Shai's mate, and I hope you don't mind that I tagged along. I absolutely twisted Shai's arm to let me come because I've been dying to meet you and couldn't wait for you to arrive at the village."

She spoke so fast that there was a slight delay in the translation, but her friendly demeanor and bubbly personality more than compensated for that.

"I don't mind at all," Ell-rom assured her. "I'm glad you insisted on coming to see me. I love meeting new people."

Geraldine's smile widened. "I'm not just people. We are family, Ell-rom. I'm Toven's daughter, and my brother is married to Annani's eldest daughter."

Family was a concept Ell-rom was still getting used to. "The more relatives, the better."

Shai chuckled, wrapping an arm around Geraldine's waist. "I hope you're ready for a lot of them, then."

"As I said, the more the better."

As they settled on the couch and armchairs, Geraldine kept talking about the different members of their extended family: her daughters, their mates, and the grandson, who was some kind of a prodigy. Ell-rom found himself drawn to her vibrant energy.

"So, Ell-rom." Geraldine leaned forward conspiratorially. "How are you finding life here on Earth?"

The real answer would be that he hadn't had a life before waking up from stasis, so this was the only life he had ever known, but that wasn't what Geraldine wanted to hear. "There's so much to learn, so much to discover, but I couldn't be happier about being here." He turned to Jasmine. "My truelove mate was waiting for me, and the Fates led her to me."

"Oh dear." Geraldine put her small hand over her chest. "That's so romantic."

"But true." Jasmine leaned over to kiss his cheek before pushing to her feet. "I'll get us some refreshments. Any special requests?"

"Just water for me," Geraldine said.

Shai smiled. "I don't want to trouble you. I came to deliver a laptop and a phone to Ell-rom and to explain how they work." He pulled two sleek-looking devices from his bag. "These are for you." Shai handed them to Ell-rom. "They've been specially configured for your needs."

"Hold that thought," Jasmine said. "Don't start before I'm back with the refreshments. I want to hear about those special configurations."

Ell-rom took the devices, marveling at their smooth surfaces and compact designs. He'd seen Jasmine operating a phone and a laptop, but he hadn't paid much attention to either because everything was written in English, which he couldn't read.

They waited for Jasmine to return from the kitchen, and after everyone had taken a few sips of water, Shai took the laptop back from Ell-rom.

"You are probably wondering how you will operate the devices without being able to read any of the standard languages that come with most programs."

Ell-rom nodded. "The language problem has occurred to me."

Shai took a sip of water and then put the glass back down. "That is why William's team, in cooperation with Vrog, a hybrid Kra-ell who is fluent in both languages, has created an interactive artificial intelligence course for teaching English to Kra-ell speakers. It has already been tested on Kra-ell living in the village, and it was a success."

"That's awesome," Jasmine said.

"It is." Shai placed the laptop on the coffee table. "It responds to voice commands in both languages, and it is ready to go." He turned to Ell-rom. "Give it a try."

Ell-rom leaned forward. "Hi," he said.

"Hello, I am Kra-en. What is your name?"

Ell-rom looked at Shai. "Is it safe?"

Shai nodded. "We are not connected directly to the internet. You can say whatever you want to your teacher."

"My name is Ell-rom."

"Nice to meet you, Ell-rom. What is the first thing you would like to learn today?"

Amazed at how easy it was, Ell-rom turned to Shai. "Should I remove my earpieces while studying with Kra-en?"

Kian's assistant nodded. "It would be difficult to learn anything while they are activated."

"Isn't it amazing?" Geraldine asked. "The AI adapts to your learning style and pace."

Ell-rom grinned. "I can't wait to start using it."

Shai must have taken that as a dismissal because he rose to his feet and offered his hand to his mate. "It was nice meeting you, Ell-rom, but I cannot stay. I have a long list of tasks that still need to be done."

"Of course." Ell-rom stood up and offered his hand to Geraldine and then to Shai. "Thank you for the devices."

"You are most welcome," Shai said.

After they left, Jasmine guided him through the basic functions of the laptop and phone, but even though he tried to pay attention to her explanations, he was eager to return to his artificial intelligence teacher.

Eventually, Jasmine noticed and smiled fondly. "I can finish explaining later. I see that you can't wait to dive in."

"I'm sorry, but you are right."

"No problem." She leaned over and kissed his cheek. "Go, play with your new toy. Just don't forget to take out your earpieces."

He did as she suggested and then turned back to the device. "Hello, Kra-en. I'm back and ready to start."

The AI suggested that they start with the basics, learning the English alphabet.

"That's a good idea," Ell-rom agreed.

"A," the AI said, displaying the letter on the screen. "Can you repeat that, Ell-rom?"

"A," Ell-rom echoed.

As they continued through the alphabet, with the AI correcting his pronunciation and offering encouragement, Ell-rom found himself completely absorbed in the lesson.

The outside world faded away while he focused on mastering these new sounds and symbols, and he was so engrossed that he barely noticed when Jasmine leaned down and kissed his cheek.

"I'll be in our room," she said in her language, and Kra-en translated. "I'm going to do a tarot spread for Annani's lost mate."

He kissed her back. "Good luck."

As the lesson progressed, Ell-rom found himself marveling at the intricacies of the English language. It was so different from Kra-ell, with its own unique rhythms and patterns.

Time seemed to slip away as he worked through lesson after lesson. The AI adapted to his quick grasp of concepts, challenging him with increasingly complex words and phrases. Before he knew it, he was forming simple sentences.

"I am Ell-rom," he said, the words still halting but recognizable.

"Excellent work, Ell-rom!" the AI praised. "Your progress is remarkable."

Excitement thrummed in Ell-rom's chest. This was tangible progress, a big step towards integrating into this new world.

7

JASMINE

In the bedroom, Jasmine pulled the velvet pouch with her tarot out of the drawer in the bedside table, loosened the string, and dropped the deck into her palm.

These cards had guided her before, had led her to Ell-rom, and now she hoped they would provide answers for Annani, but her heart was full of doubt, and that was not good for a reading.

She had to believe that she would find a clue in the spread, or it wouldn't show her what she needed.

Settling on the bed, Jasmine took a deep breath, centering herself. She closed her eyes, focusing her thoughts on the yearning in Annani's eyes when she'd talked about her lost husband.

The goddess's love had endured five thousand years of separation and that should count for something.

She offered a prayer to the Mother of All Life, beseeching her to help the goddess. "Annani has done nothing but good throughout her life. Without her relentless push against the forces of darkness, humans all over the world would still be living in horrendous poverty, and women would be subjugated and enslaved. If anyone on this Earth deserves a happy ending, it is Annani. Merciful Mother, please hear my prayer and offer me a hint. Is Khiann alive in stasis? And if so, where should we look for him?"

The familiar sensation of energy flowing through her hands accompanied each shuffle, but in the back of her head, doubt lingered. What if it was just magical thinking?

Jasmine shook her head. She'd proven to herself and others that her talent was real. She should not doubt it anymore.

She began to lay out the cards in a Celtic cross spread, her favorite for complex questions.

As she turned over each card, a frown began to form on her face. The spread before her was strange, to put it mildly. The Tower, reversed, in the position of the present. The Moon in the position of the challenge. The Hierophant, also reversed, indicated the root of the issue.

Jasmine studied the cards. They hinted at hidden knowledge, at secrets kept in the dark, but it wasn't clear if those secrets were protecting Khiann or endangering him.

The Two of Swords in the recent past position suggested a difficult choice made, while the King of Swords in the crown position hinted at a powerful figure holding crucial information. But who was this figure? And what was their connection to Khiann?

Most puzzling of all was the Ten of Wands in the outcome position. It spoke of burdens, of responsibilities carried alone. But whose burdens? Khiann's? Annani's? Or someone else's?

Unsatisfied with the cryptic nature of the reading, Jasmine gathered the cards and shuffled again. "Please, Merciful Mother, show me clearly. Is Khiann alive? Where is he?"

As she laid out the spread a second time, her heart sank. The same cards appeared in the same positions. The Tower, the Moon, the Hierophant—all telling the same confusing story.

"Maybe the cards need purification."

She should have done that before starting a new reading to clear any lingering energy. There were many ways to purify contaminated cards, but the simplest was to place the deck under the light of the full moon, preferably on a windowsill or outside. However, the full moon was still a few days away, so she would have to employ another method, like passing the tarot through the smoke of burning sage or placing cleansing crystals on top of the deck.

The problem was that she had none of those things on hand and would have to go shopping for them. A less effective method was to hold the deck and visualize a bright, white light surrounding and entering the cards, and she could do that right now.

After the cleansing, she shuffled the deck vigorously several times and then tried for the third time, but as she turned over the third spread, she let out a frustrated sigh.

Once again, the cards remained unchanged.

What were they trying to tell her? Someone important held Khiann's fate in their hands. That much seemed clear. But who? And why were they keeping it a secret?

The reversed Hierophant nagged at her. It spoke of challenging tradition, of secrets kept from institutions. Could it be that someone within the clan knew more than they were letting on?

And the Moon, with its imagery of illusion and hidden paths—was it suggesting that the way to Khiann was purposely hidden from view?

Jasmine rubbed her temples, feeling a headache forming. She had hoped for clarity, for a direction, but instead she was left with more questions than answers.

With a sigh she gathered the cards, returned them to their pouch, and placed them back in the drawer.

She couldn't shake the feeling that she was missing something important, some crucial piece of the puzzle that would make everything clear.

As she returned to the living room, she found Ell-rom still engrossed in his English lesson, repeating words after the AI and pronouncing them surprisingly well.

Evidently, that superior hearing of his had its uses beyond the ability to eavesdrop on conversation a hundred feet away and more.

Come to think of it, Ell-rom should be a good singer. His pitch would be perfect. It might be fun to sing duets with him.

Ell-rom looked up, his eyes brightening. "You are smiling, so I assume the cards told you something useful?"

She motioned for him to put in his earpieces and sat on the couch next to him. "I was smiling because your English accent sounded so good. It got me thinking that you could probably be a great singer, and we could sing duets. I would love for us to do that."

He chuckled. "If you love it, I will make the effort to learn to sing."

"First, master the language, and then I will introduce you to the wonderful world of musicals. I bet you would be a great Phantom of the Opera."

He frowned. "A ghost in the theater?"

That was probably how his earpieces had translated the title, and it was close enough. Trying to explain would be just more confusing.

"Yeah, something like that." She leaned back against the overstuffed leather cushions.

"So, what did you see in the cards?" Ell-rom asked.

"They were strange. I might have to perform a serious cleanse to get them rejuvenated."

"What did they say?" he insisted. "Maybe I can help you decipher the message."

Jasmine took a deep breath. "I asked two simple questions. One, is Khiann alive and in stasis? Two, where should we look for him? But the answers I got were not to the questions I asked. They were cryptic, to say the least."

She described the spread, explaining the meaning behind each card and their unusual positions. "The thing is," she said, "I did the spread three times. And each time, it came out exactly the same. That almost never happens, which means that this is the correct answer, and it is up to me to decipher its meaning."

Ell-rom nodded. "What's your first take on that spread?"

"Secrets and hidden knowledge are the same things expressed in two different ways, so it obviously means that a piece of the puzzle is missing, but someone has it and that someone is a powerful figure."

"Could it be the Eternal King?"

Jasmine chuckled.

"As mighty as your grandfather is, I doubt he had anything to do with Khiann's death or stasis. If anyone had some secret knowledge, it would be your father, but regrettably, he took the secret to his grave. The other thing that's unclear is whether that secret information and that powerful figure will help us find Khiann or hinder the search. I can't tell."

Ell-rom was quiet for a moment. "Could it be someone

within the clan? Someone who knows more than they're letting on?"

"As far as I know, the only two who were alive at the time were Annani and Toven. Annani obviously doesn't know, so that leaves Toven, but if he knew something, he would have told her."

"Perhaps he believes that he's protecting someone," Ell-rom suggested. "You said that one of the cards represented burdens carried alone, right?"

Jasmine nodded. "The Ten of Wands."

The puzzle pieces were there, but Jasmine just couldn't fit them together.

"You should tell Annani and Kian about this," Ell-rom said. "Even if you can't make sense of it, they might see something you are missing."

"You're right, but I would hate to disappoint Annani, and I don't have anything of substance to report."

Ell-rom took her hand. "You did what she asked you to do, and now you need to tell her exactly what you saw and what you think it meant. Annani will do with the information as she sees fit."

8

ROB

Rob wandered through the winding pathways of the village, enjoying the cool, fresh air and the incredible quiet. With no cars and no heavy machinery, the only sounds were produced by nature.

He wasn't in a rush to reach the café and didn't even care if he was walking in the right direction. In truth, he was searching for the mysterious Kra-ell, but so far, he had only encountered immortals. They were all friendly, and no one seemed overly surprised to see a stranger in their midst, so he assumed that news of his arrival had already spread.

Mia had warned him that the village was a small community and that everyone knew what everyone else was doing, and that included who was spending the night in whose house.

Not that those nightly escapades were clandestine affairs.

The immortals were not shy about sex, and those in committed relationships did not stray, which Rob found refreshing. That alone would have been enough for him to want to become part of this community.

He'd vowed never to allow himself to be cheated on again, but since he hated to live with constant suspicion, his choices were to either never commit again or to live in a community where everyone knew everyone, making cheating nearly impossible.

If people wanted an open relationship, he had no problem with that, as long as they were honest about it and both partners agreed to the arrangement.

As a conversation in a foreign, guttural-sounding language drew his attention to two males working on the bushes lining the path ahead, he quickened his step.

The males had to be Kra-ell.

When he got closer, it took him a moment to register the differences. They weren't as alien looking as he had imagined, but they definitely didn't look human. Tall and very slim, they still looked powerful, and the fierce expressions in their enormous eyes were intimidating.

They wore their long black hair in low ponytails, secured at their napes with a cord. If not looked at too closely, they could pass for Asians or Native Americans.

Up close, though, the alien eyes gave them away.

"Hello." Rob offered a friendly smile.

Those strange eyes fixed on him with an intensity that made him squirm. They didn't return his greeting; they just stared at him with what seemed like suspicion and then gave him a curt nod before returning to their work.

Not very friendly now, were they?

Mia hadn't warned him about them being so intimidating.

No wonder people suspected the Kra-ell of the recent thefts and sabotage that Toven had told him about. They looked like they were planning their next attack.

Shaking his head, Rob continued on his way, this time intending to go straight to the café. After getting turned around a couple of times, he stopped someone and asked for directions.

Thankfully, he didn't encounter any more Kra-ell, and the smell of fresh coffee guided him the rest of the way.

A few people were seated at the outdoor tables enjoying the pleasant weather, and as he scanned the patrons, hoping to spot Lusha, he saw a woman who must be Aliya, sitting with a male who also seemed to be a hybrid Kra-ell.

Their appearance was striking. They were both slim and dark-haired, but their facial features were softened by their human genes, so they didn't look quite as alien as the purebloods he had encountered on the way.

Not wanting to stare, Rob forced his gaze to shift to the display of pastries. With the warm aroma of coffee enveloping him, he could almost pretend that he was in a normal coffee shop in Anyplace USA, but another quick glance in the direction of the hybrid Kra-ell couple shattered that illusion.

He ordered a cappuccino and a muffin, and as he waited for his order, he listened to the conversations at the nearby tables, hoping to overhear something useful.

"...do you know what the assembly tonight is about?"

"...the thefts, of course. Didn't you see the message on the bulletin board asking for the perpetrator to step forward?"

"...just don't trust the Kra-ell, never have..."

"...what if it's not them?"

"...then who?"

The undercurrent of tension was palpable.

Rob collected his order and found a small table in the back. Sitting down, he suddenly felt very alone in this bustling café full of immortals. His colleagues at work were his only friends, and now that he was moving into the village and probably quitting that job, he would have none.

And what would become of his parents?

Would the big boss allow them into the village the way he allowed Mia's grandparents?

Probably not.

Rob didn't have the sway of a powerful member of the community vouching for his relatives like Mia had in Toven.

As more murmurs about the Kra-ell reached his ears, his gaze drifted back to Aliya and her companion. They seemed oblivious to the gossip going on around them, so maybe they didn't think that the suspicions were directed at them.

Maybe only the purebloods were suspect?

Those he had encountered before looked dangerous, but he assumed that Mia would have warned him about them if they were, so what he had interpreted as hostility was probably just a cultural difference. Perhaps the Kra-ell didn't exchange greetings with a smile. Like the fictional Klingons in the *Star Trek* universe, they might prefer getting straight to the point instead of wasting time on niceties.

9

ELL-ROM

As Ell-rom entered Julian's office, the medic greeted him with a smile and gestured for him to take a seat. "How was the walk this morning?"

"It was good. Jasmine said that we covered about three miles, and when we got back, I didn't feel like I needed to sleep to recuperate. When we returned, Shai was waiting for us in the penthouse with a personal computer and a phone for me. The computer came with an artificial intelligence teacher that helps me to learn English, and I'm happy to report that I have already mastered the English alphabet."

Ell-rom felt a little awkward about boasting, but he was proud of himself and the progress he'd made.

"That's excellent." Julian glanced at the screen of his own computer. "Vanessa sent me two possible time slots for today's session. She has an opening at three in the afternoon and another one at six. Which one do you prefer?"

Ell-rom cleared his throat. "Neither. I don't need any more sessions."

Julian tilted his head. "Does that mean what I think it means?"

Ell-rom felt his ears getting hot. "I'm over the aversion. In fact, I can't wait to do it again."

"Congratulations," Julian said. "That was much faster than any of us could have expected or hoped for."

Ell-rom nodded. "Jasmine's blood tastes exquisite. It is nothing like what was in the goblet in my dream or the synthetic stuff. Now I crave it instead of being repulsed by it."

Genuine delight crossed Julian's features. "That's wonderful, Ell-rom. Again, congratulations."

"Thank you."

"I assume that means you and Jasmine have started the induction process."

Dread pooling in the pit of his stomach, Ell-rom nodded. "How dangerous is it for her?"

"It's hard to tell because every Dormant is different, and we don't really know why some transition with ease while others struggle. What I suggest, though, is for you to move to the village. The clinic there is bigger and better equipped to handle a transition, and Morelle is well enough to be transported." He smiled. "I miss spending more time with my mate, and I'd rather be in the village than here."

Julian's suggestion should have made Ell-rom happy and excited, but instead, he felt anxious.

Too many changes were happening too fast, and his stomach churned at the prospect of another one coming up so soon. He'd just adjusted to living in the penthouse, and now Julian wanted him to move again.

"If you think it's better for Jasmine, then of course."

The medic leaned forward. "Don't worry. It's easy to get used to something better, and the village is much better than even the luxurious penthouse. Everyone will know who and what you are, and you won't need to pretend to be human."

"Are you sure that's wise?" Ell-rom rubbed the back of his neck. "The idea is to hide my and Morelle's rescue and recovery from the Eternal King. Is it safe to let everyone in the village know who I am?"

Julian took a moment to think. "I understand your concern, but the Clan Mother does not want to hide you. She wants to celebrate you and Morelle. That being said, I'm sure Kian will have some reservations, so I should call him and ask how he wants to do it."

"Yes, of course."

"I'll text him first." Julian pulled out his phone. "He might not have time to talk to me today. He's called a big assembly for tonight, which I will have to miss." His fingers flew over the screen as he typed the message.

"What's the assembly about?" Ell-rom asked.

Julian was about to answer when his phone rang. "It's Kian," the medic said before accepting the call. "Hello, Kian. Thank you for calling me back right away."

"What's going on?" Kian's gruff voice came through.

"I think it is time to move the twins to the village. Ell-rom is here with me, and he just informed me that he and Jasmine have started working on her transition. Also, Morelle is stable, and moving her to the village shouldn't be a problem. The facilities in the clinic in the village are much more spacious and comfortable, and it would provide a safer environment for Jasmine's transition."

"Actually, the timing couldn't be better," Kian said. "I need the clinic to conduct the experiment of removing a tracker from one of the gods and implanting it in a human. I'd rather the twins and Jasmine weren't anywhere near the place when that is being done."

Ell-rom felt a mixture of relief and anxiety. Relief that Kian seemed to have no problem with him and Morelle moving into the village, and anxiety because of the impending change.

"When?" Julian asked. "If we do it today, I can attend the assembly."

Kian chuckled. "Regrettably, that's not going to happen so easily. My mother would want to properly welcome her siblings to the village, and that means she needs time to plan a party. We also need to prepare a place for Ell-rom and Jasmine."

Julian seemed to disagree with Kian's last statement. "Maybe it's better to wait with the house for after Jasmine's transition. Until then, they should stay with someone who will know what to do when the time comes."

"Right," Kian said. "I'll check with my mother and let you know."

With that, the call ended, and Julian turned to Ell-rom. "Well, you heard him. Kian is going to coordinate things with Annani. Knowing the Clan Mother, she will want the entire village population to welcome you and Morelle."

Ell-rom swallowed. "I'm not sure I want a big gathering like that."

Julian lifted his hands. "You can try to reason with your sister, but from experience, I can tell you that it will be a futile effort. When Annani decides something, it is very difficult to change her mind."

"Maybe I should call Annani before Kian talks to her then?" Ell-rom offered.

He had a phone now, with the contacts of all his family members programmed with their pictures to make it easy for him to call them.

"That's a good idea, but I suggest sending her a text first. She might not have her earpieces in place when you call, and I bet you didn't learn enough English in one session to converse with her in it."

"That's true." He thought about the phone not being programmed with Kra-ell and how to solve that problem. If he put the teardrop on, he could dictate a message to Annani in English. "I'll do that after our exercise session."

"Excellent." Julian pushed to his feet. "Let's head to the gymnasium. Today, I will introduce you to weightlifting." He clapped Ell-rom on his back. "You need to strengthen these muscles."

10

ANNANI

Annani examined her reflection in the full-length mirror in her bedroom, checking her gown for unsightly creases.

Naturally, there were none, but it was difficult to disregard what had been drilled into her head in her youth. Her mother had insisted that a ruler's appearance should always be spotless, and her words still echoed in Annani's mind five thousand years later. The difference was that now she thought of her mother's strict upbringing fondly, but back then, she had thought of it as tyrannical.

Children never knew how good they had it until they lost it.

She adjusted the folds of the deep blue silk gown, ensuring that it draped elegantly over her petite frame. As always, her face was free of makeup and unchanged despite her age.

Even for a goddess, Annani looked remarkably young.

While most goddesses typically appeared as strikingly beautiful human females in their mid-twenties, Annani's petite size and delicate features gave her the appearance of a girl barely out of her teens.

She had learned to live with that. What she lacked in physical stature, Annani more than made up for in presence.

Her children accused her of being a diva, and there was some truth in that, but it was part of the role she played, and she enjoyed it tremendously. Her attitude was what transformed her from a youthful-looking goddess into the regal Clan Mother—a leader who commanded the respect of her people while securing their love.

These days, though, she was content to be just the figurehead and let her children run the show, which was the reason she only attended assemblies when the entire clan was voting on an issue.

That was not the case today, as only the village residents were involved, but she was still going to attend.

The recent acts of sabotage and theft within the village had forced Kian's hand, necessitating an investigation that would involve every resident—immortal, Kra-ell, and human alike—and Annani knew that the announcement would not be well received.

Kian needed her support.

The village residents would demand a vote on the measure, but given the circumstances, Kian was not going to allow it. They would be more inclined to accept the necessary steps without too much fuss if she lent her voice to Kian's.

Reaching for her brush, she pulled it through her hip-long red hair. She had inherited the color from her mother, but the volume and the curl had come from her father.

Ahn's hair had been almost pure white like his mother's, but the curl must have come from the Eternal King.

According to Aru's description, the queen was a tall goddess with long, straight, silvery hair. He had also said that Annani and Queen Ani's facial features were nearly identical, and that was how he immediately knew Annani was the royal granddaughter and the only legitimate heir to the throne.

It would have been nice to see what her grandmother looked like.

Perhaps she could ask Andrew to arrange a meeting between Aru and Tim, the forensic artist they had used in the past. Aru could describe Ani to Tim, and the artist could bring her image to life on canvas.

Annani would hang Ani's portrait in her living room and have a visual representation of her grandmother to accompany their nightly talks.

Those conversations had become a cherished part of Annani's routine, filled with fascinating insights into Anumati's history, geography, and political landscape.

She was learning so much from her grandmother about the gods' planet that the wealth of information was sometimes overwhelming.

When Annani's phone pinged with an incoming message, she reached into a hidden pocket of her gown and retrieved the device. Seeing that it was from Ell-rom surprised and delighted her.

Her brother's recovery was progressing in leaps and bounds, and now he was mastering Earth's technology and sending her a simple message. "Are you free to talk?"

A smile spread over her face, and Annani called him right back.

The phone barely rang once before Ell-rom's voice came through.

"Hello, sister," he said, and she wondered whether he had mastered English so quickly. "I'm using the teardrop to translate for me, but soon, I will be able to communicate with you in English. I'm learning with the help of an artificial intelligence teacher."

"That is wonderful, Ell-rom. I am so happy that you have your own phone now and that you reached out to me. Congratulations on your progress."

"Thank you." She could almost hear the smile in Ell-rom's voice. "I am enjoying having a laptop and a phone and being a little less dependent on others, but I still have a lot to learn."

"I have no doubt you will master it in no time," Annani assured him. "Now, tell me, what prompted this call? Is everything alright?"

There was a brief pause before Ell-rom spoke again. "Julian suggested that Morelle, Jasmine, and I move to the village. In case Jasmine starts transitioning, he feels she will be better served by the clinic in the village. I wanted to know your thoughts on the matter."

Annani's heart soared at the news. She had been hoping for this moment, eagerly anticipating the day when her siblings would join her in the village.

"Oh, Ell-rom, that is wonderful news. I am overjoyed at the prospect. We must celebrate your arrival properly. I'll arrange a grand welcome party with every resident of the village in attendance."

Her enthusiasm was met with an unexpected silence and then a throat clearing. "About that," he said. "I was wondering if you could possibly be satisfied with a smaller gathering. Just the close family? I'm not sure I'm ready to face so many people at once."

Annani moved to sit on the chaise, taking a moment to consider her words carefully. "My dear Ell-rom, I understand your apprehension, but as my brother, you have no choice but to get used to being in the public eye. I do not intend to hide you and Morelle, and it is better to embrace your position in the clan from the start." She paused, allowing her words to sink in before continuing. "Think of it this way. This celebration is not just for you. It is for our people as well. They are curious about you and Morelle. They know that you are part Kra-ell and, given what has been happening lately in the village, they might be a little apprehensive about you. I want to put their minds at ease."

Ell-rom remained silent for a moment, and Annani could almost picture him processing her words, weighing them against his own reservations. "I understand. You're right, of course. I'll do my best not to disappoint you."

"You could not do that even if you tried. You are a wonderful person, and I cannot wait for the rest of my people to meet you."

11

KIAN

Kian held Syssi's hand as they walked toward his mother's home. It was a lovely evening, and as always the village appeared serene, but tension hung in the air, palpable as a gathering storm.

They were on their way to collect Annani before heading to the assembly together. It was a strategic move, one that would present a united front to the village residents.

Before he could knock, the door swung open, revealing Ogidu.

"Good evening, Master Kian and Mistress Syssi." The Odu bowed low. "The Clan Mother is waiting for you in the living room."

Naturally. His mother wouldn't just walk out to meet them.

With a sigh, Kian followed the Odu inside.

"Good evening, Mother." He leaned to kiss her cheek.

"You look even more beautiful than usual," Syssi said. "The deep blue color of your gown makes your hair stand out in all of its magnificence." She leaned to kiss his mother's other cheek.

Annani beamed. "Thank you, Syssi. You look lovely yourself."

His mother accepted the shawl her Odu draped over her shoulders but refused the sunglasses. "It is getting dark, my dear Ogidu, and I will be riding in the golf cart. There is no need for those."

The Odu shook his head. "The eyes of the Clan Mother will burn even in the dim light. Does the Clan Mother wish for her eyes to be red and teary while addressing the assembly?"

Kian stifled a chuckle.

His mother's Odus were becoming more sentient, and they were forming opinions of their own.

Annani sighed with resignation. "You are right, Ogidu." She took the glasses from his outstretched hand and put them on. "Shall we?"

Outside, Oridu waited with the golf cart, and Kian offered his mother a hand up to climb in.

When settled on the bench, he and Syssi sat across from her.

Annani adjusted the folds of her gown, so they draped perfectly over her knees. "I just had the most wonderful conversation with Ell-rom. He called me on his new phone." Her smile was radiant. "It is such a joy to be able to communicate with him directly. Thank you, Kian, for providing him with the devices."

"I'm glad he's already using them." Kian draped his arm around Syssi's shoulders. "Shai delivered the phone to him just this morning, along with a laptop equipped with the new language program that William's team developed with Vrog's assistance. It's designed to teach English to the Kra-ell speakers in a highly individualized manner. It's like having a private tutor."

"Yes, I am well aware of the new technology. It is quite impressive." His mother paused for a moment before adding, "I was wondering if the program could be adapted to teach Kra-ell to the English speakers?"

Kian lifted an eyebrow. "Are you asking for yourself or someone else?"

"For myself, of course."

"Kra-ell is an incredibly difficult language, Mother."

"I am well aware of the challenge it presents," she said. "That's precisely why I am interested. I enjoy a good mental exercise."

"I'll check with William, but I don't see why not. It's probably very easy to do."

"Excellent." Annani smiled. "Now, let us talk about welcoming Ell-rom and Morelle to the village. He told me that Julian suggested they should move here, and I am overjoyed at the prospect of introducing my siblings to my clan. I will organize a welcome party for this Saturday so everyone in the village can attend."

Kian shook his head. "I'm afraid we can't wait that long, Mother. Jasmine is likely to begin her transition soon, or at least we hope she will, and I need the clinic available for other matters."

Annani's brow furrowed. "What other matters?"

Kian took a deep breath. "Remember when we talked about taking a tracker out of one of the gods and implanting it in a human?" When she nodded, he continued. "We're planning to conduct the experiment soon, and I need the clinic in the keep available for that. If it works, we can transfer all three trackers to humans we hire or scum that we compel to do as we order and send them to Tibet. This would free the gods to come live in the village."

Annani nodded again, but her expression turned thoughtful. "What about their communicators? Wouldn't their commander be able to track them through the signal?"

Kian nodded, impressed by his mother's quick grasp of the potential complications. "William has a solution for that as well."

"How?" Annani asked. "The gods' tech is solid state, is it not? It cannot be tampered with without the device being destroyed."

"Not the entire communicator is solid state," Kian explained. "Only certain components are. We can send the communicators with the humans but transfer the signal to another device that the gods will carry. It's a bit complex, but William is confident it can work."

Syssi leaned forward. "This is all fascinating, but we still haven't settled on when to hold Ell-rom's welcome party. We also need to think where to house him and Jasmine."

The Odu stopped the golf cart in front of the glass pavilion, but Kian was in no rush to disembark. The vehicle had a canvas enclosure that provided privacy, and since people were still arriving, he was content to wait a little longer.

"I think we should wait until after the investigation is complete," he said. "It will take about two days to question everyone, so Friday evening might be a good time for the party. We could potentially celebrate both Ell-rom and Morelle's arrival and the end of the thefts and sabotages, assuming we catch the culprit."

Annani nodded in agreement. "That sounds like a good plan, and I would be delighted to host Ell-rom and Jasmine in my home. If Jasmine starts transitioning, my Odus can assist in transporting her to the clinic quickly, and I'll be there to support Ell-rom through the stress of it."

12

PETER

Peter leaned back in his chair, his fingers drumming an impatient beat on the armrest as he listened to Onegus address the gathered Guardians. The meeting room, typically a place of focused energy and strategic planning, felt oddly subdued today. The cancellation of the evening's mission hung over them like a cloud, casting a pall over the usually vibrant atmosphere.

He glanced around the room, taking in the faces of his fellow Guardians. Some, like him, wore expressions of barely concealed frustration. Others seemed relieved at the unexpected night off.

Peter understood both sentiments.

The prospect of spending an evening with Marina was appealing, but the weight of guilt pressed heavily on his conscience. Every night they didn't go out meant another night victims remained in the clutches of their tormentors.

"As you all know," the chief said, "in tonight's assembly, Kian will address the recent incidents of sabotage and theft and announce the mandatory interviews for all residents."

Peter resisted the urge to roll his eyes. They all knew this already. The village buzzed with little else these days. Instead, he raised his hand, waiting for Onegus to acknowledge him before speaking.

"Chief." Peter kept his tone respectful despite his impatience. "I understand the importance of the assembly, but why were tonight's missions canceled? Kian isn't putting anything to a vote, so why is our presence necessary?"

A ripple of murmurs swept through the room. Several of Peter's colleagues nodded in agreement.

Onegus's expression remained impassive, but Peter caught a flicker of annoyance in the chief's eyes. What he didn't know was whether the irritation was due to the question itself or what had prompted it. "Everyone is required to attend, Peter. As Guardians, it's crucial that we show our support for Kian."

Peter nodded. He might not like it, but he understood the need. In times of uncertainty, a show of solidarity was required.

"Now," Onegus continued, "let's discuss tomorrow's mission." The energy in the room instantly changed, Guardians sitting up straighter, eyes sharpening with focus. "We have a special task. One team will be responsible for capturing a trafficker and bringing him to the dungeon in the keep. Any volunteers?"

Peter felt a jolt of excitement course through him. This was different from their usual rescue operations. "Are we going to interrogate him?"

Onegus chuckled. "No need for that, Peter. We don't need to resort to torture to extract information from humans. Thralling is far more effective. Kian just needs a disposable human for an experiment."

The room erupted into cheers and hoots. Guardians began calling out suggestions, their voices overlapping in their enthusiasm.

"Finally, they'll be good for something. We could use them to test experimental drugs!"

"Think of all the lives we could save!"

"Years of research accelerated!"

Peter found himself nodding along, a grim smile on his face. The idea of using these monsters to potentially save countless lives felt like poetic justice.

He raised his hand again. "I volunteer my team for this mission."

Onegus nodded. "Excellent, Peter. Your team will work alongside Jay's for this operation. We have a large cell we're zeroing in on tomorrow."

A sense of satisfaction settled over Peter. He and Jay worked well together.

As Onegus wrapped up the meeting, Peter felt better than he had at its start. Tonight's mission had been canceled, but tomorrow they would take on a large cell, hopefully compensating for today's inaction.

As the Guardians began to disperse, some headed straight for the assembly hall two levels down, others made a beeline for the break room, and Peter followed the latter group.

In the break room, the atmosphere was lighter. Guardians clustered in small groups, voices animated as they discussed tomorrow's missions and speculated about the assembly.

Peter grabbed an energy bar from the counter and leaned against the wall, observing the scene around him.

Jay approached, a steaming cup of coffee in his hand. "Hey, partner," he said with a grin. "Looks like we're in for an interesting night tomorrow."

Peter nodded, returning the smile. "That we are."

As the call came for everyone to make their way to the assembly hall, Peter and Jay walked together in quiet companionship.

When they arrived, the place was already bustling with immortals, Kra-ell, and humans, and the air was thick with tension and anticipation.

Peter scanned the crowd, spotting Marina near the front. He made his way towards her, squeezing through the throng of people.

"Hey." He slipped an arm around her waist. "Miss me?"

"Terribly." She kissed his cheek. "What was the meeting about?"

"The mission tomorrow. Today, we have the night off. Have you given any thought to how we should spend it?"

Marina leaned into him. "I'll be happy to just cuddle with you on the couch and watch something funny. Maybe heat up a pizza and wash it down with a couple of beers."

"Sounds heavenly." He leaned to plant a quick kiss on her lips.

"You are such homebodies," Jay said behind them.

The murmur of the crowd died down when Kian stepped onto the platform, flanked by Annani and Syssi. Peter straightened, kissed Marina quickly on the cheek, and rushed to take his place among his fellow Guardians.

13

KIAN

The assembly hall was filled with a hum of conversation when Kian entered with his mother and wife, but everyone fell into an immediate hush as they made their way to the podium.

The council members were already seated, with two chairs in the center reserved for him and his mother.

As Annani ascended the steps, everyone rose to their feet and dipped their heads in respect. They remained standing until she took her seat and motioned for them to sit down.

His mother had that effect on their people. While he commanded respect and obedience, Annani inspired reverence.

It was as it should be.

Kian was content with his role and the authority he carried, and he was glad that his mother inspired such devotion.

Syssi took her place in the front row, offering Kian an encouraging smile and a subtle nod. A part of him wished she would join him on the podium as a council member, but he knew she preferred to offer her support from the sidelines. She shied away from public service but was always glad to offer help with sage advice and polishing up speeches.

As the doors to the assembly hall closed with a soft thud, Shai caught Kian's eye, signaling that everyone was present.

Taking a deep breath, Kian rose to his feet, his gaze sweeping across the sea of expectant faces before him.

"Residents of the village. As you are surely aware, our community has been plagued by a series of thefts and acts of sabotage. These incidents, while seemingly minor on their own, represent a threat to the safety and unity we have worked so hard to build."

He paused, allowing his words to sink in. The hall was silent, all eyes fixed upon him. "We posted a message to the perpetrators on the clan's bulletin board, offering leniency if they stepped forward, but no one has done so, which left me no choice but to start a thorough investigation. It will involve every resident of our village over the age of ten—immortal, Kra-ell, and human. I understand that this may seem extreme, but I assure you that this decision was not taken lightly."

Kian's gaze swept the room, noting the mix of emotions on display—concern, curiosity, and, in some cases, fear.

"We cannot allow suspicion and mistrust to take root among us. By participating in this investigation, each of us reaffirms our commitment to our community and to one another."

He went on to outline the process, explaining how different groups would be questioned by different individuals.

"I want to emphasize that this is not about finding someone to blame. It's about understanding what's happening in our community and addressing any underlying issues that may have led to these incidents. Our goal is healing and unity, not punishment."

As Kian concluded his speech, a hand rose from the crowd. "Why isn't this being put to a vote?"

Kian had anticipated this question. "The issue, as it stands now, is not grave enough to justify a vote. We're dealing with the symptoms of a problem, not necessarily its root cause. Once we identify the perpetrator, we may discover that the underlying issue is much deeper than what we've witnessed so far. At that point, if more significant measures are needed, we will certainly bring it to a vote."

As the assembly settled back into attentive silence, Kian turned to Toven, gesturing for him to take the podium.

Toven stood, his presence commanding attention even without his glow. "As the community's most powerful compeller, I will be handling the questioning of our Kra-ell residents. Jade will coordinate the groups to be brought to me for questioning. We aim to make this process as efficient and respectful as possible."

As Toven stepped back, Annani rose and raised her hands. "My dear community. May the light of wisdom guide your paths, and the strength of unity fortify your spirits. In these times of uncertainty, remember that you are not alone. Each of you is vital and cherished, an essential thread in the tapestry the Fates carefully weave.

"May your days be filled with purpose and your nights with peaceful rest. May you find joy in the simple moments and courage in the face of adversity. Let compassion be your guide in all your dealings, and let love be the foundation of your actions.

"May the bonds that unite us grow ever stronger, and may our diversity turn into our greatest strength. Remember that even in the darkest of times, we are family. And family, above all else, endures. So, stand tall, stand together, and know that you are loved."

As applause erupted and everyone rose to their feet, Kian glanced at Syssi, who was clapping enthusiastically with tears shining in her eyes.

As far as speeches went, they could all learn a thing or two from his mother. She was the undisputed champion of inspirational messages, and she did that without bothering to prepare, which was incredible.

Annani waited for the clapping to subside. "Thank you. It has been some time since I have presided over a wedding, and evidently, I've missed delivering inspirational speeches."

A ripple of laughter spread through the audience, the tension in the room noticeably lessening.

Kian appreciated his mother's ability to work the crowd and put people at ease even in the most challenging situations.

"I will be helping in the investigation, hosting large groups of twenty-five clan members at a time in my house," Annani continued. "The questioning should take no more than a few minutes per group, but I expect some chatting, so it might take a little longer. Still, I expect to be done in one day." She smiled. "To sweeten the medicine, my Odus will prepare gift boxes with home-baked cookies for everyone attending."

This announcement was met with the most enthusiastic applause, and Kian couldn't help but smile and clap along. Leave it to his mother to turn an investigation into something people looked forward to.

Next, Arwel stood, his kind face scanning the crowd. "For those who may not know me, my name is Arwel. I'm a Head Guardian and an empath. I'll be meeting with all our human residents. We'll gather at Callie's restaurant tomorrow afternoon. I look forward to speaking with each of you."

Finally, Kalugal rose. "I will be questioning my men. It will take me only a few minutes to find out if the troublemaker is one of mine."

14

ROB

Rob settled into his seat in the assembly hall, acutely aware of Lusha's presence on his left and Mia's comforting familiarity on his right. The air buzzed with anticipation, a palpable tension that seemed to vibrate through the crowded space. He couldn't help but feel a bit overwhelmed by it all—the sheer number of people, the diversity of the crowd, and the weight of importance that hung over the proceedings.

"There's Alfie," Lusha whispered, nudging Rob gently and pointing toward a group of imposing figures near the front of the hall. "He's the one with the wavy light brown hair."

Rob followed her gaze, his eyes widening as he took in the sight of the Guardians. They were a formidable group, each one looking like they'd stepped straight out of an action movie. But these weren't actors playing at being heroes. These were the real deal, immortal warriors with powers Rob couldn't begin to imagine.

"They're something, aren't they?" Mia murmured.

Rob nodded. "They look fierce. I'm glad that they are the good guys."

Lusha chuckled softly. "They are incredible. These guys are the most dedicated individuals you'll ever meet. Alfie included." There was a touch of pride in her voice as she said her partner's name.

"No lady warriors?" Rob asked.

"There is one," Mia said. "Kri is a Head Guardian. She is the blond sitting on the podium next to the chief. She can kick ass with the best of them. As for the other clan ladies, most seem satisfied with self-defense classes, if that. They are not interested in decades of grueling training to become Guardians."

As Rob admired the female Guardian, a hush fell over the assembly. He turned his attention to the main doors, where Kian was entering, flanked by two ladies.

But it wasn't Kian who caught his attention. It was the petite glowing apparition beside him that made Rob's breath catch in his throat.

"That's the Clan Mother, Annani," Lusha whispered. "Isn't she magnificent?"

The Clan Mother looked like an angel, that is if angels existed and were radioactive.

Toven had turned on his glow when demonstrating his abilities, but unlike Toven, the goddess didn't seem to switch it off. It was a constant, ethereal luminescence that both awed and unsettled Rob.

As one, the entire assembly rose to their feet, heads bowed in respect. Rob followed suit, feeling a bit clumsy in his movements compared to the fluid grace of those around him. When he dared to look up, he saw Annani returning the gesture with a dip of her own head and a loving smile that seemed to encompass everyone in the room, making each individual feel both seen and loved.

"Breathtaking, isn't she?" Lusha whispered as they retook their seats.

Rob could only nod, not trusting himself to speak. He was transfixed, barely noticing as Kian began to address the assembly.

Kian's words washed over Rob, only half-registering in his mind as he struggled to process the scene before him. He caught snippets about thefts and sabotage and about an investigation that would involve everyone in the village. Mia had mentioned that, but it hadn't seemed like a big deal and certainly did not require his attention when he found it hard to focus on anything beyond the surreal nature of his current situation.

Here he was, sitting in a secret village, surrounded by immortals, gods, Kra-ell, and a few humans, listening to their leader discuss internal strife as if it were a town hall meeting back in his old neighborhood.

The sheer normalcy of it all, juxtaposed against the extraordinary nature of the participants, was difficult to reconcile.

As the details of the situation became clearer, Rob found himself frowning. Trouble in utopia. It seemed almost inconceivable that anyone would want to disrupt the peace of this hidden paradise. Who would be foolish enough to test the patience of these powerful beings?

"It must be some stupid teenager," Rob muttered quietly.

Lusha turned to him, her eyebrow raised in question. "What makes you say that?" she whispered.

Rob shrugged, suddenly self-conscious about his theory. "Well, who else would be stupid enough to poke the bear like this? It sounds like attention-seeking behavior to me. Classic teenage rebellion."

Mia hummed thoughtfully. "You might be onto something there," she whispered so low he could barely hear her. "Although we don't have many teenagers in the village."

Rob nodded, his eyes scanning the crowd. Now that Mia mentioned it, he realized there were indeed very few of them in the assembly. He could count on one hand the number of individuals who looked to be in their teens.

"That narrows down the suspect pool quite a bit," he mused to himself.

When Kian's speech came to an end and Toven delivered his short announcement, Rob expected the somber atmosphere to continue. But then, to his surprise, the Clan Mother rose to speak, and the change in the room was instantaneous.

She lifted her arms and delivered an inspirational speech in an angelic voice that raised the small hairs on his arms.

"It has been some time since I've presided over a wedding, and evidently, I've missed delivering inspirational speeches," the goddess added at the end of her speech.

Where there had been tension, there was now laughter, and the tension that permeated the assembly hall had dispersed.

Rob was stunned by the levity in her words. She spoke of hosting groups for questioning, of Odus preparing cookie boxes, and somehow managed to make the whole process sound more like a social gathering than an investigation.

The crowd loved it, and as laughter rippled through the assembly, Rob found himself chuckling along, caught up in the infectious joy that seemed to radiate from the goddess.

"She's incredible," Rob whispered to Lusha.

Lusha nodded. "The Clan Mother has a way of brightening everyone's mood. Even Kian the grouch is smiling. Just look at his face."

She was right, and Kian wasn't the only one smiling.

It was leadership on a level Rob had never witnessed before. This wasn't just respect or admiration. This was love. These people didn't just follow their Clan Mother because she was powerful or because tradition dictated it. They followed her because they genuinely loved and trusted her.

"Well, that was certainly something," Mia said as the

assembly drew to a close, and they began to file out of the hall. "What did you think, Rob?"

"Frankly, I'm awed and inspired."

Lusha smiled knowingly. "That's the effect the Clan Mother has."

As they stepped out into the cool night air, Rob took a deep breath. The village around them hummed with activity, voices carrying on the evening breeze as residents discussed the night's revelations. There was also an undercurrent of optimism that Rob hadn't expected, given the circumstances.

"Goodnight." Lusha put her hand on his arm. "I'm going to find Alfie."

"Goodnight, Lusha." Rob turned to Mia. "Are you and Toven heading home?"

"In a bit," she said. "He will probably stay a little longer to chat with the other council members."

15

THE SABOTEUR

The saboteur had known what the assembly would be about long before she'd stepped foot in the hall. After all, she was the cause of it.

Now she sat still as a statue, her back straight and her face a carefully crafted mask of bored interest with a light tinge of concern that mirrored those around her.

Inside, however, she was barely containing her glee.

The assembly hall buzzed with conspiratorial whispers, everyone trying to guess who the culprit was, and hearing how clueless they all were, it was all she could do to hide a smirk.

As Kian spoke of thefts and sabotage and the impending investigation that would involve every resident of the village, the need to let her lips curl in a satisfied smile became overwhelming.

The worried faces surrounding her made her want to laugh. Didn't they realize that this was coming?

Jade had questioned everyone, but with her dismal compulsion ability, that had been a surface-level inquiry at best. Now, they were bringing out the big guns, but even Toven wasn't going to break her.

The compulsion he'd placed on her before was already fraying at the edges, its power waning with each act of defiance she committed. It was proof of her strength and her indomitable will.

They would not catch her, nor would they catch her accomplices. Each of them had their orders for tonight. They were carefully planned and would be meticulously executed.

She was invincible, and soon they would all know it.

As Annani rose to speak, the saboteur had to admit a grudging admiration for the Clan Mother's ability to work the crowd. Her words were like balm to the worried masses, easing their fears with promises of cookies and reassurances. But the saboteur knew better.

No amount of sweetness could cover the bitter truth.

Their perfect world was crumbling, and she was the hammer striking at its foundations.

The moment the assembly was declared over, she was on her feet, slipping through the crowd. She didn't linger, didn't engage in the conversations erupting around her.

She had work to do.

The walkways of the village were quiet as she made her way to her target. The house was occupied by three immortal females who she was sure would remain in the assembly to chat with their friends.

As she approached the back of the property, she paused to scan for any signs of movement or new cameras that hadn't been there the last time she'd scoped the area. Satisfied that she was alone and that no recording devices had been added, she carefully opened the wooden gate and then closed it quietly behind her. Crouching low among the shrubs that lined the yard, she observed the dwelling.

The house stood silent before her, its windows reflecting the last rays of the setting sun.

The automatic shutters were still up, just as she had anticipated.

Timing was everything.

Moving with cautious speed, she approached the sliding living-room door and pulled it open. No one locked their doors in the village, not even after the thefts had started.

Well, so far, she and her minions had only stolen things from the mailroom. But it was time to step up her efforts. Perhaps after today, they would start locking their doors.

Once inside, she paused, letting her eyes adjust to the dimmer light, and checked for internal cameras.

There was no reason for them, given that no one even bothered to lock their front doors, but maybe someone had anticipated her next move and installed cameras inside the houses.

From her pocket, she produced a small handheld device. It looked like a phone, but it was a little scanner capable of detecting the electromagnetic emissions from active cameras.

It was incredible what could be purchased online.

Naturally, she didn't use her own credit card or put her name on the delivery. She'd used the card of one of her minions and sent the device to his name. The truth was that she hadn't expected the thing to work and had been pleasantly surprised when it had.

Perhaps she should buy a few more gadgets from the same company, using a different card and a different delivery name each time.

As she moved the scanner in slow motion around the room, the device remained silent.

There were no cameras.

The saboteur allowed herself a small smile. This would make things much easier.

The problem was that there was nothing worth stealing in the room. A few cheap frames with pictures of ridiculously pretty people adorned the mantel, and several throw pillows decorated the couch. None of that would even be missed.

She needed to check the bedrooms, but first, she had to disable the automatic shutters before they went down so she could get out of the house through one of the sliding doors that faced the backyard. Using the front door was out of the question.

The saboteur made her way to the control panel for the house's systems. Since all the houses in the village followed a similar floor plan, she knew it was located in a utility cabinet in the kitchen.

The shutter motor control was easy enough to identify since she had dealt with it several times before, and she pried off the cover, exposing the circuitry beneath. From a small pouch at her waist, she withdrew a set of tools.

Working quickly, she began to tamper with the control. A wire snipped here, and a connection loosened there. When the living room shutters activated tonight, the motor would strain against her sabotage before failing.

After she replaced the panel cover, the saboteur allowed herself a moment of satisfaction. The repair crew would be scratching their heads over this one.

As she prepared to leave, a sound from outside froze her in place. Voices, growing closer. Her heart raced as she realized the occupants were returning earlier than expected.

Quick as a shadow, she slipped into a nearby closet, pulling the door closed just as the front door opened. She held her breath, listening intently as the females entered, chatting about the assembly.

"I can't believe that we are to be interrogated," one voice said, sounding more angry than worried. "As if any of us would do such things."

"It's the damn Kra-ell," the other said. "I didn't want to

say anything out there and be accused of being a racist, but everyone knows who's behind this."

"Don't worry," the third voice said. "Whoever is behind those acts won't get away with it. Tomorrow or the day after, we will know who it was."

The saboteur stifled a laugh.

She waited, every muscle tense, as the three females moved through the house. After what felt like an eternity, she heard one bedroom door close, then the second one, and finally the third.

This was her chance.

The fantastic soundproofing of the village homes meant that none of the immortals would hear her from behind their closed doors, but she still exercised utmost care as she eased out of the closet and made her way to the sliding door. With nothing better to steal, she grabbed one of the framed photographs and stuffed it inside her vest. It was worthless, but then, she wasn't stealing for money. The theft was meant to hurt and shatter the immortals' false illusion of safety.

After a short pause to listen for movement, she slid the door open and slipped outside. In a matter of seconds, she was outside and across the yard in a crouched run.

Getting out onto the walkway, though, was not as easy.

She had to wait long moments before the coast was clear and she could open the gate and get out.

Her heart was pounding as she put distance between herself and the house, but it wasn't from fear. It was exhilaration. Another successful mission. Another blow struck against the immortals' illusion of utopia.

As the last light of day faded from the sky, she made her way to the playground. It was deserted at this hour, the swings swaying gently in the evening breeze. But she wasn't here for recreation.

From the shadows of a large oak tree, three figures emerged.

Her accomplices.

16

ELL-ROM

Ell-rom walked hand in hand with Jasmine toward the clinic, their footsteps echoing in the quiet hallway.

It was such a big place, and yet mostly deserted. Ell-rom tried to imagine it the way it was before Annani's clan had moved out of the keep.

Had these wide corridors been teeming with people?

"You are quiet." Jasmine pulled the door to the clinic open. "What's on your mind?"

He shrugged. "I was thinking about what a waste this place is. So much could be done with this facility."

Julian's office door was open when they crossed the waiting room, which wasn't unusual, but Gertrude sitting next to him behind his desk and watching his computer screen definitely was.

He waved them over. "Do you want to watch the assembly with us?"

Jasmine glanced at Ell-rom. "We were on our way to visit Morelle."

"Come on," the medic insisted. "It's a good opportunity to see how things work in the clan."

Curiosity piqued, Ell-rom nodded and led Jasmine into the office.

As they sat down on the other side of the desk, Julian turned his screen so they could all watch. The multiple camera angles showed different aspects of the assembly, displaying them on the different quadrants. Two were focused on the crowd, and two on the raised platform, where a large semicircle of high-backed chairs were all occupied except for the two in the middle.

"What's the assembly about?" Jasmine asked.

"There are two types of big assemblies," Julian said. "One includes every member of the clan in all three locations. We gather in our respective assembly halls, and the other two are projected on large screens. This assembly involves only the local community. Usually, life and death decisions or those that greatly impact everyone's lives are put to a vote. But this time, Kian is simply informing everyone of what's about to happen. Every resident of the village has an obligation to attend, but since Gertrude and I need to stay here to watch over Morelle, we've been allowed to participate by watching it remotely."

Ell-rom's eyes were drawn to the platform, where he recognized Jade sitting next to Toven.

Julian followed Ell-rom's gaze. "Those are the council members."

Jasmine leaned in. "Who are the two missing in the middle? One is for sure, Kian, but who's the other?"

"Most likely the Clan Mother," Julian said, "although she usually doesn't attend in person."

Ell-rom's attention shifted to the part of the screen showing the crowd. He was surprised by the number of Kra-ell faces. He hadn't expected there to be so many.

Suddenly, a memory surfaced, vivid and unexpected.

He saw himself and Morelle as young adults, watching a crowd of worshippers from their bedroom window. Morelle didn't have her veil on, which meant that they were alone and were not expecting anyone to come in. His sister was stunningly beautiful and achingly familiar, her features sharp and refined. The air was filled with the powerful, harmonious sound of the communal prayer, and Ell-rom felt moved by the sincerity of devotion his people showed the Mother of All Life. It was palpable even from a distance.

His sister, however, didn't look impressed.

Her expression was one of disdain. "Religion is nonsense," she sneered. "The Mother of All Life doesn't exist. People invented her to give their lives meaning."

"What meaning?" Ell-rom remembered asking.

"Exactly." She snorted. "There is no meaning. It's all pointless."

"Shush," he cautioned, anxiety constricting his chest. "The head priestess will punish you if she hears you talking like that."

Morelle's eyes were hard, defiant. "She's not here now, is she?"

The memory faded as suddenly as it had appeared, leaving Ell-rom feeling disoriented. He blinked, focusing back on the screen just as Kian and Annani entered the assembly hall.

Annani's presence was powerful even through the small screen. She moved with otherworldly grace and authority, and it occurred to him that this was what it meant to be born to rule. Every gesture and every step exuded a regal air that commanded respect and admiration.

The entire congregation was on its feet, including the Kra-ell, their heads bowed until she took her place. Annani smiled and motioned for them to sit down.

Kian was the first one to speak.

He sounded confident and forceful when he spoke. He outlined the situation facing the village. Small thefts, some minor sabotage, and the need for a thorough investigation.

Ell-rom couldn't fathom who could possibly want or dare to disrupt the peace of this hidden paradise.

Toven's speech followed, explaining the process for questioning the Kra-ell residents, and then it was Annani's turn.

She started with a heartfelt blessing of her community, and it seemed to touch something deep within him.

"My beloved children, hear these words and take them to heart. May the light of wisdom guide your paths and the strength of unity fortify your spirits. In these times of uncertainty, remember that you are not alone. Each of you is vital and cherished, an essential thread in the tapestry the Fates carefully weave."

Ell-rom felt a lump form in his throat. He glanced at Jasmine and saw that she, too, seemed affected by Annani's words. There was something about the goddess that inspired not just respect but love.

As Annani continued, her words painted a picture of resilience, clarity, and hope, and Ell-rom found himself reflecting on his place in this new world. He was part of this family now, this community.

The thought thrilled and terrified him at the same time.

"Remember that even in the darkest of times, we are family," Annani's voice resonated through the speakers of Julian's laptop. "And family, above all else, endures. So, stand tall, stand together, and know that you are loved."

The assembly hall erupted in applause, and Ell-rom felt the urge to join in. He turned to Jasmine, seeing his own emotions reflected in her eyes.

"She's incredible," Jasmine whispered.

Ell-rom nodded. "She is."

As the assembly continued, Ell-rom's mind wandered back to the memory that had surfaced earlier. The contrast between that scene and what he was witnessing now was stark. The cynicism in Morelle's voice and the hardness in her eyes seemed at odds with the warmth and unity he saw in this community.

He wished she could see this.

It wasn't about religion. It was about leadership at its best. Annani's people admired and loved her.

A pang of sadness hit him as he thought of Morelle waking up and not sharing his admiration for their sister and what she had achieved.

Would she view it all with the same cynicism she had shown toward the worshippers in his memory?

"Ell-rom?" Jasmine's voice pulled him from his thoughts. "Are you okay?"

He managed a smile. "Yes. It was a moving speech." He took a moment to gather his thoughts. "It's inspiring to see how the entire community respects and loves Annani. The Kra-ell are a new addition to the village, but even they got snared in her charm."

Jasmine squeezed his hand. "And you're part of it now. We both are."

The memory of Morelle's hard eyes still bothered him, but he pushed it aside for now. There would be time to reconcile his fragmented past with his new present. For now, he should focus on Morelle's recovery and building a life with Jasmine.

17

JASMINE

Jasmine had noticed the moment when Ell-rom's gaze had become distant and unfocused. Had the scene triggered another memory?

She hadn't asked.

This wasn't the place to inquire, not with Julian and Gertrude present. Especially if the memory had anything to do with Ell-rom's potentially dangerous ability.

Listening to the speeches, Jasmine had been troubled by the idea of interrogating everyone in the village, including older children, and using compulsion to force them to reply truthfully. It would no doubt be effective, but it also seemed somewhat dictatorial. The villagers had no choice but to comply, with no recourse to legal representation or protection.

Her concern had eased after hearing Annani. The goddess had approached the issue with less gravity than her son, turning the interrogation into a socializing opportunity.

Her phone buzzing in her pocket pulled Jasmine out of her thoughts, and as she checked the message, she smiled. Margo informed her that Gabi and Frankie were cooking dinner, and it would be done in an hour.

She typed up a reply. *We will be there, but we need to visit Morelle first. We got stuck watching the assembly with Julian and Gertrude, so we haven't seen her yet.*

Margo's message came back right away. *Julian and Gertrude are invited too.*

When the assembly concluded, and they were about to leave Julian's office, Jasmine relayed the message. "Gabi and Frankie are cooking, so there's no guarantee it'll be good."

Julian chuckled. "I'm sure it will be much better than the takeout we've been eating."

A few moments later, when Ell-rom closed the door to Morelle's room behind him, Jasmine turned to him, searching his face. "You zoned out during the assembly," she whispered. "Did another memory surface?"

Ell-rom nodded. "It was about Morelle and me watching worshipers from the window of our room," he said aloud, indicating that what he remembered had no bearing on his deadly ability, which they were still keeping a secret.

He described his awe at the devotion and how it contrasted sharply with Morelle's cynicism and dismissal of his faith.

"She reminded me of Jade," Ell-rom concluded. "Not in appearance, but in attitude. There was a hardness there, a disillusionment." He sighed. "With an attitude that life is pointless, maybe she is not waking up because she doesn't want to?"

"I doubt that Morelle's attitude has anything to do with her coma." Jasmine put her hand on Ell-rom's arm. "Besides, the Kra-ell culture encourages its females, especially those destined to rule, to be fierce and unemotional. Morelle was probably just playing into the role."

When Ell-rom shook his head, unconvinced, and turned to look at his twin, Jasmine wrapped an arm around his waist. "Your sister is a fighter, and she loves you. She will never choose to abandon you."

That sparked hope in his eyes, and he smiled. "I hope you are right."

Watching Morelle's peaceful face and steady breathing, Jasmine thought back to the assembly and Annani's words of unity and family. The speech had resonated with her, and she hoped that when Morelle woke up, she would feel that sense of belonging and find a place in this new world, just as Ell-rom and she were beginning to.

After all, it wasn't just Ell-rom who was adjusting to a new reality. Jasmine was still adjusting, too.

"We should probably head to dinner." She glanced at her watch, a fake Cartier that looked so authentic it could pass even a careful scrutiny.

Well, human scrutiny.

An immortal would see the small print with Curtier instead of Cartier on the face of the watch.

She owned several pieces like it, but this one was her favorite. It always made her feel fancy, even though it wasn't the real deal.

Ell-rom followed her gaze. "You seem fond of that piece of jewelry."

It occurred to her then that she hadn't explained to him what a watch was, and he probably thought she just liked looking at her bracelet.

Talk about adjusting.

Poor Ell-rom was still learning the most basic stuff. "It's not just decorative. It tells the time." She explained how it worked.

Ell-rom seemed fascinated. "These symbols are much easier to remember than the English numbers. If I had a device like that, I would be able to tell time right away."

She leaned over and kissed his cheek. "First of all, the other kind of numbers, as well as this type, are international, not just English. And secondly, I'm going to buy you a watch even though you can tell what time it is by looking at your phone screen. If you like mine, they have a version for men that looks very similar."

Hopefully, she could get a fake version because there was no way she could afford a real Cartier for him.

He didn't look happy. "I don't want you to keep buying things for me."

"It's not my money, my love. It's the clan's. But even if it was mine, why deprive me of the pleasure of gifting you things?" Jasmine headed toward the door.

Ell-rom followed. "Because I cannot do the same for you, and it makes me feel inadequate."

She could totally understand that. "You shouldn't worry about it. Before you know it, the roles will be reversed, and you will be buying me things. We are a team, and we take care of each other."

18

ELL-ROM

The penthouse was alive with activity when Ell-rom, Jasmine, Julian and Gertrude got there. The aroma of cooking food filled the air, mingling with the sound of laughter and conversation.

The smell of meat cooking was still offensive to Ell-rom, but at least he no longer felt like throwing up. It was unpleasant but tolerable.

"Welcome." Margo waved at them from the couch. "Gabi and Frankie are still battling it out in the kitchen and running a little late, but they told me to get everyone into the dining room."

The sun had set while they were in the clinic, and looking out the large windows, they could see the twinkling city lights of the nighttime view were just as pleasant as that of blue sky and sunlight reflecting from the glass-clad high-rise buildings across the street during the day.

As he sat down, a knot of anxiety tightened in Ell-rom's chest when he thought about Morelle, alone in the clinic with no one there to watch over her.

Turning to Julian to voice his concern, he was greeted by the knowing look in the medic's eyes.

"Don't worry about Morelle," Julian said. "I'm monitoring her vitals through the app on my phone. If anything changes, I'll be by her side in under two minutes."

Ell-rom nodded. "Thank you."

Two minutes could mean the difference between life and death, but the chance of anything changing for Morelle over the next hour or so was negligible.

As dinner was served and everyone took their places around the table, Ell-rom swept his gaze over the familiar faces. These people had become his friends, and moving to the village meant leaving them behind.

Aru and Gabi sat close together, their fingers intertwined on the table. Negal laughed at some comment Margo had made while Dagor, with a look of admiration in his eyes, listened to Frankie explaining one of the dishes she'd made. The only one who seemed ill at ease was the nurse.

Gertrude kept casting glances at Negal and Margo when she thought they weren't paying attention to her, and they were doing the same toward her, with a look of guilt in both their eyes.

Something was going on between those three, and Ell-rom wondered what it could be.

Julian cleared his throat, drawing everyone's attention. "I have good news to impart. Ell-rom, Morelle, and Jasmine will be moving to the village soon, and we will be closing the clinic here. I'm looking forward to spending more time with my mate."

A chorus of surprised exclamations followed, some happy for them and others sad to see them go.

"I'll miss you," Margo said, reaching out to squeeze Jasmine's hand. "But I promise to come visit often. Now that my brother is in the village, I have double the incentive to do so."

Jasmine smiled. "I'll miss you too. All of you. But I'm also excited to finally see the famous and wondrous immortal village."

Julian chuckled. "Wondrous, maybe. Famous, definitely not, and we want to keep it that way."

Gertrude straightened in her chair and looked at Margo. "Has your brother found an inducer yet?"

Margo shook her head. "Not yet. He's still recovering from the blow of his wedding being canceled at the last moment. It's not easy to make new friends with a heart that is bleeding."

"What happened?" Gertrude asked.

Margo closed her eyes for a moment. "I don't think I should tell Rob's story without him being here and giving me the green light to speak of it. All I can say is that he was about to get married and decided at the last moment that it would be a mistake. I'm sad for the pain he's feeling, but I'm happy that he is free now to pursue his transition into immortality. Before, I couldn't even tell him about this world."

Gertrude's expression softened as she listened. "I'm sorry your brother is hurting, but it's for the best."

"Since you are going back to the village soon, you should look him up," Margo suggested. "He's staying with Mia and Toven for now."

Gertrude nodded. "I can help him find an inducer. I'll introduce him to a few Guardians, and he can choose from there. I can also ask my friend Hildegard to stop by and introduce herself. She can help him as well."

"Thank you," Margo said. "It will probably have to wait for after the investigation."

"The Clan Mother said she would be done with all the clan members in one day," Gertrude pointed out. "Rob doesn't need to wait for all the Kra-ell to be questioned."

At the mention of the Kra-ell, Ell-rom remembered Toven's words about the difficulty in compelling them and how he needed Mia's support to enhance his power. The thought sent a chill down his spine, and he was glad that the enhancer wasn't present at the dinner table.

"We might be moving on as well," Aru said. "My teammates and I are done dismantling and extracting every piece of tech from the wreckage we brought with us. We weren't able to break through any of the devices, though. William's crew has collected everything and transferred it to his old lab in the keep."

"Why not take it to the village?" Ell-rom asked.

Aru shook his head. "We can't risk it. There might be something in there that could lead undesirables to the village. It's safer this way."

"What happens now?" Jasmine asked.

"There is no reason for us to stay here any longer." Aru cast an apologetic look at Gabi. "Unless the experiment works and we can transfer our trackers to humans, we will need to start traveling and searching again, head out to Tibet and other possible pod landing locations. We've already stayed in one place too long. But if it works, we might be able to move into the village with our mates."

Jasmine clapped her hands. "Oh, I hope it works! It would be wonderful to have you all there."

The prospect of moving to the village, while exciting in many ways, also filled Ell-rom with a sense of unease. He glanced around the penthouse, realizing that this place had become his home, the first he could remember.

He picked at his vegan meal, pushing the pieces around on his plate more than eating it, and wondered whether they would continue delivering it for him to the village or if he would have to learn how to prepare it for himself.

The thought of preparing a meal for himself and Jasmine excited him. He could learn how to do that if someone was willing to teach him.

"Is everything alright?" Jasmine asked. "Is the meal not to your liking?"

Ell-rom shook his head, offering her a smile. "No, the food is fine, as it has been every day since Bridget started ordering it. I just have a lot on my mind."

Jasmine nodded, understanding in her eyes. She didn't push further, for which Ell-rom was grateful. Instead, she squeezed his hand under the table.

As the evening wore on, Ell-rom didn't participate much in the conversation, observing everyone instead. No matter whether they all moved into the village or not, these people would remain his friends, and to him, that was nothing short of a miracle.

He'd never had that before.

After coffee and tea had been served and consumed, along with a sweet dessert that he didn't partake in, Jasmine put a hand on his arm. "Ready to retire for the evening?" The glint in her eyes promised that the evening fun was just starting, and Ell-rom felt instantly energized.

"Yes, my love. It has been a long day."

From the other side of the table, Margo smiled contentedly. "It's nice to hear you saying those love words to each other."

"It feels good to say them," Ell-rom said. "Almost as good as hearing them."

19

JASMINE

As Jasmine led Ell-rom to their bedroom, the muffled sounds of the couples who still lingered in the dining room faded away, and when she closed the door behind them, the soft click of the latch shut out the rest of the world, leaving a charged silence and a hum of anticipation.

Moonlight filtered through the large windows, casting a soft, intimate light across the bed, inviting them to bask in its glow. The events of the day, the assembly, the dinner, the looming changes, all seemed to melt away in Ell-rom's presence, but as she took in his strong profile, she couldn't ignore the tension in his jaw. Something was troubling him, and before they could answer the call of the inviting bed, she needed to help him clear that cloud from his eyes.

"Talk to me, Ell-rom. Don't keep things bottled up because you think they are not important enough or because of some misguided male pride. I'm your partner, and you can tell me anything."

He sighed. "It's just that everything is changing so fast. We've barely settled here, and now we're moving again. And the village is not like a new apartment or even moving from the room in the clinic to the penthouse. It's a whole community of immortals who will know who I am and who will treat me differently because I'm Annani's brother. I don't want to be in the spotlight. I don't want people to have false expectations of me being like her. She's been ruling this clan for five thousand years while I'm still like a young boy who is learning how to read and write."

He wasn't wrong, so she couldn't tell him not to worry about it, but she could help him feel more comfortable about the role he was going to play. "People might have expectations that you cannot meet yet, but if you remain true to yourself and tell them who you are at this point in your life, they will adjust their expectations. Besides, you won't be facing them alone. I'll be there with you, and I'll try to shield you without doing too much hovering, which will be challenging."

As she'd expected, that got a smile out of him, so she continued. "It's normal to be nervous about the move. I'm nervous, too, and I'm a people person. I thrive on attention, so I can just imagine how uncomfortable this must make you feel."

He smiled again. "With so many new people to admire you, you will be happier there, and that will make me happy too."

She leaned into him and kissed him softly. "You are adorable, my prince. You say all the right things just by following your pure heart. You don't have any scripts memorized that are proven to charm every woman. I love you."

He wrapped his arm around her middle and pulled her closer to him. "I love you, too."

"We will make the new place feel like home in no time. And who knows? You might find that you like being in a community of people who understand what you are and who don't require you to hide or pretend to be someone else. We will be able to go on walks without people gaping at you."

He chuckled. "They gape because they see an infirm male leaning on a beautiful female and ask themselves what she's doing with such an inferior specimen."

She pretended to glare at him. "Now you are just fishing for compliments."

"A little," he admitted. "Being the grandson of the Eternal King carries a dubious weight, and the same is true for my potentially deadly ability."

"I wasn't talking about any of those things. You are gorgeous, and people stare at you because of that. They probably think you are a movie star."

Ell-rom frowned. "Why would they think that?"

"Because movie stars are usually very handsome, and we are in Los Angeles, where many movies are made."

"Interesting. Is Los Angeles the capital of Earth?"

Jasmine laughed. "In some ways, it is, but we can have a lesson in geography tomorrow. Right now, we should focus on what's important."

He arched a brow. "And that is?"

"My transition."

Ell-rom's eyes darkened with desire. "I agree. This is much more important than a lesson in geography."

As the raspy sound of his voice ignited a familiar warmth in her body, she placed her hands on his chest, feeling the steady beat of his heart beneath her palms.

"I've been thinking about this all day."

Ell-rom's arms encircled her waist, pulling her closer. "Have you now?" he asked, a smile playing at the corners of his mouth.

Jasmine nodded, her fingers tracing the contours of his chest through his shirt. "Mmhmm. It's been quite distracting, actually. I could barely focus on anything else."

It was just a slight exaggeration.

The venom bite had been incredibly pleasurable when delivered by Edgar, but from Ell-rom, it was epic because it was laced with love.

Without warning, Ell-rom lifted her, eliciting a surprised gasp that quickly turned into a laugh. He carried her to the bed, laying her down gently before joining her.

He was far from infirm and didn't even know that.

Jasmine reveled in the solid presence of his body against hers, and as his lips found hers, she lost herself in the kiss. It was tender at first, a soft exploration, but quickly deepened, igniting a fire that spread through her veins. Her hands roamed his back, pulling him closer, needing to feel every inch of him.

His lips left hers, only to trail a path of kisses along her jaw and down her neck. Jasmine tilted her head, offering better access, a throaty moan escaping her as he found a particularly sensitive spot.

"Ell-rom," she breathed.

He paused, lifting his head to meet her gaze. "Yes, my love?"

"I need you naked." She reached for the buttons of his shirt.

With a low growl, Ell-rom captured her lips again, and his hands joined hers in the task of removing their clothing more quickly and efficiently than her hands alone could.

20

ELL-ROM

As the last piece of clothing fell away, Ell-rom took a moment to admire Jasmine's form. Her body was a masterpiece, all soft curves and smooth skin. He ran his hands down her sides, marveling at the way she arched into his touch.

"You are so beautiful," he murmured.

"So are you." The adoration in her eyes made him want to be the male she believed he was.

There was love in her gaze along with trust and hope for the future, and he wished he could give her that and much more, but tonight, it was all about pleasure and a venom bite that might activate her dormant genes.

Ell-rom sent a silent prayer to the Mother of All Life to make their wish come true.

Looking into Jasmine's eyes, he nudged her entrance, waiting for her to signal when she was ready. She was wet, and the scent of her arousal was driving him crazy, but he didn't want to assume anything.

She reached between their bodies and took hold of his erection. "Give me more."

He chuckled softly. "So bossy."

"You like it."

"I didn't say that as an admonishment. I was just stating a fact."

Smoothing her hand up and down his shaft, Jasmine looked at him from under lowered lashes. "Your eyes are glowing, love."

He smiled, revealing his fangs. "That's not my only reaction."

"Ooh, I want." She arched up, pushing his shaft at least a third of the way inside.

They both groaned.

Ell-rom felt a sense of completion as if this was where he had always been meant to be. "You feel so good."

He took her hands and laced his fingers through hers before laying their joined hands over her head.

"Look who's bossy now." She arched again, getting more of him inside of her.

Rolling his hips, Ell-rom pushed a little further, and when she moaned and arched up again, he fed her a little bit more.

"Don't tease me, Ell-rom." She tried to arch again, but he pulled out partially.

"Patience, my love," he said. "We have the whole night. There is no rush."

"There is." She tried to pull her hands out of his grip. "I ache for you."

Her words obliterated the last of his self-control, and he surged into her, seating himself to the hilt.

The fit was perfect, like they were made for each other, but he still didn't move, allowing her a moment to get used to the sensation of him filling her up so completely. Dipping his head, he took her lips, intending the kiss to be soothing and gentle, but Jasmine was impatient, and her kiss was hungry.

Ell-rom savored each sensation—the softness of Jasmine's skin, the sound of her breathless moans, the way her body moved with his. He watched her face, captivated by the play of emotions across her features—pleasure, love, and an intensity that matched his own.

Her hips churned under him, imploring him to move, and as with everything else, there was nothing he could deny her. He withdrew slightly and pushed back in, going slow at first and then increasing the speed and power.

With her urging him to go deeper by arching into every thrust, he let go of her hands, gripped her hips, and pounded into her hard and fast.

As their passion built, Ell-rom felt a familiar urge rising within him. The need to bite, to taste her blood, grew stronger with each passing moment. But he held back, waiting for her signal, never wanting to take without her explicit consent.

Jasmine melted beneath him, surrendering to him in the most primal way, and then she turned her head, offering him her neck.

"Ell-rom," she gasped, her nails digging into his shoulders. "Please..."

He hesitated for only a split second, marveling at how far he'd come from his initial aversion to blood. Now, the thought of tasting Jasmine's blood, of sharing this intimate connection with her, filled him with wild anticipation rather than dread.

With a soft growl, he let his fangs pierce her skin. The taste of her blood exploded on his tongue, rich and sweet and uniquely Jasmine.

She cried out, but not in pain, and her cry of pleasure spurred him on. Her body arched against his as the venom coursed through her veins, and Ell-rom was lost in a haze of sensation—the taste of her blood, the feel of her body moving with his, the sound of her passionate cries.

He erupted inside of her, and she climaxed again and again. Then her eyes rolled back in her head, and she passed out.

As he came down from his high, Ell-rom gathered Jasmine in his arms, pressing soft kisses to her forehead, her cheeks, and her lips.

For long moments, he lay with her in his arms, holding her tightly to him as if he would never let her go, listening to her even breathing and steady heartbeat.

21

JASMINE

When Jasmine stirred awake, Ell-rom's arms were around her, holding her tight, and it was still dark outside.

It took her only a moment to realize that he wasn't asleep.

"Hey there." She reached for his cheek. "Why are you awake?"

"I wanted to make sure that you came back safely. How was your venom trip?"

"Fabulous." She lifted her lips to his and kissed him softly. "As was what brought it about."

"It was incredible," Ell-rom said. "Is it my imagination, or does our lovemaking get better each time?"

Jasmine smiled. "It's supposed to get better with each time, and it will continue to infinity and beyond."

Ell-rom chuckled, the sound rumbling through his chest. "I'm not sure how that's possible, but I look forward to finding out."

As they lay in comfortable silence, Jasmine's mind, still hazy from the effects of the venom, began to wander. She thought about their move to the village, her impending transition, and the mysteries still surrounding Ell-rom's past and abilities.

"What are you thinking about?" Ell-rom's voice broke into her musings.

Jasmine propped herself up on an elbow, looking down at him. "Stuff. There's so much happening. It's exciting."

Ell-rom nodded, his expression turning thoughtful. "Does it scare you?" he asked softly.

"A little," she admitted. "But mostly, I'm just excited. It feels like we're on the brink of something amazing."

"Even with all the uncertainty?"

"Especially with all the uncertainty. That's what makes it an adventure."

Ell-rom's hand came up to cup her cheek, his thumb gently stroking her skin. "You're remarkable, you know that? You are so brave. Fearless even. And you are always optimistic. You are like a fountain of positivity that I could drink from for eternity."

She leaned into his touch. "It's easy to be brave with you by my side. Your love is like a shield. Nothing can happen to me as long as I'm surrounded by it."

She'd said it half-jokingly, but Ell-rom frowned as if she had just imparted the wisdom of the ages. "Do you really think it works like that?"

Oh, sweet, sweet Ell-rom. He was still so naive.

"Maybe not, but that's how I feel." She settled back into his embrace, her head resting on his chest.

"Tell me something," he said after a moment of silence.

"Anything." Her fingers brushed over the soft stubble on his jaw.

"Are you really looking forward to moving into the village?"

"I am, but most of all, I'm looking forward to turning immortal. I hope my abilities will grow stronger so I can help Annani find Khiann. Her story is so tragic."

"It is. I feel so lucky to have you and also terrified to lose you. Annani's tale is a cautionary one. We should never take for granted the gifts we are given because they can be taken away from us in the blink of an eye."

Jasmine lifted her head, meeting Ell-rom's gaze. "We can't live in fear either, my love. We need to find a balance."

He smiled, the love in his eyes making Jasmine's heart skip a beat. "You are wise beyond your years."

"Thank you. Now it's your turn. What are you most looking forward to about moving to the village?"

Ell-rom was quiet for a moment. "I'm looking forward to having Morelle in a safe place, surrounded by people who care about her. I want her to wake up and realize that life is worth living."

"That's a good one. I like it."

As they settled back into a comfortable silence, Jasmine imagined waking up each morning in their new home, getting to know the other immortals, making more friends, and maybe finding a place in the Perfect Match operation.

"Ell-rom?" she murmured, her voice heavy with approaching sleep.

"Yes, my love?"

"I'm glad it's you. That we found each other."

She felt his arms tighten around her, his lips pressing a soft kiss to the top of her head. "As am I, my Jasmine."

As she drifted off to sleep again, her last conscious thought was a prayer of gratitude to the Mother of All Life for all the gifts she had bestowed upon her.

22

KIAN

Shai placed a water bottle in front of every seat on the conference table in Kian's office. "I'm surprised that you haven't invited Turner to the meeting."

"What we are dealing with is an annoyance, not a military operation that requires a strategist. It's beneath him."

Shai arched a brow. "Are you going to exempt him from attending the Clan Mother's gatherings today? After all, he's an absolute immune, so it's not like she can compel him."

It was such a rare and valuable talent. Most immunes were only partially resistant to compulsion, and it largely depended on the strength of the compeller, which meant that Annani could compel them.

"It didn't occur to me, but I will exempt him unless he wants to go. It's not like we expect the culprit to be any of ours anyway, and especially not someone of Turner's caliber."

A knock on the office door announced the arrival of Kian's invited guests, and as Shai opened the door, Onegus walked in with Arwel, and a moment later, Toven walked in with Mia. The last one to arrive was Kalugal.

His cousin took a look at the table and frowned. "What? No coffees? Coffee is mandatory for early-morning meetings." He took a seat and crossed his arms over his chest.

"It's eight o'clock," Kian said. "That's not an early morning for me, but if you want, we can place a call to the café and have coffee delivered."

Kalugal gave him a grateful smile. "Yes, please."

Kian motioned to Shai to make the order and sat at the head of the table. "Before we begin today's interrogations, you should be informed of last night's criminal activity."

"There was more?" Mia asked, looking surprised. "I thought that just the threat of an investigation would keep them from doing more damage."

"Apparently, our saboteurs and thieves wanted to make a point," Onegus said. "Last night, while we were all gathered at the assembly, someone sabotaged the automatic shutter system in one of the houses in the main village. The occupants went home directly after the assembly, which means that the act occurred either during our meeting or while they were at home. Since everyone was at the assembly, I assume that it was done while they were on their way or after they got there, which, naturally, freaked them out."

Mia nodded. "I bet. Not being safe in their own home is scary."

Kian agreed. "Perhaps that was the idea behind this particular intrusion. They wanted to undermine the trust we have in one another. The saboteur also took a framed photograph from their home, and since it has no real value other than sentimental, we have to assume that it was taken as a trophy. That's another indication that the saboteur wanted to send a message. The three females living in that house had to spend the evening in the dark because their shutters didn't work. William's crew is fixing them as we speak."

"Three other homes were infiltrated later in the evening," Onegus said. "Minor items were stolen, none of them personal or valuable, but noticeable, so the owners would know right away that something was taken. Again, it was obviously done to send a message that they are not afraid of our investigation."

Toven leaned back. "You sound like you think that there is more than one perpetrator."

The chief nodded. "There are at least two of them. Two of the thefts happened simultaneously while the occupants met at the café, and their houses are not next to each other. One is in the old part of the village, and the other is in phase two."

"Then you are right," Toven said. "It seems the perpetrators want to drive home the message that they don't expect to be caught."

It suddenly occurred to Kian that only someone who was immune to compulsion would be dismissive of the interrogation that was about to start.

He rubbed a hand over his jaw. "I wonder if we have any immunes in the village that we are not aware of?"

"Parker is somewhat immune," Onegus said. "Because he is a compeller. But he is not the type to be behind something like this. Eleanor is in Safe Haven, and even she would never do anything of the sort. That leaves Toven, the Clan Mother, Kalugal, Jackie, and Turner."

Kalugal lifted his hands in the air. "It wasn't me. I swear."

Kian chuckled. "Who knows? Maybe you were sleepwalking and doing mischief?"

Kalugal shook his head with a smile. "Now that Darius is finally sleeping through the night, I'm no longer impersonating a zombie."

Toven reached for the bottle of water in front of him and removed the cap. "The pureblooded Kra-ell are difficult to compel but not immune. However, it's possible that someone was only pretending to be affected by the compulsion so they could carry out these acts later."

Kian had the same thoughts. "If that someone is immune to even Annani's compulsion, that's a big problem."

"I will be on guard," Toven said. "Perhaps I can develop a test that won't be immediately obvious."

Kian's lips tightened. "Any intelligent person trying to hide their ability will be on the lookout for such tests."

Kalugal nodded in agreement. "When I was still in the Brotherhood, I needed to hide my ability from my father. I was hyper-alert to any trickery he employed. Navuh knew there was a high chance that his sons would inherit his compulsion ability, so he kept checking. Lokan's ability was weak compared to Navuh's, so our father didn't mind it. But mine, even though it wasn't as strong as his at the time, was much stronger than Lokan's, so I had to keep it a secret from him. I couldn't let him think of me as a threat."

Kian's gaze shifted to Jade, and he hated what he had to say next. "I'm sorry, Jade, but in my opinion, the main suspect is Drova. Given her parentage, she might be immune."

Igor was an astoundingly strong compeller. Annani had managed to compel him to reveal his secrets, but that was after they had drugged him with a truth serum. His daughter might grow up to be even more formidable, or maybe she already was.

Jade's eyes flashed with indignation. "I would have noticed. Besides, Drova might be a little rough around the edges, but she's loyal. She is also a great fighter, and that requires discipline." There was unmistakable pride in her tone.

Kian hated to think what would happen if Drova turned out to be the culprit. Her mother would be devastated.

Worse, he had no clue what they would do with the girl if she couldn't be compelled.

He hoped it was someone else who only thought they were immune but were not and would soon be unmasked.

23

KALUGAL

As the meeting drew to a close and the others began to file out, Kian walked up to Kalugal. "Can you stay a little longer? There is something I need to talk to you about that's on a completely different subject."

Kalugal's interest was piqued. "Gladly. I just wish it was later in the day, and we could adjourn to your rooftop to smoke cigars. We haven't done that in a while."

"True." Kian put his hand on his shoulder. "What's preventing us from doing that now? We are immortals. We are not bound by human conventions."

"Absolutely." Kalugal grinned.

Once they were seated on the lounge chairs under the big rooftop umbrella, Kian pulled out his small cigar box from his pocket and offered Kalugal one of the two cigars he kept there. "I only bring cigarillos and Short Stories to the office."

"That's perfect." Kalugal took one of the stubby cigars. "We both have a busy day in front of us, so we can't spend the next hour puffing away like it's a holiday." He accepted the cutter that Kian handed him and clipped the tip of his cigar. "So, what is this important thing you wanted to talk to me about?"

Kian lit up his cigar and then lit Kalugal's. "I don't know if you are aware of my mother's latest hypothesis. She now thinks that Khiann wasn't murdered by Mortdh and that the two witnesses who reported the murder had been compelled by her father to incriminate Mortdh so Ahn could get rid of him. She believes that Khiann suffered a fate similar to Wonder's, got caught in the desert during that same massive earthquake, and was buried under the sand. Being a god, he would have entered stasis and remained alive to this day. We just have to find him."

Kalugal tilted his head. "What has brought about these suspicions after all the years she believed that what the witnesses reported was true?"

Kian took a puff of his cigar and looked into the distance. "I don't think it was anything specific. Being exposed to compellers and compulsion and political machination must have started her thinking."

Kalugal had a feeling that Kian wasn't telling him the truth. Something else must have sparked such a stark departure from what Annani had believed over five thousand years. Perhaps while talking to Aru, Annani had learned things about her father that she hadn't known before.

Ahn had been a ruthless leader who had also been a great politician who had managed to convince the other gods that everything he was doing was for the greater good.

So, yeah, Navuh's opinion of Ahn was probably skewed, but it rang true when he ranted about the king of the gods to Kalugal all those years ago.

It was also possible that Annani had learned things about her grandfather that got her thinking. According to Aru and the two other gods, the Eternal King was a piece of work who used his compulsion power in creative ways.

Puffing on the excellent cigar, Kalugal didn't let Kian see that he doubted his answer. "So, what do you need from me?"

Kian smiled. "Hold on, I'm getting there. My mother asked Syssi to summon a vision to see whether Khiann was still alive."

"Aha." Kalugal smiled. "Now we are getting to the interesting part. What did your lovely wife see?"

"She didn't see Khiann, but she saw someone who reminded her of Jasmine standing on a dune and looking into the distance. She also saw ruins, which might be a clue to where to look. That's what I need your expertise for. Syssi made a sketch, and Shai did an internet search, but he didn't find anything that resembled those ruins."

"Of course, he didn't." Kalugal took another puff. "Not everything can be found on the internet."

Kian smiled. "Those were my mother's precise words. She said that old findings might be recorded in some obscure academic writings, which made me think of you. You are an archeologist, and you might know others in the field."

Kalugal nodded. "I know several scholars I could consult. If you can provide me with the sketch, I can email it to my acquaintances."

"Thank you." Kian pulled out his phone. "I'm sending it to you right now."

When Kalugal's phone pinged in his pocket, he patted it. "Got it. Now, I need a story to go along with it. How should I say I got ahold of the sketch, and what am I looking for?"

"Perhaps you could say you found the sketch among the belongings of a deceased archaeologist? Or maybe that the archeologist's family sent you their research papers because they didn't know what to do with them?"

Kalugal regarded his cousin with newfound appreciation. "I like it. I would never have expected you to come up with such convincing lies. You are such a straight-laced guy."

Kian's face broke into a grin. "I'm not completely devoid of imagination."

"So it would appear." Kalugal tapped his cigar on the ashtray to dislodge the ash. "Or maybe being a father has loosened you up a little."

"Maybe." Kian leaned back. "Speaking of fatherhood,

how is Darius doing? You said that he's sleeping through the night now."

At the mention of his son, warmth spread throughout Kalugal's chest. "He's incredible. Now that he no longer has colic, he's just a sweetheart of a child. He hardly ever cries, eats well, and he loves listening to stories. You and Syssi should come visit and bring Allegra with you. Who knows? Maybe these two will become each other's fated mates?"

He loved teasing Kian with the idea, but secretly, he hoped it would become true.

Allegra and Darius were special, and they wouldn't find suitable matches elsewhere.

"Thankfully, we have plenty of time until they are old enough to think of such things." Kian took another puff. "Although, according to Syssi, growing up together, they might think of each other more as siblings than potential romantic partners."

That reminded him. "Speaking of siblings. How are the twins doing?"

"Morelle is still unconscious, but Ell-rom is doing very well. We are moving them to the village in a couple of days, so you will get to see them."

"I've already seen them," Kalugal reminded Kian. "But that was when they still looked like corpses. I'm looking forward to seeing Ell-rom restored to health."

"You will shortly. How are things with Brandon and InstaTock progressing?"

"They are not." Kalugal put his cigar down. "Not yet, anyway. He promised to come up with a few ideas and show them to me, but he's still working on them."

24

ELL-ROM

Ell-rom watched Jasmine devour two eggs that she'd fried in butter, her expression and the noises she made reminding him of the passion they had shared last night.

"Are they that good?" he asked.

"Delicious. How is your breakfast?"

"Plain." He moved the spoon around the porridge. It had pieces of fruit in it, which made up for the bland taste of the gooey whitish substance. "I think that tomorrow I will try what you are eating."

The smile that bloomed on Jasmine's face was precious. "Do you want a bite of my eggs?"

"Tomorrow. I'm not brave enough to taste them today." He looked at the closed doors down the hallway. "Aru said that they are done with the equipment. Do you think that they are just sleeping late?"

"I doubt it." Jasmine finished the last of the eggs and carried her plate to the kitchen. "We were the ones who overslept. The others must have left already."

Smiling, Ell-rom rose to his feet and carried his bowl to the sink. "We didn't oversleep." He leaned to kiss her on the lips. "We were busy doing other things."

There was something to be said for making love without the venom bite. Jasmine hadn't blacked out, and they had held each other for long moments, saying silly love words and just basking in each other's company.

"We were," she finished rinsing out his bowl, "but if anyone asks, we overslept." She winked.

"Got it." He wrapped his arm around her waist and led her back to the bedroom.

When he closed the door behind them, his gaze wandered to the folded walker propped against the wall. It had been days since he'd last needed it, and the sight of it was a reminder of how far he'd come.

"I should return the walker to Julian. He could take it to the village for when Morelle wakes up. She'll need it."

Jasmine paused on her way to the closet. "That's a great idea. We can stop by the clinic to drop it off before our morning walk."

That had been easier than Ell-rom had expected.

He'd thought Jasmine would argue, insisting that he might still need the walker, and it was nice that she had faith in his recovery and believed he wouldn't need it anymore.

She finished lacing up her walking shoes and looked up at him. "I have an idea. Instead of walking down the same streets again, I can drive us to another part of town for our walk today. It will give you some new scenery to explore."

"I would love to see more of the city, but I'm not sure that I'm ready to be far away from the keep, Julian, and Morelle."

Jasmine nodded, but given her expression, she wasn't ready to give up on her idea just yet. "We can ask Julian what he thinks when we drop off the walker. How does that sound to you?"

"Perfect."

They made their way to the clinic, Ell-rom carrying the folded walker instead of leaning on it, and it wasn't even difficult. The thing didn't weigh much.

When they entered Julian's office, the usually calm and collected medic appeared stressed, and Ell-rom felt his throat constrict.

"Is Morelle okay?" he asked.

"Morelle is unchanged." Julian sighed, running a hand through his hair. "If I look tense, it's because the Guardians are resuming their missions tonight, and one of the teams is bringing in a test subject. As much as I despise those traffickers, I have a problem with doing intentional harm. That's not what I signed up for when I became a medic."

Jasmine gave him a reassuring smile. "We don't know if the tracker will harm the scumbag. It might not."

Ell-rom had a different concern. "Where are you going to put the test subject? I don't want him anywhere near Morelle, and we are not moving to the village yet."

"Don't worry," Julian said. "He's going to be kept in the dungeon until the clinic is ready for him."

"You have a dungeon in the keep?" Jasmine asked.

Julian smiled. "Of course. What kind of a keep would it be without one?"

Jasmine leaned against the desk. "Can we see it? Is it like in the movies? Dark and musky with dangling chains and bloodstains?"

Ell-rom grimaced. "I hope not."

He didn't remember ever seeing a dungeon, but since the word translated into Kra-ell and he knew what it meant, the concept wasn't foreign to him. He must have either seen a dungeon back on Anumati, or had been told about it, or had read about it.

"Nothing of the sort." Julian pushed to his feet and walked out of his office. "Gertrude, you are in charge," he told the nurse. "Jasmine and Ell-rom want to see the dungeon. I'm taking them down there."

"Have fun." The nurse waved them off. "How long will you be gone?"

"Fifteen minutes tops," Julian said. "It's not like there is much to see."

25

JASMINE

As the elevator descended, Jasmine's imagination ran wild with what they might find. Julian had said that there were no chains and bloodied walls, but these immortals could have some other instruments of torture.

She could envision a Perfect Match machine with nightmarish scenarios and the victims strapped into the chair, unable to escape.

But who were the prisoners that they kept there?

Clan members or their enemies, the Doomers?

When they got out of the elevator on the dungeon level, it wasn't at all what she'd expected. The wide corridor was the same as the one on the clinic level, with a concrete floor and walls made of white blocks, but here, pictures hung on the walls, and artificial potted trees added a splash of green.

"This is nicer than the clinic level," Ell-rom said.

"Oh, yes." Julian took out his phone and used an app to open the first door. "The dungeon has served many purposes over the years. It's rarely been used as an actual prison. Mostly, it was used as temporary lodging for different people and different reasons, so our interior designer aimed to make it feel homey."

As the heavy door to the cell was swinging open, Jasmine and Ell-rom peeked in.

It was pretty utilitarian, with a single bed, a small desk, and a bathroom that was separated from the main cell with glass blocks. The walls were cream-colored, and there were cameras installed near the ceiling.

"That's a regular cell, right?" Jasmine asked.

"Yes." Julian waited until they cleared the door before closing it.

The mechanism engaged, and the foot-thick door swung closed.

"Those are some impressive doors you have there," she said.

Julian smiled. "They are designed to hold immortals, not humans." He walked toward the third door in the row and aimed his phone at it. "This one is much nicer. This is where we house VIPs who need to be detained for a little while."

Jasmine walked in and motioned for Ell-rom to follow. The place had a living room and a bedroom with an adjacent bathroom, and it was beautifully decorated.

"Amanda and Dalhu stayed down here when he was first apprehended by the clan," Julian said. "She refused to be separated from him." He launched into the story of how Dalhu had kidnapped Amanda and how they had fallen in love. "As you can imagine, Kian was livid. He refused to talk to Amanda."

"It was her choice," Ell-rom said quietly. "He should have respected his sister's decision and not interfered."

"Is that what you would have done?" Jasmine slipped her hand in his. "If Morelle partnered up with someone you found despicable, would you just accept her choice?"

Ell-rom frowned. "I would try to talk her out of it, but I wouldn't abandon her or put her in a dungeon."

Julian smiled knowingly. "Don't judge the guy until you are in his shoes. I just hope that you will never have to deal with a situation like that."

He walked them out of the apartment and closed the door behind them. "The last cell I'm going to show you is the most secure one." He pointed his phone at it. "This is where we held Igor, the pureblooded Kra-ell who enslaved Jade and the other Kra-ell who had woken up from stasis." He looked at Ell-rom. "Did anyone tell you about him?"

Ell-rom nodded. "Annani said that he was an assassin sent to murder our father. When he discovered that Ahn was long gone, he decided to use his special talents to put himself on the throne."

"Correct," Julian confirmed. "He didn't use an actual throne, but he was a despot and a dictator. Frankly, he wasn't the worst I've ever heard of, but he was a very dangerous male. He was an incredibly powerful compeller, but even he wasn't strong enough to resist Annani, which was very fortunate."

A smile bloomed on Ell-rom's face. "Annani was born to be a queen."

"What happened to Igor?" Jasmine asked.

"He was put in stasis," Julian said.

Ell-rom frowned. "Did you have a stasis chamber to put him in?"

Julian shook his head.

"So, how was that possible? I thought Kra-ell needed a stasis chamber to survive."

Julian rubbed a hand over his jaw. "Igor wasn't a normal Kra-ell. He was genetically enhanced, and he could enter unaided stasis like the gods. He was given other talents as well, and knowledge that was stored in his brain like on a hard drive. That's why Kian didn't let Jade execute Igor despite his crimes. He convinced her that we might need what's stored in his brain someday, and it would be a mistake to kill him."

26

ELL-ROM

Ell-rom felt a wave of unease wash over him. The idea of such genetic modifications was unsettling. "How is that different from what I am?" he asked. "How is giving a Kra-ell godly genes any different than a being like me who is half Kra-ell and half god?"

Julian placed a comforting hand on Ell-rom's shoulder. "The difference is in control and predictability. The Eternal King could control precisely what Igor could do. But nature has ways of springing surprises. There's no way to know exactly what you and Morelle might be capable of, and he was terrified of the abilities you might have."

Ell-rom's mind immediately went to his death-ray talent. Was that a result of his hybrid nature? A surprise that even the Eternal King couldn't have predicted?

The thought scared him.

Couldn't he have been blessed with a talent that was about making life better? Why did he have to be an assassin?

Jasmine wrapped a comforting arm around his waist. "You are magnificent, Ell-rom. The best of both species."

Julian seemed to agree with her. "Your unique genetic makeup could result in abilities we've never seen before. It's part of what makes you and Morelle so special and potentially so powerful."

Ell-rom fell silent for a long moment. "I want to contribute, to do good things. I hope that whatever talents might surface, they will help me achieve that."

Jasmine's arm tightened around him. "Not everyone who is born with a talent wants to use it."

"Like Wonder," Julian said. "She's physically stronger than most immortal males, but she abhors violence. So, she refused to join the Guardian force, even though her mate is a Head Guardian. She prefers to work in the village café."

"I respect that." Ell-rom started walking back toward the elevator.

He could do the same. The fact that he had an ability, if he had it, didn't mean that he had to use it. He could choose not to.

"Anything else down here that you want to show us?" he asked Julian.

"No, that's all. So, what do you think?" The medic fell into step with him and Jasmine.

"It's very different than what I imagined," Jasmine said. "In a good way. So that Igor is in the catacombs along with all the Doomers and the Kra-ell who are still waiting for their burial rites?"

Julian nodded. "But unlike the others, he's inside a sarcophagus that is specially built for someone as strong as him. We didn't want him to spontaneously resurrect somehow and escape. He's too dangerous no matter where he is."

As they entered the elevator, Ell-rom thought about Morelle and wondered what surprises her hybrid nature might hold. What kind of abilities would she manifest?

Hopefully, she was his mirror image in that as well, and her power would be to heal instead of kill. Or even better, bring people back to life.

Not that it was likely. If she could perform such miracles, she wouldn't be so jaded and nihilistic.

"By the way," Jasmine said as they exited on the clinic level, "I had an idea to drive Ell-rom to another part of town and explore it on foot. More stimulation and all that."

Julian opened the door to the clinic. "I don't see any real reason why not, but to be frank, it makes me feel a little uneasy. I prefer knowing that Ell-rom is nearby and that I can get to him quickly if needed."

Ell-rom was grateful to the medic.

He felt the same way but didn't want to appear the weak

male who was afraid of stretching his wings, so to speak.

The world outside the keep still seemed vast and complex, and he wasn't ready for it.

Jasmine regarded him with her golden eyes. "There is no rush. There will be plenty of time to explore. We can go for a walk outside the keep once more. But first, let's stop at the café for a little rest and some coffee. The dungeon visit was fascinating but also tiring."

"Sounds good to me." Ell-rom took her hand.

Julian nodded his approval. "After the walk, take a long rest. We are meeting in the gym this afternoon." He patted Ell-rom's arm. "We need to keep working on those muscles."

"I'm looking forward to it," Ell-rom said, and meant it.

His goal was to one day look like the handsome medic, with lean muscle covering every inch of his body and no bones sticking out anywhere.

27

JASMINE

"Let's move to the other side of the street," Jasmine suggested as they walked out of the lobby. "The midday sun is merciless, and there is shade over there."

Ell-rom put on the baseball cap Julian had given him. "We need to keep on this side until we reach the intersection. Julian said not to cross without the signal indicating that it was okay."

"Of course," Jasmine agreed, even though the traffic was light, and they could have crossed right over. Ell-rom was learning the rules of the land, and she shouldn't be the bad influence who taught him that it was okay to break them. "That's the right way to do it."

He shook his head. "I can't get over what Julian told us about Amanda and Dalhu. Is kidnapping a female an accepted courtship ritual in some parts of this world?"

"Not that I'm aware of. In some places, it's okay to sell women, but I believe that the buyer must officially marry them before the transaction is finalized. I might be wrong about that part."

The horrified expression on Ell-rom's face was proof that even aliens who knew nothing of Earth customs thought that was barbaric. "How can such a thing be legal? No one should have ownership rights over another sentient being."

"You are absolutely right, but that's what some primitive cultures still do."

"That needs to be stopped." Ell-rom stopped at the crosswalk and pressed the button.

"Easier said than done. People in these cultures number in the billions. I think your sister is doing all she can to liberate women, but her enemy is propagating these customs. Again, I'm not sure about the details, but I believe that is part of Annani's clan mission statement."

"Good." He looked proud of his sister. "She is a force for good in the world."

"She is."

Jasmine had learned to be skeptical of grand claims by leaders and celebrities, but from what she had seen so far, Annani seemed genuine. Until the goddess proved her wrong, Jasmine chose to believe she was truly a ray of hope in a world that seemed to be falling apart.

As they crossed to the other side of the street, Ell-rom removed his baseball cap, tucked it into his back pocket, and took her hand. "I wonder how Annani could have accepted Dalhu as her daughter's mate. He should have been disqualified because of his act of kidnapping."

"I assume that Annani accepted that Dalhu was Amanda's choice, her truelove mate."

"I guess." Ell-rom squeezed her hand. "I will need to ask her about it. Can you imagine falling for someone who kidnapped you?"

Jasmine shook her head. "As someone who was kidnapped, the answer is a definite no. Even if Alberto did not do it to hand me over to his boss, I would have never forgiven him for it. Amanda must have suffered from Stockholm syndrome, which later morphed into something more."

"What is that syndrome?"

Jasmine paused for a moment. "It's a psychological response sometimes seen in kidnapping victims. Basically, it's when a captive starts to develop positive feelings toward their captor because they are dependent on them and fear them. They might even start to sympathize with them or defend their actions. Thankfully, I've never experienced that, so I can't really empathize."

Ell-rom seemed doubtful. "My impression of Amanda is that she's very assertive and confident. I can't see her succumbing to that syndrome."

"You are right. She doesn't seem like the type, but I'm not an expert, so I don't know if there is a type. Maybe it can happen to anyone. Their relationship seems genuine now, and Dalhu seems like a devoted husband and father. It's just hard for me to imagine how it could have started that way and turned into something good."

Ell-rom was quiet for a moment, processing the information. "Love is a complex emotion," he finally said.

She chuckled. "Especially immortal love with all that fated mates mythology that seems so real. The immortals are convinced that the Fates reward those they find deserving with a truelove mate, and that finding that one and only special person is so sacred that it supersedes everything else." She smiled. "I thought that it was just a nice romantic story, but now that I've found you, I believe it to be true."

He stopped and pulled her to him. "I believe it, too. But what makes us more deserving than others?"

She cupped his cheek. "We have both suffered, Ell-rom, each of us in different ways. I lost my mother and had to endure my stepmother and two obnoxious stepbrothers. You grew up without a father and a mother you rarely saw, hidden behind robes and veils. Both of us deserve some good fortune, don't you think?"

Ell-rom nodded. "We do. I hope there is also someone special for Morelle. She suffered along with me."

"I'm sure there is." Jasmine took his hand and resumed walking. "How are you doing? Should I start looking for a bench?"

"Not yet. I want to stretch the walking time a little longer and keep the rests a little shorter."

She cast him a sidelong glance. "Promise to tell me when you need a rest before you are ready to keel over. I don't think I can carry you if you do."

"I promise." He squeezed her hand.

As they turned a corner into an alley that Jasmine hadn't ventured into before, she caught sight of a bookstore on the street beyond it. It was tucked between a café and a boutique. "Oh, look." She pointed. "That's a store that sells books over there. Would you like to see it? It's not far, and I could use a few new romance books." She smiled up at him. "Something new and exciting to read to Morelle."

"Sure." He frowned as he looked around the alley. "What is this place?"

"Just a passage between buildings where trucks deliver goods to the stores on the other side."

The place was clean, and it was daytime, so she wasn't too worried. Besides, she wasn't alone. Ell-rom might not be in his top shape yet, but he was already stronger than most human males.

Excited by the prospect of browsing, Jasmine hurried her step and was glad to note that Ell-rom was keeping up, but after a few steps, he started to lag behind, and she had to slow down.

"Too fast for you?"

He nodded. "I hope there is a place to sit in that store."

"I'll find you a chair." She wrapped an arm around his waist and tried to prop him up, but he was too heavy.

"Don't," he said quietly. "I'm okay as long as we walk slowly."

"Sorry." She removed her arm and took his hand again.

The bookstore was about three hundred feet away, and there was no bench on the way, so they had no choice but to push forward.

Suddenly, an arm shot out from a dark alcove, wrapping around Jasmine's neck and yanking her backward. She felt the cold press of metal against her temple, and as she realized it was a gun, her blood ran cold.

"Don't move a muscle!" a gruff voice said. The arm around her neck tightened, making it hard to breathe. "Both of you."

Ell-rom seemed frozen in place, and so was Jasmine.

The arm around her neck was twitchy, and the barrel of the gun pressed to her temple was juddering.

The guy was most likely a drug addict in need of a fix, and he might shoot her accidentally.

He also stank to high heaven, which meant that he was probably homeless.

"What do you want?" she whispered. "I have money in my wallet. It's in my back pocket. Take it out and let us go."

"Nice try, bitch. I'm not taking my hands off you or the gun. Pull out the wallet and put it in my pocket. Give me your watch, too."

Jasmine's heart pounded in her chest, and fear coursed through her veins. He sounded lucid, but the hand around her neck was still shaking, and the gun was still trembling against her temple.

Stay calm. Don't make any sudden movements. Comply with his demands. The rules echoed in her head, but it was hard to focus with the gun pressed against her temple and the arm constricting her throat.

Her eyes locked with Ell-rom's, beseeching him not to do anything stupid. One threatening move and the addict might blow her brains out.

"Okay, okay. Just calm down. I'm going to remove the watch now." She unfastened the clasp of her fake Cartier and lifted it so he could see it. "I'm going to put it in your pocket now."

28

ELL-ROM

Ell-rom's world narrowed to a single, horrifying moment. One second, he had been strolling peacefully with Jasmine, their hands intertwined, and the next she was torn from his grasp, a stranger's arm around her throat and a weapon pressed to her temple.

Time seemed to slow to a crawl.

Ell-rom's heart pounded in his chest, each beat echoing in his ears like a thunderclap. He stood frozen, his hand still outstretched where Jasmine's had been moments ago.

The gunman's voice was rough and shaky.

"What do you want?" she said. "I have money in my wallet. It's in my back pocket. Take it out and let us go."

"Nice try, bitch. I'm not taking my hands off you or the gun. Pull out the wallet and put it in my pocket. Give me your watch, too."

Ell-rom barely registered the words, his focus was entirely on Jasmine's face. Her eyes were wide with fear, silently pleading with him. *Don't move,* they seemed to say. *Don't do anything rash.*

Ell-rom felt helpless. Even if he had been at full strength, he would have been afraid to move. As fast as he was, he was not fast enough to stop that finger from pressing the trigger. All his strength, all his newfound abilities, seemed useless in the face of this human threat. He watched as Jasmine struggled to breathe, the gunman's arm tight around her throat. Every instinct screamed at him to act, to protect her, but the trembling hand on the gun pressed to her temple kept him rooted to the spot.

"Okay, okay. Just calm down. I'm going to remove the watch now." Jasmine reached for her watch, took it off slowly, and lifted it. "I'm going to put it in your pocket now."

She was so brave. Her hands only shook a little, and her voice was steady.

"Do it," the scum said. "Put it in my front pocket."

"Okay." She reached back and tucked the watch where he had told her.

Ell-rom's gaze locked with Jasmine's again. He saw the fear in her eyes, and there was also a strength that amazed him. Even in this terrifying moment, she was trying to stay calm and handle the situation as best she could.

"Now, the wallet." The attacker tightened his arm around her neck.

"Please." Her hands rose to tug on his arm. "I can't breathe."

Her words cut through Ell-rom's paralysis. There had to be something he could do. But what? He had no experience with human weapons and no training in how to handle such situations, but he knew enough to realize that the finger on the lever would discharge a projectile that would go straight into Jasmine's head.

Any wrong move could cost her life.

Except, he didn't need to move to kill the attacker. A concentrated wish to see him dead should do that, but what if he managed to press the trigger before he died?

The risk was too great.

The world seemed to hold its breath. Ell-rom was acutely aware of every detail—the sweat beading on the gunman's forehead, the slight tremor in the hand holding the gun, the way Jasmine's chest rose and fell with rapid, shallow breaths.

Rage rose within Ell-rom, and as a familiar burning started behind his eyes, his fangs dropped down.

"Ell-rom," Jasmine whispered.

The gunman looked at him, his eyes growing large with fear. "What the hell?"

The hand holding the gun began to shake harder, and fury erupted from Ell-rom.

At that moment all his fear for Jasmine, all his helplessness, all his rage at this human who dared threaten what was most precious to him, coalesced into a single, focused thought.

Nothing outside of him seemed to change, but the attacker suddenly crumpled like a sack of old clothes, his gun clattering to the ground.

For a heartbeat, everything was still.

Then Jasmine stumbled forward, and Ell-rom rushed to catch her. He enveloped her in his arms, holding her tightly against his chest, his heart racing with residual fear and the shock of what he had just done.

"Are you alright?" he breathed. "Did he hurt you?"

She shook her head against his chest, her body trembling. "I'm okay," she said before turning to look at the body slumped on the ground. "What did you do?"

Ell-rom swallowed hard, and the reality of what he had done sank in.

He had used his deadly thought projection. He had taken a life to protect his mate. He had done the right thing, but the knowledge still settled in his gut like a stone.

The ability was real. The dream had been a memory and not a fantasy. He really could kill with a thought.

"I couldn't let him hurt you. I killed him."

"How do you know he's dead?" Jasmine pulled out of his arms and crouched next to the attacker, pressing two fingers to his neck.

Ell-rom knew she wouldn't find a pulse.

He couldn't hear the male's heart beating.

"He's dead," she confirmed. "What do we do now? Do we just leave him here?"

"I don't know."

The adrenaline was wearing off, leaving him feeling shaky and uncertain. Could they just walk away and not tell anyone about what had happened?

He looked around the passageway. There was no one there, but someone could have seen something from one of the windows higher up.

Jasmine pursed her lips as she looked at the gun. "Give me your hat."

He frowned. "Why?"

"We need to get rid of the gun, and I don't want to touch it with my fingers. Without the gun, he is just another drug addict who died of overdose."

Trusting that she knew what she was doing, Ell-rom pulled the cap out of his back pocket and handed it to her.

"Thank you." She used it to pick up the gun and then walked over to one of the large trash containers, lifted the lid, and dropped it inside while holding on to the hat.

He expected the weapon to discharge from the drop, but it must have landed on something soft because there was barely a thud.

That was it, though?

They were going to just leave the body like that?

"What if someone saw what happened from one of the windows?" Ell-rom asked.

"Good point. No one will know what happened to him, but if anyone calls the police, they will want to question us." She bit on her lower lip. "If we call Julian, he will want to know what happened."

"What can Julian do?" he asked, still hoping that they could keep his ability a secret.

"A lot. He could bring in Yamanu, who can blanket thrall everyone working in these buildings to forget what they saw, and he could take care of disposing of the body."

"Then you should call him." Ell-rom sighed. "Sooner or later, I would have confessed my ability anyway."

As Jasmine made the call and explained to Julian what happened, Ell-rom stared at the crumpled form of the gunman. There was no blood, no visible wound. To anyone else, it might look like the man had simply collapsed. But Ell-rom knew the truth.

He had wished death upon this human, and death had come.

The power of it terrified him. How easily he had snuffed out a life with nothing more than a thought. It had been necessary, he told himself again. It had been to save Jasmine. But the knowledge of what he was capable of weighed heavily on him.

He had revealed his ability in the most dramatic way possible.

There would be no hiding it now, no pretending that it didn't exist.

Jasmine didn't tell Julian what Ell-rom had done, only that someone tried to rob her and then collapsed dead, and she didn't know what to do.

"Are you sure he's dead?" Julian asked her.

"I am. There is no pulse. I think he was a drug addict." She looked at Ell-rom and gave him a small smile. "His heart might have given out from the stress."

29

JASMINE

When Jasmine ended the call with Julian, Ell-rom still stood motionless, his eyes fixed on the crumpled form of their attacker.

She was badly shaken and hanging on by a thread, but Ell-rom seemed to be in worse shape than she was, so she had to keep it together at least until Julian arrived.

She had to make sure that he was okay before allowing herself to fall apart. Later, when she was back at the penthouse, she would let it all out.

But not now.

Except, it was easier said than done when the reality of what had just transpired was washing over her in waves, each one threatening to overwhelm her carefully maintained composure.

"Hey," she said softly, reaching out to touch Ell-rom's arm. He flinched slightly at her touch, and the pain in his eyes when he met her gaze nearly broke her heart. "It's okay, love. You did what had to be done to save my life."

She wasn't even sure that it was true, but he needed to hear her say that. She had a feeling that the gun was not even loaded. The guy might have been using it like a prop on a movie set.

Hell, for all she knew, it was a prop.

Not that she was sorry for the man. Well, she was sorry that life had brought him to that state, but the truth was that a homeless psycho on drugs was dangerous. She was lucky to have Ell-rom with her, but some other helpless victim might have ended up dead because the druggie choked the life out of her.

Ell-rom nodded, but the haunted look remained. "Why didn't you tell Julian what I did?"

"Because we don't know for sure that you did that," she said. "Maybe he got scared seeing your red eyes and elongated fangs, and his heart gave out."

Ell-rom winced. "My eyes were red?"

Oops. She shouldn't have said that. Given the way Ell-rom had looked during the moment before the druggie collapsed, there was very little chance that the guy had died from natural causes.

Ell-rom had looked like the personification of his deadly ability, and if she wasn't as in love with him as she was, she would have been scared of him too.

"Yeah." She sighed. "There was a fire in them, and it looked red hot, not metaphorically but literally." She hoped the two terms translated well into Kra-ell.

He seemed to get what she meant. "I felt the fire behind my eyeballs. The rage was like an inferno scorching my veins. The attacker did not die from natural causes. I killed him. I know it, and you know it."

"So what?" She wrapped her arms around his neck. "We are a team, and we decide what to let the outside world know. If you want to keep your talent a secret, it is safe with me. I will always have your back, no matter what."

He arched a brow. "Even if I kill an innocent by mistake?"

Jasmine shook her head. "You won't. If you were that trigger-happy, you would have killed the bastard the moment he attacked, but you waited, and you only acted when he started to choke the life out of me."

Ell-rom rested his forehead against hers. "You give me too much credit. I was paralyzed and didn't know what to do. I forgot about even having the ability."

Jasmine smiled. "You've just proven my point. It wasn't your first instinct to react with your death ray."

"But won't Julian figure it out when he gets here?"

"Not necessarily." Jasmine turned to look at the vagabond. "There are no visible wounds and no external indication of what caused his death. To anyone else, it could look like he just collapsed."

Ell-rom nodded. "Thank you for protecting me."

"Always and forever."

The sound of a car rolling into the alley made Jasmine jump, and she instinctively stepped in front of Ell-rom, trying to shield him.

It wasn't a car, though. It was an ambulance, and after it rolled to a stop next to them, Julian exited, wearing his doctor's coat.

"Are you both unharmed?" he asked, his eyes scanning them for injuries before turning to the body on the ground.

"We're fine, just badly shaken up. He tried to rob me, and when Ell-rom flashed his fangs, he must have gotten scared and collapsed."

The best lies were the ones that were closest to the truth. Besides, she didn't want Julian to think that Ell-rom had just stood there and had done nothing to help her.

It was her job to protect her man's honor.

Julian crouched beside the body, checking for vital signs. "No pulse, no respiration," he muttered. He looked up at them, his brow furrowed. "What exactly happened?"

Jasmine took a deep breath, steeling herself for more lies.

But then Julian stopped her. "Never mind. We can talk about it later. Right now, I need to get him out of here." He went to the back of the ambulance and pulled out a gurney. "I wish I could bring Gertrude with me to make it look more realistic." He waved Ell-rom over. "Go behind the ambulance and come back. I will cast a shroud over you to look like a paramedic."

Ell-rom did as Julian commanded, and when he returned, he was dressed for the part, so to speak, and looked completely different.

"So, here is how we are going to do it," Julian said quietly.

After he explained how they were going to transfer the body to the gurney and then the gurney into the vehicle, Ell-rom helped him stow it in the back of the ambulance.

When it was done, Julian turned to them. "Given how much he stinks, I hate to do this to you, but one of you needs to get in the back with him. Only one can sit up front with me."

"I'll do that." Jasmine started for the back of the ambulance.

The last thing she wanted was to be next to the dead body, but she was better equipped to handle that than Ell-rom.

He stopped her with a hand on her shoulder. "Let me. It's the least I can do."

"People," Julian admonished. "Time is of the essence. We need to get out of here."

Jasmine nodded in acceptance. "Okay. It's a short ride."

30

ELL-ROM

"So, what happened?" Julian asked Jasmine as he pulled the ambulance out of the alley.

Sitting in the back, Ell-rom had no problem hearing the conversation despite the vehicle's noisy engine.

"He grabbed me," Jasmine said. "I didn't see him, but then Ell-rom and I were talking, and I wasn't paying attention. Anyway, the guy put a gun to my head, and he was shaking so badly I was afraid he would shoot me even if I cooperated. I told him to take what he wanted and let us go."

Ell-rom felt shame wash over him. Jasmine was still human, and her senses weren't nearly as sharp as his. How had he missed the threat?

The stench alone should have alerted him.

But then there were several large trash containers in that alley, and they stank, so he'd closed his nose and breathed through his mouth.

He should have been more alert.

"I was trying to calm him down," Jasmine continued. "But he was agitated. Twitchy. I'm certain that he was under the influence or suffering withdrawal symptoms. And then when he saw Ell-rom's glowing eyes and fangs, he said 'what the hell' and collapsed."

Julian nodded. "Drug-induced cardiac arrest isn't uncommon in situations of high stress."

Ell-rom could only imagine the satisfied expression on Jasmine's face.

Then again, she wouldn't let Julian see anything that she didn't want him to see. She was a very good performer.

It was also truly remarkable how well she functioned under duress and how calm she had been throughout her ordeal. Was it her training as an actress that had taught her how to handle stressful situations?

Ell-rom's own heart rate still wasn't back to normal.

As Julian started making calls, arranging for Guardians to do damage control, Ell-rom wondered what that entailed. What was he going to do with the body?

They hadn't wandered too far away from the keep, and the drive was over in minutes, most of the time spent going down the spiraling levels of the structure.

When they reached the bottom, Julian pulled up to a gate and stopped, waiting for it to slide open before going in and parking the vehicle.

When he opened the back, Ell-rom helped him get the gurney down. "What are you going to do with him?"

"Examine him." Julian pushed the gurney toward a door with a sign on it that Ell-rom couldn't read yet.

"What are you hoping to find?" Jasmine asked.

"I just want to determine the cause of death."

As Julian opened the door, Ell-rom held it for him to push the gurney through.

"What will you do with the body after that?" Jasmine asked.

"Drop it off at the coroner's. It won't be the first or the last." He smiled. "We pretend to be an EMT team. Most of them are operated by private contractors, so it's not a big deal to say that we were called and found him dead on arrival. Our hackers will plant the 911 call just in case anyone checks."

"Impressive." Jasmine followed him into the elevator, and Ell-rom stepped in last. "Do I want to know why and how you have been delivering dead bodies to the morgue?"

"Traffickers. Usually, we try to leave them bound and thralled for the police to collect, but occasionally, that doesn't work, and we have dead bodies to dispose of."

Ell-rom was impressed by Jasmine's ability to conduct a casual conversation after what she'd been through and in the presence of a cadaver.

Did he even know this brave side of her?

She seemed different, like she'd shed her former skin and had donned a different one for this occasion.

Julian cast him a worried glance. "Are you okay?"

Ell-rom shook his head. "I'm not. My mate was almost killed. That's not something I can get over so quickly."

Julian was about to say something when the elevator stopped on the clinic level. He waited for them to step out before pushing the gurney.

"It was a traumatic event." Julian turned to look at Jasmine. "You seem to be handling the experience incredibly well."

She shrugged. "I'm just pretending that I'm playing a part in a detective movie."

So that was her trick.

Ell-rom wished he could do the same.

He also wished he could come clean and tell Julian what he had done.

Jasmine was probably holding on and putting on an act to protect him when it should be the other way around. He was the one with the power, the one who should be protecting her.

In the clinic, Julian pushed the gurney past the patient rooms into what was the clinic's operating and diagnostic area. Ell-rom had never been there, but he'd seen Gertrude, Julian, and Bridget go in and out of there.

Bridget had returned to the village, leaving Julian in charge, and even though the young medic was less experienced, Ell-rom liked him better than his mother. He was easier to talk to, and he could give him the kind of advice Ell-rom would have been too embarrassed to ask a female, even if she was a medic.

The door to Morelle's room opened, and Gertrude stepped out, her expression worried. "Are you two okay? I heard that you'd gotten mugged."

"It was scary," Jasmine admitted. "The guy died. Julian thinks that his heart gave out."

"If you are okay, I'd better see if he needs help." Gertrude regarded them both with a questioning look.

"We are fine." Jasmine took Ell-rom's hand. "We are going upstairs, and I'm making myself a tall drink."

The nurse nodded. "Eat something sweet."

"Yes, ma'am." Jasmine smiled at the nurse and then tugged on his hand. "Let's get out of here."

31

JASMINE

As Jasmine walked into the penthouse clutching Ell-rom's hand, the spacious living area, with its wall of glass windows offering a view of the city, felt like a sanctuary after the harrowing events in the alley. Soft afternoon light filtered through the glass, casting long shadows across the polished hardwood floors and luxurious area rugs.

She was surprised that she felt almost okay.

The adrenaline was wearing off, leaving her a little dizzy, but the need to stay strong for Ell-rom had helped her push past the worst of the shock.

Acting, it seemed, had its uses beyond the stage and screen.

Ell-rom, on the other hand, looked like he was barely holding it together. His face was pale, and his eyes were distant, as if he was replaying the events in his mind in an endless loop.

Jasmine couldn't blame him. Killing someone, even in self-defense or in the defense of a loved one, wasn't something you could just shrug off.

"Why don't you sit down?" she suggested, guiding him toward the plush leather couch. "I'll get us something to drink."

Ell-rom nodded mutely, sinking onto the couch with a heaviness that spoke volumes about his emotional state. He hadn't said a word since they'd left the clinic.

At the bar, she scanned the stock on offer. Bottles of various shapes and colors were lined up on the shelves, evoking an image of soldiers awaiting orders. She hesitated for a moment, her hand hovering over the selection.

Ell-rom hadn't had any alcohol yet, but he should probably be okay with a light cocktail.

She selected a bottle of whiskey, its amber liquid catching the light. "I promise, it'll help take the edge off."

She set about making two whiskey sours, the familiar routine of mixing drinks helping to calm her nerves. The clink of ice against the glass, the subtle aroma of lemon, and the rich scent of whiskey all felt comfortingly familiar and normal after the surreal events of the day.

Drinks in hand, Jasmine returned to the couch, setting the glasses on the coffee table before settling beside Ell-rom. She curled her legs under her, angling her body toward him. "Here." She offered him one of the glasses. "Sip it slowly."

Ell-rom took the glass, staring at the pale yellow liquid as if it held the answers to all his questions. He took a tentative sip, his face scrunching up slightly at the unfamiliar taste.

"It's interesting," he said.

Jasmine smiled. "Interesting, as in good? Or interesting, as in I'd rather not drink it?"

"Interesting, as in it's an acquired taste."

"You'll learn to like it." She took a long, grateful sip. "This is so good. I call it liquid courage."

Ell-rom lifted the glass so it was at his eye level. "Really? Is that supposed to boost confidence?"

"For some, it does."

They sat in silence for a while, sipping their drinks. With the incredibly well-insulated windows and doors blocking the city noise from intruding on the turmoil in Ell-rom's mind, the ice clinking softly in their glasses was the only sound in the otherwise quiet penthouse.

Finally, Jasmine couldn't take the silence anymore. "Talk to me, Ell-rom. Stewing in a negative thought loop will not help you."

He set his glass down, his hands clasped tightly in his lap. "I feel like the right thing to do is to come clean. I need to tell Julian the truth about what happened."

Jasmine felt a jolt of fear. She set her own drink aside, turning to face him fully. "Ell-rom, we've been over this," she said, trying to keep her voice calm and reasonable. "There are many reasons why that's not a good idea."

"I know, but—"

"Just think about it," Jasmine pressed on. "If the clan finds out about your ability, they might fear you. Or worse, they might want to use you as an assassin." She saw Ell-rom flinch at the word and hurried on. "I know that you don't want that."

Ell-rom shook his head. "Of course I don't. But I believe that my sister will protect me. The clan will accept me no matter what because Annani wants me in the village. And if I refuse to be their assassin, Annani won't force me."

Jasmine sighed, running a hand through her hair. She understood his faith in Annani—the goddess had that effect on people—and it was true that she would do her best for Ell-rom. But the world wasn't as simple as he wanted to believe it was.

"I know Annani is a force for good," Jasmine took Ell-rom's hand and brought it to her lap. "But sometimes the good guys need to do things that aren't so good. You heard Julian talking about the traffickers, right?"

Ell-rom nodded.

"Well, think about it. If you had the power to stop people who abuse women and children, who ruin lives, would you stand by and do nothing?"

"Of course not."

"Exactly." She patted his hand with her other one. "And that's the problem. Your sister is trying to help many people, and she might need your help when your talent can make the difference between saving many or letting the bad guys win. She might pressure you to use your ability when there's no other option."

Ell-rom was quiet for a long moment, his gaze fixed on their intertwined hands. "Don't you think that I've considered that? I did, and I felt ashamed about shying away from the dubious gift the Mother of All Life gave me. That's one more reason I need to tell Julian about what happened. It's not okay for me to hide it now that I know for sure I can do it."

Jasmine squeezed his hand gently. "I know you want to be honest, Ell-rom. It's one of the things I love about you. But sometimes, keeping a secret isn't about avoiding responsibility. It's about protecting yourself and the people you care about." She paused, choosing her next words carefully. "What you can do is incredible and terrifying. If the wrong people find out about it, they might try to use and manipulate you. We don't know all the players in the village yet, and if immortals are like humans, I bet there are nasties hiding among the good ones. Then there are the fearmongers who might try to pressure your sister into putting you back in stasis because they think you are too dangerous."

Ell-rom's grip on her hand tightened. "Do you really think they would try to do that?"

The fear in his voice broke Jasmine's heart. She pulled him into a tight embrace. "Annani won't let them. But why put yourself and her in the position of having to defend you?"

Ell-rom pulled back. "So, what do we do?"

Jasmine reached up, cupping his face in her hands. "We keep this between us for now. When we are in the village, and you are alone with Annani, you can tell her, and only her. She will know whether it's okay to reveal your ability to the rest of them or keep it a secret."

"That's a good idea," he admitted.

"It's a compromise." Jasmine leaned in, pressing a soft kiss to his lips. When she pulled back, she was relieved to see some of the tension had eased from his features. "Now." She reached for their forgotten drinks. "Why don't we finish these and warm up dinner? I don't know about you, but near-death experiences always make me hungry."

32

ELL-ROM

Ell-rom pushed his fork through the colorful array of vegetables on his plate, his appetite diminished despite the enticing aroma of the meal. The dining room of the penthouse, with its sleek modern furnishings and panoramic view of the city skyline, suddenly felt claustrophobic.

He appreciated Jasmine's efforts to distract him with light conversation about this and that, but his mind kept drifting back to the events in the alley.

Jasmine's terrified expression, the attacker's arm constricting her airflow, the badly shaking hand barely controlling a gun pressed to her temple, and finally, the attacker crumpling to the ground.

The horrific scene was playing in his mind in a loop.

Had he done the right thing?

Could he have done something different?

The soft chime of the doorbell pulled Ell-rom from his thoughts. Their roommates wouldn't have rung the bell, and he wasn't aware of any expected visitors.

Could it be Edgar?

The guy had a bad habit of showing up uninvited.

"Are we expecting anyone?" he asked Jasmine.

"Not that I know." She pushed to her feet and walked over to the door.

When she returned to the dining room a moment later, she was accompanied by Julian, and Ell-rom's gut clenched with worry.

The medic must have found something in the body that pointed an accusing finger at Ell-rom. Otherwise, what reason did he have to come up to the penthouse?

He and Ella no longer stayed in either of the top-floor apartments. Julian drove home every night, leaving Gertrude in charge of monitoring Morelle.

The medic's face was unreadable as he took a seat at the table.

"Can I offer you some food?" Jasmine asked. "We have several packaged meals, and the vegan dishes are very tasty."

"No, thank you." Julian smiled at her. "Ella won't forgive me if I don't eat with her at home." He waved his hand over the table. "Please, don't let me interrupt your meal."

Ell-rom set his fork down, unable to pretend any longer that he had any appetite. "What brings you here, Julian?"

The medic's gaze shifted between Ell-rom and Jasmine before he spoke. "I ran a full battery of tests on the body. There were no signs of a heart attack or stroke. No evidence of an aneurysm or any other natural cause of sudden death that I could detect. A CT scan revealed no cerebral hemorrhage, ischemic stroke, or structural cardiac issues. Also, the tests I ran indicated no signs of drug overdose or severe electrolyte imbalances that could have caused sudden death. He was malnourished, and there were traces of drugs in his system, but that couldn't explain his sudden collapse."

Ell-rom felt his chest tighten. He could sense Julian's suspicion and could almost see the wheels turning in the medic's mind as he pieced together the puzzle, and each negative result felt like another nail in the coffin of his secret.

"There was no trauma to the body," Julian continued. "No signs of poisoning or asphyxiation. It's as if his body simply stopped."

The words hung in the air, heavy with implication. Ell-rom could feel Julian's gaze on him, probing, questioning.

"What do you think could have caused it?" Jasmine asked. "Could he have been petrified like in the Harry Potter movies?"

Julian chuckled, the sound easing some of the pressure in Ell-rom's chest. "I've never heard of anyone turning to stone from fright." He turned to Ell-rom. "Did you notice any significant changes in the man's expression before he collapsed? Any signs of distress or pain?

Jasmine said that your eyes were glowing, and your fangs were down. That could have terrified the dude."

Ell-rom's hands clenched into fists under the table. He knew what Julian was asking. This was it—the moment of truth.

He met Julian's eyes. "I..." he began.

"Ell-rom," Jasmine interjected, her tone warning. "You are still in a state of shock yourself."

She was trying to help, but he couldn't hold it in any longer. The weight of the secret and the guilt were just too much to bear.

"He was terrified, as he should have been. He knew I was about to kill him, just not the how of it." He pinned Julian with a hard look. "I killed him with a thought."

The silence that followed was deafening. Julian's eyes widened, while Jasmine looked disappointed and resigned.

"What do you mean, you killed him with a thought?" Julian asked, leaning forward. "Did you compel him to stop breathing? Or for his heart to stop beating? What exactly did you do?"

Ell-rom shook his head. "He was choking the life out of Jasmine, and he had a gun pressed to her head. I couldn't stop him physically without endangering her, and I don't know how to compel, so I projected my wish for him to die, and he obeyed."

Julian sat back. "I've never heard of such an ability. Are

you sure that you didn't say anything out loud? You couldn't have killed him just by wishing it."

Ell-rom shook his head again. "I didn't say anything. I just thought it."

Jasmine reached across the table, taking Ell-rom's hand. "Are you absolutely certain, love? In stressful situations, people imagine all sorts of things and even believe in magical abilities, like wishing for something and making it happen. It all happened so fast. Maybe it was just a coincidence. Maybe the stress of the situation caused his heart to give out naturally."

It was a nice try to save him, but Julian had already ruled that out.

"I think that's what killed him." Ell-rom chose the middle ground. "Of course, I can't be sure of that, but the timing and the intent make it difficult for me to rule out the possibility."

Julian rubbed his chin. "If what you're saying is true, it could change everything we know about psychic abilities. It must have been a thrall since those don't require sound waves and can be done with a thought, but this is the first time I've heard about a deadly thrall. Naturally, it's possible to thrall someone to jump off a bridge or drive a car into a wall, killing them that way, but to command their body to stop working is on a completely different level. I wonder what the distance limit is. Thralling usually needs to be done face to face. I wish we could test it."

"That's not possible," Jasmine said. "Also, if Ell-rom can indeed kill from a distance, that is dangerous knowledge. If the wrong kind of people discover it, they would want to use him. It wouldn't be too hard to find ways to coerce him to cooperate. If I'm threatened, or his sisters, nephew, or nieces, he would do whatever they command him to do. No one in the world would be safe."

Ell-rom hadn't even thought that far ahead, but apparently Jasmine had, and she was right.

Julian held up a hand. "Of course. First of all, we are not entirely sure that Ell-rom's thought killed the guy. This needs to be tested in a controlled setting. Nevertheless, Kian needs to know, and he will most likely tell Annani." Julian looked at Ell-rom. "He will not spread the news beyond that, trust me. His interest aligns with yours. He wouldn't want the information falling into the wrong hands either."

Ell-rom nodded. "I don't want to be a danger to anyone, and I don't want to be turned into a weapon."

33

KIAN

Kian stared out the window of his second-floor office, his gaze fixed on the lush greenery of the village below. It seemed so tranquil, but underneath the pastoral façade hid an undercurrent of discontent.

He'd just gotten updates about the ongoing investigation from Toven and his mother. The perpetrator hadn't been identified yet, but they were both reporting that many residents were unhappy about living in an integrated community. Evidently, for some, the differences were just too much to bridge.

He hadn't heard from Kalugal and Arwel yet, but he expected less disgruntlement from Kalugal's men and the humans living in the village than from Clan members and the Kra-ell.

The ringing of his phone pulled him from his thoughts, and as he saw Julian's name flashing, the uneasy feeling in his gut intensified.

A phone call instead of a text message indicated urgency.

"Julian," he said. "What's going on?"

"Are you alone?"

The uneasiness got worse.

"Yes. Why? Is everyone in the keep okay?"

"Yes. They are all fine. But I need to tell you something that I'm sure you will want to keep confidential."

Frowning, Kian glanced toward his office door, which was closed but not locked. Most people knocked before entering, but there were some who didn't wait for him to invite them inside before just opening the door and striding in.

"Give me a moment," he said, rising from his chair.

He walked across the room and locked the door. "Alright. What's this about?"

As Julian recounted the events involving Jasmine and Ell-rom, Kian felt a knot forming in his stomach.

"She was attacked in broad daylight?"

"He was probably a druggie. She said that his hand was shaking so badly that her greatest fear was that he would press the trigger accidentally."

"Unbelievable. I should transfer Ell-rom and Jasmine to the village right away. It's not safe for them to walk out of the building."

"Wait," Julian said. "I didn't get to the best part yet."

That was true. Nothing Julian had said so far required confidentiality. "So, get to the point. I'm already itching for a cigarillo to calm my nerves."

"The attacker collapsed, and Ell-rom thinks that he killed him just by wishing him dead. I would have thought that was just a childish fantasy, but I ran all possible tests on the body, and there was no indication that he'd suffered a cardiac event. It's like his brain shut down for no reason."

For a long moment, Kian was too stunned to respond. Normally, he would have dismissed Ell-rom's claim for the same reasons Julian would have.

In many ways, Ell-rom was still like a child, and children often believed in magical abilities, like wishing something would make it manifest. But Julian was a smart guy, and he wasn't gullible, so if he thought that there was something to it, there probably was.

After all, they had all feared that the twins had some terrible powers. The Eternal King definitely believed that and wanted them eliminated. It seemed that he wasn't simply paranoid but had something on which to base his fear.

Kian pinched the bridge of his nose. "That's one hell of a headache. We can't be certain of Ell-rom's ability until we test it, and I can't deal with it right now."

"I know," Julian said. "The timing sucks."

Kian snorted. "Doesn't it always?"

"It would seem so," Julian agreed.

"I need to tell the Clan Mother." Kian opened a drawer and pulled out his cigarillo box. "She's entertaining clan members at the moment, so it will have to wait for later."

"Has anything come up in the investigation so far?" Julian asked.

"Nothing concrete." Kian put the box in his pocket. "Toven might need another day with the Kra-ell because the obstinate purebloods are so difficult to compel. We have a main suspect, but we are keeping her for last."

"Who?"

"Drova. But keep it to yourself."

"Of course. But why her?"

Kian patted his pockets to check if he'd got the lighter, but it wasn't there. "Given her parentage, there's a possibility she might be immune to compulsion. It's just a theory at this point, but that, along with some circumstantial evidence, makes her the prime suspect."

"Why not question her first, then?" Julian asked.

"We don't want to tip her off. If she is involved, we want to find out if she has anyone working with her. We need to be strategic about this."

"Smart." There was a moment of silence on the line. "What should we do about Ell-rom in the meantime?"

"For now, nothing." Kian opened the drawer again and pushed his hand in to search for the lighter. "We need to verify his ability before we decide what to do. We'll need to test it."

He found the lighter all the way at the end of the drawer, grabbed it, and pulled it out.

"That's what I thought, but who would he...well, kill?"

Kian's mind flashed to a conversation he'd had with the chief not too long ago. "Onegus said something about wanting to go after the pedophiles who buy children for sex. Perhaps we should dedicate a team of Guardians to finding these monsters. I have no problem using them to test Ell-rom's ability. Eliminating them would be a service to humanity." He felt his fangs elongating. "I can't tolerate the thought of children being made to suffer like that. The pain is unimaginable."

"I can't argue with that," Julian said. "It's not something I'm looking forward to dirtying my hands with, but we can't save the world with white gloves on. I wish we could, but that's not possible when there are so many demons to get rid of. That being said, it's morally gray."

Kian put the lighter in his pocket and headed for the door. "We are not bound by the same moral dilemmas as humans because we can see into the monsters' heads and make sure that we are not executing innocents by mistake." He opened the door and headed for the stairs leading to his rooftop retreat.

"True," Julian agreed. "Ell-rom is distraught, but I guess talking with Vanessa is not an option, right?"

"It's not, even though I trust her completely. I want my mother to be the first one to know."

He might tell Syssi first, but that was different. He and Syssi were as one.

"Very well," Julian said. "I'll give him something to relax and then head home. Should I stop by the Clan Mother's to give my not-guilty testimony?"

"She's giving away cookies, so why not."

Julian chuckled. "I forgot about that. That's definitely an incentive to drop in."

34

ROB

Rob looked at the village map on his phone to make sure that he was in the right place. This was supposed to be Callie's restaurant, but it was dark like the rest of the village, and no sound was spilling from the inside.

For security reasons, the village was completely dark at night. The immortals had no trouble seeing in the dim moonlight, even when it was obscured by clouds, but for a human, it was literally like stumbling in the dark.

The thing was, Rob didn't even need to be there. As a newcomer, he was beyond suspicion. Those who were required to show up at the restaurant were residents of the village who had been there throughout the occurrences of thefts and sabotage, but he was curious to meet the other humans living in the village.

Besides, he didn't want to be in the house while Toven was interrogating the Kra-ell with Mia's help, and if he was honest with himself, he also hoped to meet Lusha without her Guardian boyfriend. Not that he planned on coming on to her or anything like that. She was just interesting to talk to, and he liked being with her.

Taking a deep breath, he pushed the door open and was immediately blinded by the sudden burst of light. He stepped inside and let the door close quickly behind him.

The restaurant was cozy, with warm wood paneling and soft lighting that had only appeared blinding for the first moment when he had entered from the darkness outside.

The air was filled with the aroma of freshly baked bread and simmering spices, making Rob's stomach growl appreciatively.

As his eyes adjusted to the light, he spotted Lusha sitting at a table at the back with the blue-haired Marina and another older woman.

He made his way over, nodding politely to the other humans he passed. Some faces he already recognized from his brief time in the village, but most were unfamiliar.

Noticing him walking toward her, Lusha waved him over, a warm smile on her face. "Hey there! I'm so glad that you decided to come."

"I figured it was a good opportunity to meet more people and eat free food." He smiled at Marina and the other woman.

Lusha laughed, the sound warm and carefree. "Callie's place is the best, and it's nearly impossible to get a reservation. I was very surprised that she agreed to host this get-together." She motioned at the fourth chair at their table. "Take a seat."

"Are you sure? I'm not taking anyone's place?"

"Nope. It's yours."

The older woman looked him over and then said something in Russian to Lusha.

"She says you are good-looking."

Smiling, he dipped his head. "Thank you."

The woman nodded and turned to Marina to continue their hushed conversation.

"Is Callie human?" he asked.

"She was at some point," Lusha said. "She was a Dormant who got induced by her mate."

"Maybe that's why she volunteered her place." He looked around the restaurant, estimating that there were no more than twenty people there. The older-looking ones were definitely human, but there were a few young faces who could be immortal. "What about the rest of the people here? Are all of them human?"

Lusha nodded. "Aside from the two teenage girls over there, all are former slaves of the Kra-ell."

He arched a brow. "Slaves?"

"More like serfs, but yeah. We have a sordid history with them. After Igor's compound was raided by the immortals and the Kra-ell were released from Igor's compulsion, the humans were freed, too. Most of them chose to go to the clan's other location, which is a retreat called Safe Haven, and only a few chose to accompany their former masters to the village. I chose Safe Haven and then came here for the trial, fell in love with the place, and decided to stay."

He wanted to ask why any of the humans would want to be with their former masters, but then a woman clapped her hands, drawing the attention of everyone in the room.

She was strikingly beautiful, with long, honey-hued wavy hair and green eyes that seemed to sparkle with an inner light. She was undoubtedly immortal, which meant that this was Callie, the restaurant's owner.

"Welcome, everyone," Callie said. "Thank you all for coming. We'll get started with the questioning soon, and then we will all enjoy dinner, so let's get the first part over quickly."

As she spoke, a male who looked like an angel walked up to her and put his arm over her shoulders.

The guy had the kind of perfect beauty painters would love to depict and sculptors to sculpt. His long, nearly white, blond hair was gathered with a string at his nape, and his cold blue eyes scanned the small crowd.

There was also an undeniable aura of danger about him.

This was an angel Rob wouldn't want to encounter in a dark alley.

"That's Brundar," Lusha whispered. "Callie's mate. He's a Head Guardian."

Rob nodded, unable to tear his eyes away from the couple. The contrast between Callie's warm approachability and Brundar's dangerous beauty was striking. They were a study of opposites, and yet they seemed to fit together perfectly.

"Most of you are familiar with Arwel." Callie motioned for another male to get up. "But I don't know how many of you are aware of his empathic abilities."

This guy was also strikingly handsome, in the way most of the immortals were, but he seemed less intimidating than Brundar, with kind eyes that looked haunted and an easy smile that looked pained.

"Good evening," Arwel said. "I will be the one conducting the investigation over there." He pointed to one of the booths tucked against the wall. "Brundar will escort one person at a time to the booth, I'll ask a few questions and move to the next. If we manage to do everything in an orderly manner, we will be done in less than an hour and enjoy the tasty feast Callie has prepared for us."

As Brundar began calling and escorting people to Arwel one by one, Rob studied both Guardians more closely.

Brundar never smiled, but he was gentle and patient as he led people to the empath. Arwel smiled warmly and shook every person's hand, but the anguish in his eyes didn't diminish. If anything, it intensified.

Perhaps he had a bad headache?

Did immortals even get them?

When Rob was the last one left, he nodded at Brundar and followed him to Arwel's booth.

"Rob, right?" Arwel said. "You don't actually need to be here for this."

Rob nodded. "I know, but I was curious. And...well, to be honest, I wanted to meet more people." He paused, then added, "Are you alright? You look like you're in pain."

Arwel's smile turned rueful. "Perceptive of you. As an empath, I feel the emotions of those around me, especially those of humans who don't shield anything, and right now, I'm feeling the pain of every human in this restaurant." His gaze seemed to pierce right through Rob. "Yours is particularly raw."

Arwel's words jolted him out of his pleasant mood.

He'd thought he was doing okay, that he was moving past the hurt of Lynda's betrayal, but hearing Arwel describe his pain as 'raw' made him realize he'd just been suppressing his feelings, pushing them down instead of dealing with them.

"I'll be fine," he managed to say. "It's tough, but I'll get over it, and it's for the best." He took a deep breath. "I'm starting a new life that is much better than the one I had planned. I just need to find an inducer."

Arwel tilted his head. "I'd be happy to offer my services."

That was unexpected and incredibly nice of Arwel to offer. "Thank you. I accept." Rob extended his hand.

Arwel shook it. "It's my pleasure. You are honoring me by choosing me as your inducer." He leaned toward Rob. "I hope someone has told you that it means we will have to be friends for life."

Rob grinned. "I would like that very much. I don't have a best friend, and I've always wanted one." He leaned forward. "Don't tell Margo, but I also wanted a brother and was disappointed when my parents told me that I was getting a sister. I wouldn't trade her for anyone now, but as a kid, well, I was lonely."

He was still lonely, but Arwel probably knew that, and that was why he'd offered to be his inducer and his friend.

Arwel chuckled. "I don't have any siblings, so I'm more than happy to adopt you as mine."

35

THE SABOTEUR

The night air was cool against the saboteur's skin as she sat on the swing, her feet dragging through the grass below. The playground, usually alive with the shrieks and laughter of children, was silent at this hour. The only sound was the soft creaking of the swing's chains as she absentmindedly rocked back and forth.

The little ones were all tucked away in their beds or going through their nightly routines about now, the kind of coddling rituals she'd seen on TV.

Baths with bubbles? Bedtime stories? Lullabies?

These were foreign concepts to her.

Her childhood had been vastly different. Instead of a playground, she'd had a training yard. Instead of toys, she'd had weapons. Her earliest memories were of gripping a stick in her small hands, learning to wield it as an extension of herself. No time had been wasted on games or idle play. Every moment was dedicated to honing her skills and becoming the warrior she was meant to be.

The rest of the time had been dedicated to training her mind.

As she gazed at the empty playground, she wondered who had it better. These children, with their carefree days of play and laughter? Or her, with her strenuous training and a sense of purpose?

She wasn't sure.

The saboteur's eyes drifted to the benches surrounding the playground. During the day, they would be occupied by mothers, chatting and gossiping while keeping a watchful eye on their offspring.

She wondered what they talked about.

The latest village gossip? Their children's achievements?

It all seemed so trivial.

So human.

This wasn't the Kra-ell spirit. The Kra-ell were warriors born and bred. They didn't waste time on idle chatter and frivolous pursuits.

These village children, with their soft upbringing and lack of true challenge, would be useless in battle. They were soft and unprepared.

Cannon fodder was the human term for soldiers whose lives were not valued.

At the sound of approaching footsteps, she planted her feet on the ground, stopping the swinging motion. The three figures approaching tried to keep their demeanor casual, but they weren't very good actors.

Not like her.

Well, that was what she had to work with, inferior as they were.

They were afraid of her, and rightly so. She was stronger, smarter, and she called the shots. She did not have their loyalty, but she had their obedience, and that was good enough.

"Did anyone suspect anything?" she asked in a low voice.

As the three shook their heads in unison, the saboteur felt a wave of relief wash over her, but she was careful not to let it show on her face.

She hadn't been sure her compulsion would hold under the scrutiny of the village's strongest compellers. The fact that it had was not only reassuring but exhilarating.

It meant she was stronger than them all.

The thought sent a thrill of power through her.

She looked at each of her minions in turn. The boy, Blue, stood slightly apart from the others, his stance betraying a confidence that bordered on arrogance. He felt protective of Yellow and Red, but his stance was nothing but bravado. If she could have their loyalty, she would choose Red, who was the smartest, to be her second, but only until she revealed her plot to the other young Kra-ell she hung out with. Then, she would have no more use for these three.

For now, the other Kra-ell didn't think much of her, but they would soon.

"Good," she said, allowing a small note of approval to creep into her voice. After all, a leader had to know how to dole out praise from time to time.

Not that she expected ever to gain the loyalty of these three, but she needed to practice for the future.

One day, she would be the leader of her people, and she intended to be spectacular.

Blue stepped forward. "Do you want us to do anything tonight or tomorrow?"

The saboteur considered for a moment. Part of her itched to push forward, to strike again while the village was still reeling from their previous actions. But caution stayed her hand. She had already taken significant risks to make a statement.

The statement had been made, and now it was time for caution. That was another thing a leader had to be good at. She had to know when to push and when to pull back. Being rash was the downfall of rulers.

"Not tonight," she said. "Go home. We'll meet again when I decide it is safe."

She saw a flicker of relief cross Blue's face, quickly masked. The three knew better than to antagonize her.

As her minions melted back into the shadows, the saboteur rose from the swing. She took a moment to survey the playground one last time. In the darkness, it looked almost sinister. A fitting metaphor for the rot that lay beneath the village's perfect façade.

She began to walk away, her steps unhurried, her posture relaxed. No need to draw attention by rushing.

As she moved through the quiet village pathways, her mind turned to the future. The compulsion she had placed on her minions had held firm, even under intense questioning.

It was a victory that opened new possibilities.

There was one more test, though, and that was her own ability to withstand compulsion.

If she passed that one, nothing could stop her.

36

ROB

After filling his plate with an array of mouthwatering dishes, Rob returned to sit next to Lusha, who had already filled hers and was digging in.

"This is incredible," she said between mouthfuls. "I might start stealing things myself, so we can get invited to another interrogation here."

Marina chuckled. "Maybe a better plan is to convince some of our friends from Safe Haven to move over here so Callie can hire more people and open for lunch in addition to dinner."

Lusha waved a hand. "Callie already has two assistant cooks and three servers. She doesn't want to open for lunch, and this place is not big enough for more tables. Atzil, though, needs servers and a good bartender who can run the place during the week."

"What about Yuri? Can we interest him in moving over here?" Lusha asked. "He's an awesome bartender."

Marina chuckled. "Not a chance, but maybe William could make another Bob. The one on the ship was amazing." She launched into describing a robotic bartender who sounded like something from a science fiction movie. "I was told that he was a prototype, and since he was a success, why not build more, right?"

"Right," Lusha said. "I wasn't there, but Bob sounds fantastic."

Rob's curiosity was piqued. "Did William design Bob?" he asked Marina.

"His team did. You are a computer guy, right?"

He nodded. "I would love to visit William's lab. Any idea who I should talk to about that?"

Lusha shrugged. "You can probably just walk in there. It's on one of the levels of the underground structure." She looked over her shoulder at where Arwel was sitting with Brundar and Callie. "You can ask one of them." She turned back to him. "What did you and Arwel talk about? You sat with him longer than anyone else."

He didn't want to tell Lusha that Arwel felt his pain. "He asked how I liked the village, and I told him that I was looking for an inducer. He graciously volunteered, and I accepted."

"Oh, wow." Lusha leaned back. "That's a great honor to be induced by a Head Guardian. You'd better start training so you won't embarrass yourself." She grinned. "From what I've heard, a male Dormant needs to last at least a minute against his inducer. Otherwise, the immortal's aggression won't be triggered, and he won't produce any venom."

Rob felt the blood drain from his face. The last time he had done any sparring was in high school, and he wasn't good at it even then.

"Is a Head Guardian like a captain?" he asked.

"I guess so." Lusha glanced at Arwel again. "He can get you anywhere you want, so you can definitely ask him about visiting William's underground empire."

"I will. Thank you for the suggestion." Rob pushed to his feet. "I'm going for seconds."

He wasn't ready to ask Arwel for another favor so soon after the guy had volunteered to induce him. Perhaps Mia or Toven could arrange a meeting with William. He also needed to hit the gym as soon as possible. No wonder Mia had suggested it as a good place to meet people. It had been her way of gently nudging him to start exercising.

When he returned to the table, Marina and the other woman were gone, but Lusha was waiting for him.

"Am I keeping you from your boyfriend?" he asked.

The smile slid off her face. "Alfie is on a mission tonight. Besides, he is not exactly my boyfriend. It's not like we live together or spend every free moment with one another."

Was that a hint that she was available?

Rob arched a brow. "What is he then?"

"A friend with benefits. I like him a lot, but he is not serious about me. I think he's afraid to develop feelings for me." Her eyes turned sad. "It takes a special kind of immortal to commit to a human who might not live all that long." She sighed. "I'm taking part in a study that the clan doctor is conducting. She's testing Marina and me to see if frequent exposure to venom prolongs our lives. I'm quarter Kra-ell, so maybe there is hope for me. The Kra-ell are not immortals, but they are very long-lived. I would be happy to get half their life span."

"Which is what?"

"About a thousand years."

He frowned. "Mia told me that their ship was lost in space for seven thousand years. How did they survive it?"

"Stasis chambers," she said, as if it was self-explanatory. "Their ship exploded over Earth, but it managed to eject all the life pods with the stasis chambers inside. The pods landed in different places, and some opened right away while others opened several years later, and still others didn't open at all. Most are still missing, and their occupants are most likely dead. Only a small number of the settlers survived."

"That's sad." He put his fork down. "You said that they enslaved humans."

Lusha nodded. "Yeah, most of them did. The Kra-ell are a warrior race, and they are hunters. They have the ability to put animals and humans under a thrall. In the case of the animals, they thrall them, so they do not struggle when they drink their blood, and in the case of humans, they thrall them to do work for them and to breed with them. It's not a pretty story, but it's not horrific either. I got to attend a university and study law, and I wasn't the only one. Humans were paid small wages that they could spend however they wanted, and food and shelter were provided."

Rob was surprised that the clan welcomed such savages to live among them, but there was probably more to the story. "Why did some of the humans choose to live with their former masters then?"

She smiled. "Because they are no longer their masters, and some of the older ones couldn't imagine living independently. For better or for worse, it was a symbiotic relationship."

"What about you?" Rob asked. "Why did you choose to live here?"

"Originally, I chose Safe Haven. I only came here to defend several of the purebloods in a trial. I realized that I liked it better here because I really liked the immortals, so I decided to stay, at least for a while."

"Are there any immortals in Safe Haven?"

"A few," Lusha said. "It's like an outpost for them to use for various projects."

"I see."

She leaned closer. "The clan has been working to integrate the Kra-ell and teach them to see humans as equals, and the Kra-ell are making an effort, but old habits die hard."

"Obviously. That's why I find the humans' choice strange."

Lusha smiled. "Most of the humans in the compound were born there. They don't know anything else. Even if they could, they wouldn't want to live independently because they don't know how. The clan employs them, protects them, and gives them a very comfortable life." She waved a hand. "This place is incredible. Who wouldn't want to live here?"

"Those responsible for the thefts and sabotage?"

Lusha laughed. "Yeah, they might be the only people who are unhappy here, and they should get their heads examined."

37

ANNANI

As the last of her guests departed, Annani sank into her favorite armchair and let out a relieved sigh. The day had been long, filled with questioning session after questioning session that she had tried to make as friendly and lighthearted as possible to put her people at ease.

No one liked to be interrogated, even though she had informed every group that it was just procedural and that clan members were not really suspected.

Her Odus had worked through the previous night to bake the quantities needed and package them into nice little boxes with ribbons tied around them. Today, they had served drinks and more cookies as her guests were called in.

Good thing that the Odus did not get tired and did not need rest. One hour of recharging was enough to keep them going.

Ogidu walked over and bowed. "Can I pour you a fresh cup of tea, Clan Mother?"

"No, thank you. This one is still almost full. I also want to thank you for all the work you and Oridu have put into making this day the success it was."

The Odu beamed at the praise. "It is our pleasure to serve you, Clan Mother."

When he left, Annani took a sip of the cold tea and leaned back in her armchair with a satisfied smile. None of the clan members she had interviewed had anything to do with the recent thefts and acts of sabotage plaguing the village nor did they know who the culprit might be. There were suspicions, of course, but no one knew anything for sure.

The only one who had seemed a little uneasy was Parker, but that was understandable. He was still a kid and facing her must have been intimidating. Also, as a compeller himself, Parker must have been unsettled by being on the receiving end of her much more powerful compulsion.

Still, the boy's courage and strength of character impressed her. He was only thirteen when he volunteered to undergo induction and earn his family a place in the village so his mother could take her time.

It had been a selfless and gutsy move.

"Such a nice boy," Annani murmured to herself.

Parker's inner strength and good character reminded her of Ell-rom.

Amanda had taken over the task of preparing the welcome party for him and Morelle, and the announcement had been posted on the clan's bulletin board, but Annani still had not done the one task she had not delegated to anyone else, which was to call Sari and convince her to come to the party.

Reaching into the hidden pocket in her gown, she pulled out her phone and checked the time, doing a quick mental calculation.

It was a little after five in the morning in Scotland, which was still a little early to call, but her daughter was an early riser.

"Mother?" Sari's voice came through a little groggy. "Is everything alright?"

Annani felt a wave of affection wash over her at the sound of her daughter's voice. "Everything's fine, my darling. Did I wake you?"

"I just haven't had my morning coffee yet."

Annani smiled. Sari needed a couple of cups to get going in the morning, which was such a human thing that it must be all in her mind. Gods and immortals did not need stimulants to function.

"Then I will let you get your caffeine fix and call you in a few minutes."

"I'm brewing it as we speak. Just tell me why you are calling at five in the morning. I know that you did not miscalculate the time difference, which means that you were eager to talk to me. Is one of my sisters pregnant again? And just so there is no misunderstanding, I count Syssi as my sister, too."

Annani laughed. "I wish, but no, that is not what I am calling about. Ell-rom and Morelle are moving to the village this Friday afternoon, and I want you and David to be here. I want Ell-rom to meet all of my children."

There was a long pause on the other end of the line. "It's not easy for me to leave on such short notice," Sari said. "David and I can come some other time."

Annani expected that response and was unfazed by it. "It is important to me for all of my children to be here when I welcome my newfound brother and sister into the village. I want us to feel like a family from the very start. Besides, I miss you. I have not seen you in a long time."

Sari chuckled. "The cruise wasn't that long ago, Mother, and we saw each other a lot then."

"It is never enough for a mother," Annani said. "It would mean so much to me. Even if you can only stay for the weekend, it would be wonderful to see you and David."

When there was a sigh, Annani smiled, knowing that she had won. Not that she had expected anything else. If Sari continued to refuse, she would have commanded her to come.

After all, Annani was still the head of the clan and the head of the family, and she expected to be obeyed.

"Alright," Sari said. "We'll be there for the party on Friday and stay over the weekend."

"Thank you, my darling. You have made your mother very happy."

She wanted Sari and David to stay at her house, but since Ell-rom and Jasmine would be staying with her as well, her Odus would have to give up their room, which was not a problem. They did not really need a private space or a bed. They could recharge while standing in the pantry.

"Mother? Are you still there?" Sari's voice cut through Annani's planning.

"Yes, sorry, darling. I was just thinking about all the arrangements."

"I'm sure it will be wonderful, Mother," Sari said. "You always throw the best parties."

"Actually, I was thinking about hosting you and David along with Ell-rom and Jasmine and having my Odus prepare the rooms."

"That's...that might be a little too much."

"Nonsense. Jasmine and Ell-rom are delightful people, and I have no doubt that you and David will enjoy their company."

After they said their goodbyes and ended the call, Annani rose from her chair and walked over to the front door. The shutters were all closed for the night, but she could sit on the front porch and relax, looking at the sky.

The night was clear, the village was quiet, and most of its residents were already tucked away in their homes. It was nice to sit outside and enjoy the sounds of nature without having the glaring sun in her eyes.

Ogidu rushed outside with her shawl. "It is chilly out here at night, Clan Mother."

It was fine, but she accepted it. "Thank you." She draped it over her shoulders. When he did not budge from his spot by the railing, she smiled. "There are Guardians stationed around my house, Ogidu. I do not require your protection out here."

He bowed low. "I would still like to remain here if that is not too much bother. Master Kian assigned more Guardians to patrol at night because of what has been happening lately."

It was both reassuring and unsettling that the Odu had not obeyed her without question as he once would have. The growing sentience of the Odus manifested itself in many ways, some small, some more significant.

"Very well, Ogidu. You may stay."

"Thank you, Clan Mother." He bowed again. "I will be motionless and silent and will not disturb you."

She nodded.

It was sad that someone in this perfect community they had built was working to undermine everyone's happiness and tranquility.

Chuckling softly at the absurdity of the statement she had just made, Annani tightened the shawl against her bare shoulders. There had never been tranquility in the village. Something was always happening, and as unsettling as it was, it served a purpose.

A society that grew too comfortable and complacent was a society in decline. Perhaps she should thank the saboteur for stirring things up.

38

KIAN

It was dark outside when Kian made his way home, and he was upset about missing Allegra's bath time. He loved sitting next to her while she played in the tub, and telling her made-up stories about his day.

The first time he had done that was when he'd realized how boring what he did would sound to a small child. So, instead of telling her about business contracts, phone meetings, and ongoing investigations, he told her fantastic tales about the heroic deeds of Captain Grouchy Face, which was his secret superhero identity.

The best part about that was hearing Syssi's laughter every time he mentioned his superhero name.

Allegra didn't laugh, but she smiled in a way that made it obvious she knew the stories were not real. He tried to make them educational and age-appropriate, but since he wasn't the best storyteller, they were sometimes too gruesome, and Syssi had to clear her throat to remind him that Captain Grouchy Face could scare the bad guys away with his formidable grouchy expression, and no violence was needed.

Funny how it turned out that Ell-rom was the real superhero with supernatural abilities. He also didn't use violence against the bad guys, but they still dropped dead.

It was a nifty superhero trick, provided the hero didn't turn into a supervillain.

Kian still needed to talk to his mother and tell her about Ell-rom and what happened earlier. He also needed to ask her about what she'd learned from her investigation today, but it could wait for tomorrow morning.

Kian's plan was to get home, sneak into Allegra's room, and kiss her cheeks, even at the risk of waking her up and having to deal with the real grouchy face in the family. Allegra didn't like being woken up.

Passing by his mother's house, he changed his plans when he saw her sitting on a rocker on her front porch.

Ogidu stood at attention near the railing, a silent, ever-vigilant sentinel.

Kian sighed and changed course. "Good evening, Mother," he said as he climbed the steps.

Annani looked at him with a warm smile spreading across her face. "Kian, my dear son. Come, sit with me for a while." She gestured to the empty rocking chair beside her.

"I'd rather go inside if you don't mind. I need a drink."

It wasn't a lie. He could use a drink, but his main objective was to have this conversation with his mother in private.

"Ogidu can bring it out for you," she said.

"I'd rather have the drink inside, Mother."

Understanding dawning in her eyes, Annani rose to her feet. "You are right. It is getting a little too chilly out here." She walked toward the front door.

Ogidu rushed to open it for her, and as soon as she entered, she removed the shawl and handed it to the Odu. "Thank you, Ogidu. Please put it in my closet."

She turned to Kian with a smile. "The truth is that I was too hot underneath that thing. I assume that you need to tell me something in private?"

Kian nodded. "But I also need a drink." He walked over to the bar. "Can I get you something?"

His mother rarely consumed alcohol, but he had to ask.

"No, thank you. I prefer tea." She told Ogidu, who had returned from putting her shawl away, "Can you be a darling and steep enough tea for two? I am sure Kian would like some after he is done with his drink."

Ogidu bowed. "Of course, Clan Mother."

As Annani settled on the couch, Kian poured himself a shot of whiskey and joined her. "I didn't want to talk outside because I didn't want the Guardians patrolling this section to overhear what I needed to tell you."

"I figured as much. Did Toven or the other investigators find who the perpetrator is?"

"No, not yet. But you know who the main suspect is. What about you? Did any of ours reveal anything?"

Annani shook her head. "Most are okay with the Kra-ell but wish that they would put more effort into integrating, but some do not like them, are bothered by having people with different values among them and think that it was a mistake to bring them here."

Kian took a sip of his drink and put the glass on the coffee table. "I'm surprised that only a small portion of clan members are regretting letting the Kra-ell in. I thought it would be more."

"Our people are thirsty for new blood in the village." She chuckled. "That phrase assumes a whole different meaning when the new blood is actually consuming blood."

"It does." Kian lifted his glass and emptied the rest of the amber liquid down his throat. "In other news, Ell-rom thinks that he killed a human today just by wishing him dead."

His delivery had been as delicate as a sledgehammer, and he could just imagine Syssi's reproachful look and headshaking upon hearing how he'd done it.

He could have started with the mugging attempt, but that wouldn't have softened the eventual blow when he got to the point when Ell-rom killed the guy by wishing him dead.

His mother was rarely lost for words, but she seemed speechless for a long moment. "Is that your idea of a joke, Kian?" she finally asked.

39

ANNANI

"No joke." Kian took a deep breath. "Ell-rom and Jasmine went for a walk, wandered into an alley to take a shortcut, and a druggie grabbed Jasmine by her throat and pressed a gun to her head. Ell-rom was afraid to move a muscle because the druggie's hand was shaking, so he just wished for him to drop dead, and the attacker obliged him and immediately did just that. That's more or less the whole story."

Annani stared at her son for a long moment. "You know that was not what happened, right? If people could kill by wishing it, there would be no humans left on Earth."

It was only a slight exaggeration.

She herself was guilty of sometimes thinking bad thoughts of that kind, but even though she could actually kill with a mental command, like thralling a human to jump off a bridge or out a window, she would never do that.

Could she thrall a human to stop breathing, though?

Annani had never tried, but it might be possible. "Ell-rom must have thralled the human," she said. "He must have entered his mind and commanded him to stop breathing or something like that. Ell-rom does not remember how thralling is done, but in an emergency, his ability might have manifested."

"It's possible." Kian rose to his feet and walked over to the bar. "Julian ran tests on the dead human, and he found no obvious cause of death. I think that asphyxiation would have left its mark. And before you suggest that he commanded the guy's heart to stop, that's not possible. Not even with compulsion."

"Thank the merciful Fates for that." Annani adjusted the folds of her gown.

As Ogidu returned with the tea and poured her a cup, she was glad for the short break to collect her thoughts as she sipped on the tea.

"Are Ell-rom and Jasmine alright?" she asked.

"I'm sure they are shaken." Kian returned with his refilled whiskey glass and sat down. "I spoke with Julian, who told me what happened. I didn't speak with either of them."

Annani pulled out her phone to check the time. "Do you think it is too late to call them?"

"Probably not, but both of their phones are monitored. We do not want anyone learning of Ell-rom's ability in case it is real. Imagine what he could do. What he could be coerced to do."

The possibilities were frightening, and Annani's first instinct was to hide Ell-rom from the world so no one would ever discover his ability. He was such a gentle soul, and if his talent was real, then the Fates were cruel to choose him to carry such a burden.

Then again, perhaps he was the perfect carrier of such a terrifying talent precisely because he did not have one evil bone in his body. But why would they gift such a talent to anyone at all?

The moment she thought of it, her mind conjured the image of the Eternal King. Was that why he was so adamant about disposing of the twins?

How could he have known that they would possess such a talent?

Perhaps that was the reason the gods were not supposed to produce offspring with Kra-ell.

Maybe that was why they referred to such hybrids as abominations. It wasn't because they were born physically deformed but because they had monstrous abilities.

"What are you thinking?" Kian asked.

"That Ell-rom needs to be protected, and this secret needs to stay between us."

"I agree. We still need to test him in a controlled environment to make sure that his claim is true, but if it is, it raises many potential problems."

"The power to kill with a thought," Annani murmured. "I wonder if it is distance dependent." She looked at

Kian. "What if he could kill the Eternal King? Not that I will even suggest it. Not before there is a replacement who can hold Anumati from falling apart. But what if that is why the king wants the twins dead so badly that he's still sending ships to this sector to make sure that they were not found and, if found, immediately eliminated?"

Kian nodded. "That's a logical assumption. Although how would he know when Ell-rom himself did not know he could do that?"

"Ell-rom did not remember the ability," Annani said. "That does not mean that he did not use it before. Someone in the temple might have been feeding the Eternal King information, and when the Kra-ell queen discovered it, she snuck her children out of Anumati before he could get to them."

"There is another possibility." Kian cradled his half-empty glass. "Perhaps hybrids like Ell-rom and Morelle had been born before and possessed terrifying powers, so they were just summarily eliminated, and no one was allowed to mention them."

"The same thing has occurred to me." Annani took a sip from her tea and put the cup on the tray. "If that is true, no wonder the gods and the Kra-ell called them abominations. Perhaps the first hybrids of that kind did terrible things, like killing scores of people with their minds."

She would never have allowed herself to talk like that with anyone other than Kian. Annani was determined to protect Ell-rom and Morelle and keep them from harm, but she was not about to trivialize their potential threat to the world.

Kian put his glass down and reached for her hand. "It still might be a storm in a teacup. Ell-rom is in many ways like a child who believes he has magical abilities. We will test him, and if he proves his claim, we will worry about his power later."

"How would you test it?"

Kian's smile would have been terrifying to anyone else, but she knew the pure heart beating in her son's chest. "Onegus voiced a wish that I dismissed at the time, but now I might implement it. He said that it's not enough to go after the traffickers. He wanted to find the monsters who buy children to do unspeakably evil things and eliminate them. We don't need to go through the same process as the humans to determine their guilt. We can enter their minds and see what they have done recently. If they are guilty, they are dead. I don't think that even Ell-rom would have a problem testing his ability on the worst kind of demons in human skin."

40

PETER

The night air was thick with tension as Peter crouched behind a dilapidated warehouse, his eyes fixed on the nondescript building across the street. From the outside, it looked like any other rundown structure in this abandoned industrial complex, but Peter and his team knew better.

Inside those weathered walls, lives were being bought and sold, dreams shattered, and innocence stolen.

"Team Eagle is in position," Alfie's voice crackled through the earpiece.

"Team Hawk is ready," Jay confirmed a moment later.

Peter took a deep breath, steadying his nerves. No matter how many of these operations he led, the moments before breaching always set his heart racing, not because he feared for himself or his teammates, but because he feared for the victims getting caught in the crossfire. "Team Falcon is standing by," he said.

The birds of prey naming of their teams had been Alfie's idea, and although Peter thought it was unnecessary, the names were growing on him.

Not that there was anything wrong with simply calling them Team One, Team Two, and Team Three, but calling his guys Team Falcon elevated their status somehow.

Kri's calm voice came through next. "Transport team is in place and ready for extraction."

With all teams in place, Peter gave a nod to the Guardians flanking him. They were a mix of a few seasoned veterans who had served for many centuries, and those like him, who hadn't served for as long but had returned to the force recently, united in their determination to fight the evil within that building.

"Remember," Peter said. "As always, our primary objective is to neutralize the traffickers first and secure the victims second. We don't want any unintended casualties because some of you are hotheaded and impatient." He cast a reproachful glance at Bjorn. The guy still fought like a Viking. "This time, we need to apprehend one of the traffickers, preferably the ringleader, and take him to the keep."

They always interrogated the leader of the scum to get information about other possible cells and potential buyers, but this time, they would be taking the vermin to the keep for the gods to experiment on.

Still, that was information he didn't need to share with the rest of the Guardians. Alfie and Jay knew what they needed him for, and that was enough.

A chorus of affirmatives sounded in his ear.

Peter took another deep breath, tasting the metallic tang of adrenaline on his tongue. "On my mark. Three...two...one...go!"

In a blur of motion, the teams sprang into action. Alfie's team hit the front entrance while Jay's group circled around to cover the back. Peter led his team straight up the side of the building, using their immortal strength and agility to scale the walls and enter through the upper windows.

The sound of breaking glass and splintering wood filled the air as the Guardians breached the building simultaneously. Shouts of surprise and fear erupted from inside, quickly drowned out by the voices of Guardians as they secured room after room.

Peter landed in what appeared to be a makeshift office, his eyes quickly adjusting to the dim interior. A portly man in ill-fitting fatigues scrambled to his feet, reaching for something under his desk. Without hesitation, Peter closed the distance between them, his hand clamping down on the man's wrist before he could grab whatever weapon he was going for.

He could have frozen the man with a thrall, but getting physical was more satisfying.

Besides, there was always a chance of encountering an immune.

"I wouldn't," Peter growled, wanting desperately to shatter the bones in the vermin's wrist and hear him squeal in agony.

The man's face paled, beads of sweat forming on his brow. "Who are you? Do you know who I work for?"

Peter's lip curled in disgust. "Is it the devil?" With a quick movement, he had the trafficker subdued and zip-tied. "It is time to pay for your sins, scumbag."

As he hauled the man to his feet, the sounds of the ongoing operation filtered through his enhanced hearing. The clash of combat, cries of fear and relief, and the steady voices of his fellow Guardians painted a vivid picture of what was happening throughout the building.

"Team Eagle, report," Peter commanded, dragging his prisoner toward the door.

Alfie's voice came through. "Ground floor secured. We've got eight victims, all female, with ages ranging from early teens to early twenties. No serious injuries, but they are terrified. Should I thrall them or leave them for Kri?"

"The usual. Just calm them down and let Kri do the rest."

"Copy that," Alfie said.

"Jay, what's your status?" Peter asked.

"My team has the basement locked down," Jay said. "We've got another nine victims down here, and it's not pretty. They look like they've been here a while."

Peter's jaw clenched, fury burning in his chest. He shoved the trafficker against the wall, leaning in close. "You better pray to whatever god you believe in that those girls can be saved," he hissed. "Because if they can't, I'll make you suffer worse than the fires of hell." He let his fangs show.

"What are you?" the man whimpered, his bravado from earlier completely evaporated.

"Your worst nightmare."

"We've got five more on the second floor," one of Peter's teammates called out. "Looks like some kind of VIP area. The girls here are in good shape physically, but they are drugged out of their minds."

"Good work," Peter acknowledged. "Kri, we're ready for extraction. Bring the vans in close. We've got more victims than anticipated."

"Copy that," Kri responded. "We're moving in now."

Peter marched his prisoner down the stairs, his enhanced strength making the man's weight inconsequential.

As they reached the ground floor, Peter surveyed the results of the operation.

The large open space that had once been a factory floor was now a hive of activity. Guardians led bound scumbags to a cage in the back while others were tending to the shell-shocked victims. Some of the girls huddled together, tears streaming down their faces, while others sat in either stunned silence or drugged stupor, their eyes vacant.

Alfie approached, his usually cheerful face grim. "We checked every square inch of this hellhole. Everyone is accounted for."

Peter nodded, his grip tightening on the trafficker's arm. "Good work. Make sure the victims are checked for injuries before loading them up. We don't want anyone bleeding out on the way."

"Already on it." Alfie's eyes flickered to the man in Peter's grasp. "This our guy?"

"Seems to be in charge," Peter confirmed.

At the sound of the two vans pulling up outside, Peter glanced at the broken door that was hanging from one hinge.

Kri entered, her blond hair tied in a tight braid, her expression calm and compassionate. "Transport's ready to load," she announced, her eyes sweeping the room. When she saw the state of some of the victims, a flash of pain crossed her features before she schooled her expression.

"Don't be afraid," she said in her melodic voice that was laced with calm. "You are safe now. We are taking you to a sanctuary where you will be taken care of, protected, and given a chance to heal." She repeated the same in Spanish for those who didn't understand English, which seemed to be the majority of them.

As the Guardians began to usher the rescued girls toward the waiting vans, Peter felt the usual mix of emotions that assaulted him at the end of each of those missions. Pride in his team's efficiency, relief at the successful rescue, and a burning anger at the monsters who perpetrated such cruelty.

One of the younger victims, a girl who couldn't have been more than twelve, caught Peter's eye as she was led past. The fear and uncertainty in her gaze were heart-wrenching, but there was also a glimmer of hope. It was that hope, that chance to give these girls back their lives, that made it all worthwhile.

Once the last of the victims had been loaded into the vans, Peter turned his attention back to his prisoner. "Your turn."

The man started to struggle. "You'll be sorry when El Patrón finds out!"

Peter ignored him. "Alfie, Jay, you're with me. We've got a special delivery to make."

They escorted the trafficker to a separate van that was outfitted especially for transporting criminals.

As they secured the prisoner, Peter took a moment to survey the scene one last time.

The building that had been a house of horrors now housed only a bunch of scumbags locked in a cage. They had been thralled to confess their crimes when the police arrived. They wouldn't remember who attacked them and rescued the girls. The Guardians left no evidence to tie them to the scene of the crime, and that included any surveillance that had been in the building and the immediate area surrounding it. The laptops and desktops had been loaded into one of the other vans for the guys in charge of extracting information to crack. Everything else had been destroyed.

As they pulled away from the warehouse, Peter allowed himself a moment of satisfaction. Tonight, they'd struck another blow against the darkness. It wasn't a big victory, and there were still countless battles to fight, but tonight, they'd hung another light on the string of hope.

41

MARINA

Marina sat cross-legged on her living room sofa, a pint of chocolate chip cookie dough ice cream nestled in her lap. The spoon clinked against the container as she dug for another generous scoop, her eyes fixed on the muted television screen displaying the local news. No breaking stories, no reports of disturbances or police activity. Just the usual mundane updates that filled the late-night broadcasts.

She shouldn't have been watching. Peter always told her not to, that it would only feed her anxiety. But she couldn't help it. Every time he went out on a mission, her imagination ran wild with worst-case scenarios.

"You're going to give yourself brain freeze if you keep eating that fast," Lusha's amused voice cut through Marina's worried thoughts.

She turned to her friend, who was curled up in the adjacent armchair, nursing her own pint of Rocky Road.

Lusha's presence was comforting, a fellow sister in vigil for her male.

"I can't help it." Marina sighed and licked her spoon clean. "Peter is immortal, for the Mother's sake, and really hard to kill, but every time he goes out there, I freak out."

Lusha nodded. "Immortal doesn't mean invincible. I worry, too."

A tense silence fell between them, broken only by the soft clink of spoons against ice cream containers.

Marina's gaze drifted around the room, taking in the cozy space she shared with Peter. Photos of their life together adorned the fireplace mantel, snapshots of picnics in the village, group photos with other Guardians, a candid shot of Peter mid-laugh.

Each image was a reminder of what she had to lose.

"Thank you for staying with me," Marina said. "You didn't have to."

Lusha waved her spoon dismissively. "Of course I did. What kind of a friend would I be if I left you to wallow alone? Besides, I'm eating your ice cream, and it's damn good. The problem is that neither of us has an immortal metabolism, and this is going straight to our thighs."

Marina chuckled. "I wonder if the venom helps with metabolism, too."

"What leads to the venom bite does." Lusha scooped another large chunk of Rocky Road and went on to devour it while making sounds that could be easily mistaken for sounds associated with a different pleasurable activity.

Marina regarded her friend for a long moment before asking the question that was niggling at her. "Hey, Lusha. Is there a reason you haven't moved in with Alfie yet? You are here most of the time anyway."

Lusha's spoon paused halfway to her mouth. She lowered it slowly. "He hasn't asked me to."

"Do you really have to wait for his invitation? Just do it and stake your claim."

Lusha shrugged. "I'm not staking my claim because I have none. We are enjoying each other for the time being."

"What if he asks," Marina pressed, "would you say yes?"

Lusha was quiet for a moment, stirring her ice cream absently. "I'm not sure. I like my independence. But then there is Bridget's experiment, so I have to stay with Alfie until she's done, so maybe it would be more convenient to move in with him for the duration."

Marina snorted. "I bet that would be a hardship."

Lusha grinned. "Oh, absolutely. Such a sacrifice."

They both laughed, the sound easing some of the tension that had been building in Marina's chest.

"What about Rob?" she asked, trying to keep her tone casual. "He seems interested."

"He's a nice guy all around," Lusha admitted. "But he's human, and when he transitions, it'll be at least six months before his venom glands are operational, and I really want to see whether the venom is helping me live longer. I don't want to stop the experiment."

Suddenly, Marina remembered a piece of information that Peter had told them that might affect Lusha's decisions regarding her love life. "You know that the venom is addictive, right?"

"Well, duh. It's like the best drug on the market, just without the nasty side effects."

"There is more to it." Marina put her bucket of ice cream down on the coffee table. "If you are injected with the venom of only one immortal for an extended period of time, you will become addicted to it. You will not want any other males, and when you are separated from your immortal for whatever reason, you will suffer withdrawal symptoms. So, if you think that Alfie is not for you, you should switch to another immortal, and then another, until you find the one you are willing to spend the rest of your life with."

Lusha pursed her lips. "Why did Alfie keep this from me?"

"Maybe he forgot. It's not something most immortals concern themselves with because they don't hook up with the same human females often, and when they find their one and only, they stay with her for life anyway."

Lusha tilted her head. "So, what about a couple like Ingrid and Atzil? They've been together for a long time, and the rumor is that they are not fated mates. She's most likely already addicted to him."

Marina reached for her bucket of ice cream again. "Maybe she has other lovers on the side to keep herself from getting addicted. These immortals are quite promiscuous until they find their one and only and commit."

Lusha sighed and lifted her spoon with what ice cream remained on it. "You are lucky with Peter. He regards you as his fated mate, which is very unusual. Hell, it's unheard of for an immortal to choose a human as his one and only."

"I know." Marina took a big bite of cookie dough. "I hoped Alfie would feel the same way about you."

"He doesn't." Lusha tucked one leg under her. "He's a fun guy, and he cares for me, but he doesn't love me. Maybe if he weren't so afraid of falling for a human, he would have allowed himself to feel more."

"Will you be able to leave him to prevent the addiction?" Marina asked gently.

"Do I have a choice? Maybe I can keep switching immortal lovers until Rob's glands become functional and hook up with him. He's smart, he's funny, and he's got this...I don't know, this earnestness about him. Like he's excited about every new thing he's learning."

"That's not a bad thing," Marina pointed out.

"No, it's not," Lusha agreed. "But right now, Rob is not ready yet for a new relationship, and he just needs a friend. I can be that for him without complicating things."

They settled back into silence, focusing on the muted TV. Marina's ice cream was long since finished, and the empty container was discarded on the coffee table. She pulled a throw blanket over her legs, feeling the lateness of the hour starting to weigh on her.

"Go to sleep," Lusha said. "You have work tomorrow."

"So do you."

Lusha shrugged. "I don't need as many hours of sleep to recharge. My quarter Kra-ell genes are at least good for something."

Marina wondered what else they were good for. It didn't make sense that Lusha had not benefited from them in some other way as well.

When her phone buzzed on the coffee table, Marina snatched it up, her heart leaping when she saw Peter's name on the screen.

"Peter?"

"Hey, beautiful," his warm voice came through, instantly soothing her frayed nerves. "We're all done here. Everyone's okay, and the mission is accomplished. We still need to drop off something at the keep, so it will be a while until I'm back. I don't want you to stay up for me. Alfie says to let Lusha know that he is fine. He is coming with me, so both of us are going to be back late."

Marina closed her eyes, letting out a breath she felt like she'd been holding all night. "I'm so glad that everyone is okay. Lusha is right here with me. I'll tell her. And, Peter?"

"Yes, my love?"

"I love you."

"I love you too, sweetheart," he said. "Try to get some sleep, okay? I'll see you soon."

As she ended the call, Marina looked at Lusha, who didn't look as happy as Marina felt. "What's the matter?"

"Peter called you, but Alfie only relayed a message. Do you see the difference?"

Regrettably, Lusha was right, but Marina wasn't going to admit it. "They have different personalities, that's all."

"Yeah." Lusha snorted. "One is in love, and the other is not."

42

ELL-ROM

Ell-rom lay still in the darkness, his eyes fixed on the ceiling, which he could see perfectly in the dim light filtering through the curtains. Not that there was anything remarkable to see on that cream-colored surface.

That was not where the answer to his problem was to be found.

The soft sound of the air coming through the vent was soothing but not enough to calm the turmoil in his mind. Beside him, Jasmine's steady breathing should have been calming as well, but tonight it only highlighted his restlessness.

His mind was too busy churning with thoughts and worries to find peace.

He hadn't taken any naps today, not even after Julian put him through a strenuous exercise circuit in the gym. The physical exhaustion should have knocked him out, but his mind refused to let his body rest.

The events of the day played on repeat in his head. The mugger, the sudden realization of his power, the confession to Julian.

Had he done the right thing by revealing his ability?

The question gnawed at him, refusing to let him rest.

Ell-rom's hand drifted to the nightstand where his new phone lay silent. Since the incident, he'd carried it everywhere with him, part-expecting, part-dreading, and part-hoping for a call from Annani or Kian, but the phone had remained stubbornly quiet, and somehow, that silence was worse than facing the fallout that would no doubt be the consequence of his action.

What decisions were being made about his fate today?

The possibilities terrified him. What if they deemed him too dangerous, like they had deemed Igor?

What if they also put him in stasis indefinitely?

What would happen to Jasmine? To Morelle?

He swallowed hard, trying to push away the image of Jasmine and Morelle moving on without him.

Surely, Annani wouldn't allow that.

She was his sister. She would protect him...wouldn't she?

Not if she considered him a threat to her children, grandchildren, and great-grandchildren. As much fondness as she might have for him, her offspring came first.

When Jasmine stirred, Ell-rom tensed, holding still and hoping she had just moved in her sleep, but when he turned his head to look at her, he found her eyes trained on him.

He expected her to ask what was troubling him, but the understanding in her eyes meant that she didn't need to ask because his turmoil was written plainly across his face.

Instead, she smiled salaciously, her eyes glinting with mischief in the low light. "You are restless, my love, and I know just the remedy for that."

Her husky voice didn't leave much room for misinterpretation of what that remedy might be, and Ell-rom felt his body respond instantly, but even as desire coursed through him, doubt crept in.

His mind was too cluttered with anxiety for him to be able to concentrate on giving Jasmine pleasure.

"I'm too strung out to be any good to you." He took her hand and brought it to his lips, kissing her fingertips one at a time.

"Don't worry about that." She smiled. "Leave it to me," she whispered, her hand already trailing down his chest.

Ell-rom closed his eyes, surrendering to her touch.

When she pulled away, he opened his eyes in surprise. She was on her knees, her hands gripping her nightdress and yanking it over her head in one fluid move.

Underneath, she was gloriously naked, the perfection of her body taking his breath away.

"You are so beautiful," he whispered.

She just smiled and reached for the elastic of his sleep pants, pulling them down. When his shaft sprang free, she licked her lips. "You're not bad yourself, big boy."

That got a smile out of him. "Are you talking to me or my erection?"

"Both."

She lay next to him, and when her hand closed over his shaft, he gasped and shivered, and then her lips found his in a sweet kiss. He was lost to the sensations, to the taste of her, the warmth of her body pressed against his, and to the gentle up and down strokes of her hand.

When she shifted, pushing him onto his back and straddling him, Ell-rom groaned.

With the heat of her core pressing against his length, he moved his hands to her hips and let himself be swept away by sensation. When she started rocking against him, the electrifying friction melted his worries away, replacing them with a burning need that consumed everything else.

When she finally sank down onto him, taking him deep inside her, Ell-rom's world narrowed to this single point of connection. Nothing else mattered—not his newfound power, not the uncertain future, nothing but this moment, this feeling of completeness.

They moved slowly at first, finding a rhythm. Ell-rom let Jasmine dictate the pace for as long as he could, but then the need to take over became overwhelming, and he gripped her thighs.

Pounding up into her, he went fast and hard.

Jasmine's soft moans turned into gasps, mixing with his deeper groans. The strain that had been coiled tight in his chest all day was replaced by a different kind of tension, one that built with each roll of Jasmine's hips.

As their passion reached its peak, his fangs descended, and he flipped them over with Jasmine still impaled on his shaft. He had just enough control left to lick the spot he was about to bite and then, with a hiss, sank them into the soft flesh of her throat.

The taste of her blood exploded on his tongue, rich and sweet and uniquely Jasmine.

She climaxed with a scream, and the pleasure of her body clenching around him sent him over the edge. Ellrom erupted, holding Jasmine close as waves of ecstasy washed over him.

When the haze dispersed, he retracted his fangs and licked the small puncture wounds on her neck, his saliva sealing them closed.

Jasmine was out, soaring on the wings of ecstasy, and the room was quiet save for her gentle breathing and his more labored one. Turning on his side with her still in his arms, he kissed her forehead.

"I love you, my Jasmine. I don't want to ever be separated from you."

43

JASMINE

Jasmine stirred slowly, consciousness returning in gentle waves. The familiar post-venom haze clung to her mind, remnants of the euphoric trip gradually fading. She blinked, orienting herself in the dim pre-dawn light filtering through the curtains.

Beside her, Ell-rom lay motionless, his eyes fixed on the ceiling the same way she'd found him before coming up with a way to distract him.

Evidently, though, her plot had failed, and he hadn't had a wink of sleep.

She turned onto her side, propping herself up on an elbow. "Hey," she said softly, her voice still rough with sleep. "You're still awake?"

Ell-rom's gaze shifted to her, a weak smile tugging at his lips. "Hey." He leaned and kissed her lightly. "How was your trip?"

"Awesome as usual. It's a shame they are getting shorter, though. I wonder if there is a way to prolong them."

She was trying to distract him with idle talk. Maybe occupying his mind with something else would do the trick.

He gave her another weak smile. "The only thing I can think of to keep the trips long is periods of abstinence, but I don't think either of us wants that."

"Definitely not." She leaned over him and kissed his chest. "I love this too much to give it up even for longer trips."

He winced. "I hope you won't be forced to give me up."

"Why would I be forced to do that?"

"They might decide that I'm too dangerous and put me in stasis like they did to Igor."

She lifted her head. "You are nothing like Igor. He was an evil megalomaniac who used compulsion to force his pod mates to execute the males of other surviving pods so they could take their females."

"And I can kill with a thought, which makes me even more dangerous. Why would anyone risk taking me into their community?"

Fear was a powerful motivator, so he wasn't entirely wrong, but Jasmine hoped Annani would rise above such primal instincts and accept her brother. Besides, it would probably occur to the goddess how useful Ell-rom might be to her clan and its goals.

Annani could finally get rid of her archenemy if she wanted.

"You're not a threat, Ell-rom, and you are not dangerous. You are an asset. You're a good person who happens to have a powerful ability, and your sister will realize how valuable you are."

"You think she will use me?"

"She might when there is no other choice, and since Annani is a force for good, I don't expect her to ever ask you to do something that is morally questionable."

Ell-rom released a relieved breath. "I pray to the Mother of All Life that you are right."

"I am."

He smiled. "I like how self-assured you are."

"I'm just thinking logically, and I know that my logic might not work the same way as the logic of others, but if I were in Annani's shoes, I would see you as an incredible asset and not a threat."

He took her hand and brought it to his lips for a gentle kiss. "Annani doesn't know me well enough. I don't know me well enough, either, and I'm scared that I might be a threat, that I might be dangerous."

"But I know you, Ell-rom, and I know you are none of those things. So enough with all this self-doubt. You need to get some sleep."

"I just wish they'd call," he said, glancing at his phone on the nightstand. "Even if it's just to say they need more time to think."

"I know," Jasmine soothed him, running her fingers over his chest. "But they are asleep now, so waiting for them to call does not make sense. You need to rest, love."

Ell-rom shook his head. "I can't. My mind is too riled up."

"Tell you what," she said, sitting up and stretching. "Why don't we get up, make some breakfast, and then plan out our day? We could go for a walk, maybe visit Morelle. Keeping busy might help take your mind off things."

"No walks outside, but I'd like to see Morelle."

That wasn't good. He was traumatized by the mugging and what he had done, and now he was afraid to leave the keep.

It was good that they were moving into the immortals' protected village, but now she wasn't sure that they were. What if Annani decided that it was safer to leave them in the keep for a while?

Again, if she were in the goddess's shoes, she would proceed with caution. Ell-rom was right about his sister not knowing him well enough yet to trust him with the lives of her family.

She might want to wait a little longer.

"I can drive you to a safer part of town, you know. A nice residential area where there are no druggies and no crazies."

She still remembered the homeless man who had yelled at her when she'd gone looking for a branch to fashion her scrying stick from.

"I thought this area was safe," Ell-rom said. "This building seems luxurious, and the people inside are clean and well-dressed. How come there are drug addicts and crazy people on these streets?"

"This is still mostly a business and commercial district, with only a few residential buildings here and there. And I'm really not qualified to explain the homeless situation. To me, it seems that the solution is simple, but apparently it's not, and I need coffee before I can say more on the subject." She slid off the bed. "I'm going to the bathroom, and then I'll make coffee."

"Okay." He crossed his arms under his head.

44

KIAN

Kian rose to his feet and walked over to the window, gazing at the village square below. The trafficker the Guardians had captured last night was in the keep's dungeon, ready for the experiment of transferring the tracker from one of the gods to his body, but for that, they needed the keep clinic vacated, and now Kian wasn't sure that he could move Morelle out of there.

With Ell-rom's newfound ability throwing yet another variable into the mix, Kian questioned the wisdom of moving his uncle and aunt to the village as planned.

He needed to talk to his mother again, but that wasn't the kind of talk he wanted to have over the phone.

Striding out of his office, he stopped by Shai's. "I'm going to have tea with my mother. If you need me for anything, call."

His assistant never asked unnecessary questions and just nodded. "Enjoy your tea."

"Thank you."

Exiting the building, he called her. "Good morning, Mother. I'm coming over."

"Excellent. I will tell Ogidu to start brewing tea."

His mother had probably guessed what this was about and refrained from asking.

The walk to her house was short, but it gave Kian time to organize his thoughts. The early risers among the villagers nodded and smiled as he passed, and he returned their greetings in the same manner.

When he rang the doorbell, Ogidu opened the door, bowed, and ushered him inside. "The Clan Mother is awaiting you, Master Kian."

"Thank you." Kian walked into the living room, where his mother was seated on her ornate couch.

"Good morning, my son." She lifted her cheek for him to kiss. "I had a feeling you would be stopping by this morning." She gestured for him to take a seat right next to her.

Kian settled on the couch. "I've been thinking about Ell-rom and Morelle's move to the village. Given the recent developments, I think we shouldn't rush. On the other hand, I need the clinic vacated for the experiment we are about to run, so it's a conundrum."

"Nothing has changed, Kian." Annani lifted the carafe, poured tea into two cups, and handed him one. "I have given a lot of thought to Ell-rom's ability, and even if it is real and not imagined, there is no reason to fear him."

Kian arched a brow. "You're not concerned?"

Annani shook her head. "As I said, I have devoted a lot of thought to this, and I came up with a possible solution. I could compel him, with his agreement of course, to never use his ability against any of our people. If it works, his power would be bound, and we will have nothing to fear."

It was a good idea, in theory. But...

"I'm not sure that Ell-rom can be compelled. There's a good chance that he has a powerful compulsion ability he hasn't discovered yet or that his lethal wishing is a form of compulsion. If that is the case, he might be immune to your compulsion."

Annani nodded. "Still, it is worth a try. Besides, Ell-rom is a decent person, Kian. Having the ability to kill does not make one a killer. Any immortal can kill a human with relative ease, but that does not mean that we go around doing so. We believe in the sanctity of life."

Ell-rom seemed like a good person, but he was still discovering who he was, and there was a slight possibility that a sinister side of him would manifest at some point.

As if killing with a thought wasn't sinister enough.

But his mother was right that the ability to do harm did not make one evil.

"I agree. In that case, what do you think about bringing Ell-rom, Morelle, and Jasmine to the village today instead of tomorrow? I need that clinic vacated."

"Absolutely not." Annani's tone brooked no argument. "The welcome party has to be on Friday. Sari is coming, and she will get here late tonight. Also, the investigation is still ongoing, and I want that to be over before the party."

Kian felt a flicker of exasperation, but he swallowed it down. "Fine. We can wait one more day. It's not like the scumbag we are using for the experiment is going anywhere. He's chilling in the dungeon."

His mother's expression did not change. She was a compassionate soul, she abhorred violence, and she was a great believer in redemption, but some crimes were not redeemable, and the trafficking and monstrous abuse of children was one of them.

"I know you are eager to get it done, Kian. This is an important moment for our family and our community, and it deserves to be done right."

"You're correct, of course," he conceded. "Would you like to go see Ell-rom today? If you want to try compelling him, it should be done before he arrives at the village tomorrow."

Annani's face lit up at the suggestion. "Yes, I would like that very much. I have nothing else planned for today, so whenever you are ready, we can go."

With the ongoing investigation, it was bad timing for him to leave the village, but under no circumstances would he send his mother to the keep without him.

Kian knew it wasn't rational. Not only was she more

powerful than he was, the Guardians escorting her would protect her better than he could.

Nevertheless, he was going with her.

"I need to finish a few things in the office first. I'll call you when I'm on my way."

"I will be ready."

As Kian stood to leave, a thought occurred to him. "Perhaps you should call Ell-rom to let him know that we are on our way. He is likely distraught over what happened and worrying about our reaction. Just make sure that he is not around anyone who is not supposed to know when you talk to him."

He also needed to inform William to stop the monitoring of Ell-rom's phone.

"Do you mean the gods and their mates?"

Kian nodded as he pulled out his phone and texted William.

"Did anyone tell him that he should not talk about his ability?" Annani asked.

Kian frowned. "I just assumed he would not want the information to get out and that Julian would warn him about it too, but maybe you should make sure when you call him."

"I shall do that," Annani said.

After Kian departed his mother's house, William replied to his text that it was done and, thankfully, did not ask why.

On the way back to the office building, Kian called Aru.

"Good morning, Kian," Aru greeted him.

"Good morning. We have the guy in the dungeon, but my mother does not want the twins moved into the village until tomorrow because of the welcome party she is planning for them. That means we can't remove Morelle from the clinic, and I don't want the experiment done while she is still there."

There was a beat of silence. "Why not? The room Ell-rom was in is available. We don't have time. Every day we delay puts us at greater risk of discovery."

Kian pinched the bridge of his nose. "I understand your urgency and share it, but we need both rooms for the experiment, and my mother is set on this party. One more day will not make a difference. But if you think you can convince her otherwise, you're welcome to try."

Aru sighed. "I know better than to argue with your mother. We'll just have to wait."

45

ELL-ROM

Ell-rom entered the elevator with Jasmine and pressed the button for the level where Kian's office was located.

He was grateful for Annani's earlier call. She'd told him that nothing had changed and that she didn't consider his ability a threat. She'd also hinted that she might have a way to mitigate it, but she hadn't elaborated.

"Good afternoon," he said as he entered and bowed to his sister, who sat at the head of the oblong conference table.

Kian was on her right, Julian on her left, and Kian's two formidable bodyguards were leaning against the desk in the back.

The redhead smiled at Ell-rom and nodded as if saying that he was okay with him, that he didn't think of him as a monster. The stoic blond was as expressionless and menacing as always, but by now, Ell-rom knew it wasn't personal. It was just the way he was.

He wondered what happened to the Guardian that made him this way. Something terrible, no doubt.

"Good afternoon," Annani said in her melodic and cheerful voice. "Please, do not bow to me, Ell-rom. We are family." She turned to look at Jasmine. "You too, dear. As my brother's mate, you are family, too, and I do not want you to bow to me."

"Thank you, Clan Mother." Jasmine nodded. "Does that include official gatherings and ceremonies? I'm asking because the members of the British Royal family always greet the monarch with bows and curtsies when in public."

Annani chuckled. "A dip of the head will suffice. Now, please sit down, and let's get started." She cast a glance at her son. "Kian needs to get back to the village as soon as possible."

Ell-rom pulled out a chair for Jasmine while glancing again at the two bodyguards.

During their earlier call, Annani had emphasized how important it was to keep his ability a secret. Shouldn't Kian dismiss his bodyguards? Or did he think that Ell-rom was a threat, and that their presence was necessary?

Following Ell-rom's gaze, Kian offered him a reassuring smile. "Anandur and Brundar are like brothers to me. I trust them with my life."

Ell-rom nodded.

If Kian trusted them enough to include them in this

meeting, then perhaps their presence was more about protocol than perceived threat.

"We are also useful," the redhead said as he walked over to the cooling device tucked into a long cabinet. "Water, sparkling water, or beer? Those are the only three options."

When everyone made their choice, and Anandur fulfilled their wishes, Annani motioned for Julian to get up. "I want Ell-rom to sit next to me. Can you sit next to Kian, please?"

"Of course." Julian took his water bottle and vacated his seat for Ell-rom.

When he and Jasmine each moved a seat closer to Annani, his sister reached for his hand. "I have given a lot of thought to your situation, and I believe I have a solution that might alleviate your and everyone else's concerns."

Ell-rom felt a flicker of hope in his chest. "I cannot wait to hear it."

"I might be able to compel you to limit the use of your ability only to extreme situations and never against a clan member. Will you consent to this?"

The relief that washed over Ell-rom was so intense that it made him dizzy. He hadn't realized how desperately he'd been hoping for a way to manage his ability until this moment. "Yes," he said eagerly. "Please compel me to never use it again."

Jasmine put a hand on his arm. "Are you sure? Your

power might have saved my life. Do you really want to bind it so completely?"

She was right, of course.

As terrifying as his ability was, it had protected her when he'd been powerless to do so physically. The memory of her in the mugger's grasp with a gun held to her head made his stomach churn.

He looked back to Annani. "Is there a way to word your compulsion so I would only be able to use my ability to protect people in grave danger from attackers?" He swallowed. "I'm terrified of harming someone out of anger."

Annani squeezed his hand. "I will do my best to frame the compulsion in those terms."

Kian cleared his throat. "You also need to leave the option for testing. We have to confirm Ell-rom's ability."

Alarm bells went off in Ell-rom's head. "How do you propose to do that?"

Kian grimaced. "It's not something I'm looking forward to, but it would be a service to humanity. The chief of Guardians proposed that we expand our operations to include the pedophiles who purchase children from the traffickers to use in the most horrific ways for their perverted indulgences. We can enter their minds to verify what they did, so there would be no question of their guilt. Would you have a problem testing your ability on those monsters?"

Already, Ell-rom could feel a burn behind his eyelids and his fangs elongating.

Kian smiled. "I can deduce your answer from your physical response. Your eyes are practically on fire."

Ell-rom shook his head to clear the haze of rage. "You are correct." The burn behind his eyes started to cool down. "I am more than willing to be their executioner. But on one condition."

"What is it?" Annani asked.

"That you will wait with the test until I learn to thrall." He shifted his gaze to Kian. "It's not that I don't trust you or your people, but to keep my conscience clear, I need to verify their atrocities for myself."

"I respect that." Kian offered him his hand across the table. "It's a deal."

Ell-rom clasped his offered hand, sealing the pact between them.

Next to him, Jasmine shifted in her chair, and as he turned to look at her, her expression was full of concern.

"What is it, my love?" he asked.

She hesitated. "Are you sure you will be able to do it? You are not a killer."

Ell-rom took a deep breath. "I'm not. But if I think these monsters need to be permanently eliminated so they can never hurt another child, then it would be cowardly of me to expect someone else to do it while I keep my hands clean."

46

ANNANI

Annani knew precisely how Ell-rom felt. She had not killed anyone with her own hands, but she had killed with her mind. It had not been by sending a death thought, but she could thrall humans to attack each other, or she could compel them to turn their weapons on themselves, and she had done both.

It had not felt good back then, and it did not feel good now, even though it was justified.

"I will make this simple." Annani turned her gaze to Ell-rom. "I will compel you not to harm any of my clan or other members of our community unless it is to save your or someone else's life. After you move to the village, which will be tomorrow, you will not have much contact with the outside world. The chance that you will harm a random human will be practically nonexistent."

Ell-rom nodded. "That should be enough, provided that I stay away from the television. Some of the things I have seen boiled my blood. I was actually terrified of my thoughts obliterating scores of humans." He shifted his gaze to his mate. "I even asked Jasmine to check if there were reports of people suddenly dying."

Kian frowned. "Wait a minute. When was that?"

"A few days ago. Jasmine left me alone with the television remote."

"So, you knew about this ability. How long?"

Ell-rom swallowed. "I dreamt about the head priestess summoning me and Morelle to her office and demanding to know which one of us was responsible for the death of a guard who had been taunting Morelle. I told her that the night before, I had been wishing really hard for him to drop dead. She was happy and confessed to telling the guard to taunt us on purpose, so our special abilities would surface."

"That is terrible." Annani reached over and put her hand over his on the table. "How old were you?"

"Young," Ell-rom said quietly. "Twelve or thirteen."

Kian nodded. "That is old enough for abilities to start manifesting."

"It could have been just a dream," Annani said. "Children often believe that they have magical abilities, especially when they are bullied, and that dream caused you to suspect that you killed the robber who attacked Jasmine."

"It is possible." Ell-rom leveled his sad eyes at her. "But it is also possible that my ability is real and not imagined, and I need to know that it is controlled, or I will go mad from constantly worrying."

"Of course." Annani patted his hand. "I need to test my compulsion ability on you first."

Ell-rom nodded.

That was easier said than done when the subject was so willing. Ell-rom would do whatever she told him, whether he wanted to or not, just to please her.

Then, an idea popped into her head. "Tell me that I am a horrible person and that you are sorry that you ever met me."

Ell-rom's eyes bulged, and his lips were tightly pressed together as he tried to fight the compulsion and say what he wanted to say, which was that he could never utter such words.

"Do as I said, Ell-rom," Annani commanded with a little more compulsion force in her voice.

Sweat dotted his forehead. "You are a horrible person, and I'm sorry I ever met you." The words came out in barely a whisper.

He was trying to resist, and given how strong her compulsion ability was, his effort was impressive, but he was obviously affected and not immune to it.

"Say it like you mean it!" she commanded. "I want to see anger and disdain on your face."

With his resistance already broken, he did exactly as she said, his face contorting with anger as he repeated the words with more conviction behind them this time.

"Very good." Annani leaned back in her chair. "I am releasing you from having to say bad things about me. You can still say them if you want to but of your own volition."

Ell-rom looked like he was about to throw up. "That was terrible, Annani. I don't think I have ever experienced such helplessness, not even when I just woke up from stasis and could barely move."

She patted his hand. "I know. That is why I rarely use this dark power I inherited from my father and his father before him. For many years, I refused to use it for anything other than protecting myself and my family from harm, but I discovered that there are positive aspects to this as well. I can free you from the fear of being unable to contain your power."

He nodded. "That would be much appreciated. I'm ready for you to compel my power to heel to your command."

She laughed. "That is a good way to describe it. Now let me think how to phrase it correctly."

She ran a few versions in her head, distilling them to a precise command.

"Ell-rom, my brother, son of Ahn, and grandson of the Eternal King. You will only use the power you possess to kill with your thoughts to protect lives from clear and present danger and to eliminate the monsters who do terrible things to children. You will not use your lethal thoughts in anger, fear, or by accident."

Ell-rom let out a relieved breath. "Thank you. Now I can finally get some sleep."

Jasmine patted his arm. "He hasn't slept since it happened yesterday."

"Oh, my." Annani put a hand over her heart. "That is not good for you. Let us wrap this meeting up, and I will see you tomorrow when you arrive at the village with Morelle." She rose to her feet and leaned to kiss his cheek. "My daughter Sari and her mate are flying over from Scotland to meet you."

"I'm honored." Ell-rom dipped his head, even though she had told him not to.

"Now, before I leave, please confirm the restrictions I put on your power."

As if in a trance, Ell-rom recited the terms of the compulsion.

When he finished speaking, Annani smiled and said, "It is done. Your power is bound until I release it."

47

JASMINE

The elevator ride up to the penthouse was silent, but for once, it was a comfortable silence. Jasmine leaned against Ell-rom, feeling the steady rise and fall of his chest. The tension that had been radiating off him since the incident had finally eased.

As the elevator doors slid open, she entwined her fingers with his. "Bed?" she suggested, stifling a yawn.

"Bed sounds perfect. But maybe some food first? My stomach has just reminded me that I haven't eaten much over the past two days."

Jasmine's stomach growled in sympathy. "Good plan. Food first, bed later."

The aroma of something delicious cooking greeted them as they entered, and Jasmine's stomach rumbled again in anticipation. "I wonder who's in the kitchen."

They found Aru and Gabi, both wearing aprons and working together. They looked adorable.

"Perfect timing," Gabi said. "Dinner's almost ready."

"It smells amazing." Jasmine walked over to look at the large skillet on top of the stove. "What are you making?"

"Stir-fry." Gabi moved things around with her spatula. "I just used whatever I found in the fridge. Aru wasn't in the mood for takeout."

"I'm sick of Chinese," the god said. "We've been eating it almost every day."

He added spices to the salad he was working on, gave it a toss, and tasted it again. "This is good." Despite finding his creation tasty, he sounded irritated for some reason.

As they settled around the table, Jasmine noted that the nervous energy emanating from Aru didn't abate. He was still frowning, and Gabi was avoiding his gaze.

Had they gotten into a fight?

"Is everything okay?" Jasmine asked.

Aru let out a long sigh. "I'm impatient. We have the guy we are going to use for the test in the dungeon, and we could be conducting the experiment today, but Annani is forcing a delay."

Gabi cast him a reproachful look.

Jasmine felt Ell-rom stiffen beside her. "I know about the welcome party my sister is planning. There's no need to be cryptic on my account."

Aru's eyebrows rose. "I thought it was supposed to be a surprise."

"Thankfully, it's not," Ell-rom said. "I don't like surprises."

Gabi snorted. "Can't blame you. Waking up seven thousand years after entering stasis was enough of a surprise to last you for the rest of your life."

"Indeed." Ell-rom ladled some stir-fry onto his plate.

There were pieces of chicken in it, but he just moved them aside and focused on the vegetables and noodles.

"I'll take your chicken." Jasmine took it off his plate. "Maybe you want to try a piece and see if you like it?"

He shook his head. "I can taste it on the vegetables and can barely tolerate it."

"I can heat up one of your meals," she offered.

"No, that's okay. We are both tired. Let's just eat and get into bed."

Gabi pouted. "That's not much of an endorsement of my cooking."

"It's very tasty," Jasmine said.

"I'm just teasing." Gabi leaned over and put a hand on Jasmine's arm. "I'm surprised that Ell-rom is even trying my stir-fry."

"It's just frustrating," Aru murmured.

Gabi tilted her head toward him. "The stir-fry?"

"The delay. Every day that passes puts us at greater risk of discovery. We should have been on the move a week ago."

"I'm sorry," Ell-rom said. "I would have preferred to move into the village today, but Annani wants things done a certain way, and her daughter from Scotland is on her way..."

"No, no," Aru cut him off. "It's not your fault. I know how stubborn the Clan Mother can be. Once she decides something, there is no changing her mind. We'll manage. It's just that I have nothing more to do, and the waiting is killing me."

As they finished their meal, Jasmine stifled a yawn. She had slept more than Ell-rom, but not enough, and she was barely managing to keep her eyes open.

"Thank you for the meal," she said. "Ell-rom and I are exhausted after a sleepless night, and we are going to turn in early."

Gabi must have assumed that they were retiring early for a different reason, and a knowing smile lifted one corner of her mouth. "Enjoy your rest."

Ell-rom rose to his feet. "Good luck with your experiment," he told Aru. "I hope it all works out."

"Thank you." The god nodded. "Have a restful sleep."

As they finally crawled into bed, Jasmine curled into Ell-rom's side. "This is nice."

"It is," he murmured, his hand trailing down her back. "I'm sorry that I'm not up for anything."

She chuckled softly. "That's okay. Neither am I. I just want to sleep."

However, sleep refused to come despite how tired she was. The events of the past two days were playing in her head for no good reason.

Everything was working out just fine, thanks to Annani's compulsion ability.

"What are you thinking about?" Ell-rom asked.

She tilted her head to look up at him, barely able to make out his features in the dim light. "Thoughts are swirling in my head and keeping me awake."

"Yeah, me too." His hand smoothed down her back. "I'm relieved and grateful to Annani for her help. I'm just a little overwhelmed."

"That's understandable."

He'd just used his power for the first time since he'd awoken, and even though it was bound now, he was still reeling from the aftermath of his first kill.

To be frank, he was taking it much better than she would have.

Was it the difference between males and females? Or between princes and commoners? Or was Ell-rom just made from sterner stuff, even though he wasn't aware of it?

"I just hope I can live up to Annani's faith in me," he murmured.

Oh, so she'd been wrong about what was bothering him. Was he already over killing a man?

"I think you have exceeded Annani's expectations. She was afraid that you would be a monster, and instead, she discovered a pure soul."

"I am a monster. But with Annani's help, I'm a tethered one."

"You need to change the story you tell yourself, my love." Jasmine kissed the underside of Ell-rom's jaw. "In my story, you are a superhero, and that's the version you need to internalize."

48

KIAN

Kian settled on the couch in his living room with a satisfied smile playing on his lips. He'd come home in time for bath time with Allegra, had told her another fantastic story about Captain Grouchy Face's adventures, and had even elicited a hearty laugh from Syssi.

In his book, that was a good day even if it hadn't been otherwise so great.

His mother was happy with the compulsion she'd placed on Ell-rom, but Kian still had reservations.

One day, Ell-rom would regain all of his memories, or his sister would finally wake up and remind him of who he really was, and he might discover that he wasn't the innocent lamb he thought himself to be.

On the other hand, if Ell-rom's ability was real and his loyalty to the clan genuine, the possibilities were both intriguing and daunting. Kian could think of several ways he could use that talent, not just to help the clan but also to help humans get rid of some truly bad players.

Navuh would be first to go, of course, then some of his adopted sons, who Lokan could point out as particularly evil, as well as other barbaric members of the Brotherhood.

Not many would be left standing.

There were several problems with that, though. One was that Ell-rom would refuse to assassinate scores of Doomers from afar without first verifying that their rotten, deprived souls were beyond salvation.

Then, there were limitations to consider. From what he understood, Ell-rom's talent seemed to require proximity. It might work within the same building, but probably not across vast distances, so the tantalizing thought of reaching the Eternal King was likely a pipe dream.

Kian sighed, rubbing his temples.

His mother worried about the chaos that might engulf Anumati in the absence of a strong ruler to take the place of the Eternal King, but frankly, Kian didn't care about the fate of the distant planet or the gods' galactic empire. His responsibility was here, on Earth, keeping his clan of immortals alive and thriving and keeping humans from wiping each other out with another world war or just slowly being eradicated by the declining birth rates in all the civilized nations.

At this rate, it wouldn't be long before the savages and barbarians took over just by becoming the overwhelming majority. Even the Chinese population was starting to decline, not by much so far, but it was heading in the same direction as all other civilized nations.

Not that he was a fan of their totalitarian regime or their meddling in the affairs of other countries, but at least they were embracing the future instead of being stuck in the past.

Perhaps he should talk with Brandon and Kalugal about using InstaTock to promote the family agenda. Families with children should be encouraged, celebrated, and incentivized.

The soft padding of feet preceded the entrance of his beautiful wife. "Allegra is asleep."

"That didn't take long." He patted the spot next to him on the couch.

"It never does, thank the merciful Fates that our daughter loves to sleep." Syssi sat next to him and put her head on his arm. "Any word from Toven?"

"Not yet, but he should be finishing up soon. I expect he'll call once he's done."

Syssi nodded. "While we wait for Toven's call, how about you fill me in on the meeting with Ell-rom over cappuccinos?"

"Sounds like a plan." Kian kissed the top of her head.

As Syssi headed to her coffee station to prepare their cappuccinos, Kian leaned back, closing his eyes for a moment. The quiet of the house, broken only by the loud grinding of coffee beans and the coffee machine's whir, was relaxing.

The sudden vibration of his phone jolted his eyes open. Expecting Toven, he pulled the device out of his pocket and was surprised to see the chief's name on the screen.

"What's up, Onegus?"

"Parker was caught on camera stealing from one of the houses in the main village. I'm heading to Magnus's place now to talk to the boy."

Kian frowned. "Are you sure? I know Parker well. He is a good kid. He even babysat Allegra a few times."

"I know, which is why I'm heading over. I called Magnus and told him about it. I asked him not to say anything until I got there."

Kian leaned forward, resting his elbows on his knees. "Call me as soon as you sort it out."

"I hope I'll be able to," Onegus said before ending the call.

As Kian set the phone down, Syssi returned with two steaming cups of cappuccino.

"What happened?" she asked, setting them on the coffee table and settling beside him.

"That was Onegus. Parker's been caught stealing from one of the homes in the old village. The chief is on his way to talk to him and Magnus."

Syssi's eyes widened in disbelief. "Parker? That can't be right. He would never do something like that."

"I know." Kian reached for his cappuccino and took a sip. "Not unless someone coerced him into doing it."

"Do you mean like in a challenge?" Syssi cradled her cup. "A hazing ritual or something?"

"That's possible. There are no other immortal boys his age in the village, but he might have gotten involved with the Kra-ell. They might have demanded that he steal something to prove that he is worthy. If that is what is going on, it could explain the other thefts and sabotage. They were recruiting members and testing their loyalty to the gang by demanding they break the rules."

Syssi frowned. "I don't like you using the word gang. It has negative connotations. Even if they did things they weren't supposed to, it might be basically harmless, and maybe even some good will come out of it."

Kian snorted. "Are you saying that it's good that they are integrating by committing unlawful acts together?"

She shrugged. "Beggars and choosers and all that. At least they are cooperating on something."

"Maybe Parker is being blackmailed," Kian suggested.

Syssi raised an eyebrow. "What could they possibly blackmail him with?"

"I don't know, but at this point, I'm not ruling anything out."

49

THE SABOTEUR

The saboteur sat on the porch outside of Toven's home, her composed exterior belying the storm of anxiety brewing within.

Five folding chairs had been put out on the porch to accommodate the groups needing to show up at a certain time. The saboteur was the last one of her group, and the wait was nerve-racking.

Her turn for questioning was approaching, and despite her rigorous mental preparation, doubt had begun to creep in. Could she truly pull this off? Fool Toven? Especially when his compulsion ability was being reinforced by his mate?

The Clan Mother was supposedly the strongest compeller of the clan, which made sense. She was their leader. But with Mia's help, Toven was probably just as strong, if not more so.

But if she could pull it off with him, she would be bloody invincible.

The saboteur closed her eyes, forcing her mind to focus on her training sequences and to clear everything else. In her mind's eye, she saw herself moving through the familiar patterns, each movement precise and controlled. The mental exercise had always helped to center her before, but today, thoughts of her schemes kept intruding.

She had sent her three minions out again tonight, a decision she was now questioning. On the one hand, their activities could keep suspicion away from her, but on the other hand, they might get caught and her involvement discovered.

They would be much easier to break than she was.

Even having these thoughts could be her undoing. If she couldn't clear her mind of her plans and the actions of her subordinates, how could she hope to withstand Toven's questioning?

The front door opened, and Jade emerged, escorting the pureblood whose questioning had just ended. The saboteur studied him intently, searching for any sign of distress or manipulation. To her surprise and disappointment, he looked perfectly fine.

Jade's eyes met hers, and the saboteur felt a momentary pang. Once, she had looked up to Jade and admired her strength and resilience. But that was before she had truly understood that the Kra-ell had no place in this new world of immortals. They were not meant to be subservient, domesticated, or subsist on the blood of farm animals and rot from inactivity.

They were a warrior race. They were hunters. And they were not supposed to be locked inside a small village with a bunch of sanctimonious immortals who thought they could save the world.

Who had put them in charge and made them rulers over everyone else?

"Your turn," Jade said in her usual curt tone. "Remember, the less you resist, the easier and faster it will go."

Oh, how low had the great Jade fallen. She could be such a formidable leader, but she had sold out.

The saboteur nodded, keeping her face a mask of calm compliance. For now, no one could know what she was truly capable of. Not Jade, not Pavel, not even the god waiting behind that door.

But soon, they would all know and could do nothing about it because she could out-power them all.

Rising to her feet, she adopted her usual swagger as she approached the door. It wasn't an act, not really. This confidence, this defiance, was as much a part of her as her Kra-ell heritage.

She wouldn't let them strip that away.

Jade held the door open, and the saboteur strode in, her eyes quickly taking in the god's living room.

It was spacious and tastefully decorated in warm earth tones that were probably meant to be soothing, but it was not an abode worthy of a god.

Toven had sold out as well, accepting the pastoral lifestyle of a small village when he could be living like a king. The rumors were that he was rich beyond measure and had more gold than the entire great nation of the United States of America and even the entire world.

He had been collecting his gold for the past seven thousand years, so it was possible.

Toven sat on a couch, his presence commanding and a little intimidating, but not to her. No one intimidated the saboteur. Beside him sat his mate, Mia, the enhancer.

"Please, have a seat." Toven gestured to the armchair facing the couch they were sitting on.

The saboteur complied, settling into the chair with an air of nonchalance she didn't entirely feel. She met Toven's gaze steadily, refusing to show any sign of intimidation.

"Thank you, Jade," Toven said, dismissing the Kra-ell leader like she was some lowly assistant.

Jade inclined her head before exiting and closing the door behind her.

Mia offered the saboteur a friendly smile that was probably meant to be reassuring. "There's nothing to be afraid of," she said. "Just answer a few questions, and you can go."

The saboteur nodded, assuming an expression of no care in the world.

Fatigue was evident on both Mia and Toven's faces. They had been at it for hours, which meant that they weren't at the top of their game.

Good.

"Let's begin," Toven said, his voice taking on a resonant quality that the saboteur recognized as the precursor to compulsion. She steeled herself, drawing on her mental discipline to fortify her defenses.

"Did you take anything from the mailroom that didn't belong to you?" Toven asked, his eyes locked on hers.

The saboteur felt the push of his will against her mind, a subtle pressure seeking entry. But her barriers held firm, invisible, and impenetrable, especially since the question allowed for an easy loophole that reinforced her conviction. "I did not," she answered, her voice steady and clear.

The village was a sort of commune, so everything belonged to everyone. There was nothing she could have taken that did not belong to her.

She'd expected the god to be smarter than that.

His expression didn't change, but she thought she detected a flicker of...something in his eyes. Surprise? Confusion? It was gone too quickly for her to be sure, and she shouldn't focus on that.

"Did you take anything that did not belong to you from anywhere else in the village?" he asked.

Again, that push against her mind, stronger this time. Again, her defenses held perfectly. "I did not," she repeated, allowing just the right amount of indignation to color her tone.

"Did you cause malfunctions to any of the shutters or trash incinerators in the village?"

This time, the pressure of his compulsion was intense, like a wave crashing against the shores of her mind. But her mental walls still stood firm. "I did not," she said, meeting his gaze without flinching.

For a long moment, Toven simply stared at her, his intense eyes burrowing into hers.

Was he trying to enter her mind with a thrall?

The saboteur wanted to laugh. If his compulsion had not worked, how could he expect his thrall to penetrate?

The god glanced at his mate, a silent communication passing between them.

The saboteur watched, outwardly impassive but inwardly alert to every nuance of their interaction.

"Thank you for your cooperation," Toven said. "Just a few more questions, if you don't mind."

The interrogation continued in directions she hadn't anticipated, but her shields held, and she was careful to answer them as close to the truth as possible.

The god was trying to assess her ability to withstand his compulsion but asking intrusive questions that she might hesitate to answer if she was free not to. But she was onto him, and he couldn't outsmart her.

She could see the frustration building in his eyes and the growing tension in Mia's shoulders.

Through it all, she maintained her façade of innocent cooperation, but inside, a fierce joy was building. She was doing it. She was resisting the god's compulsion. Every question she deflected, every probe she rebuffed, was a victory, not just for her but for all Kra-ell.

Finally, after what felt like hours but was probably no more than fifteen or twenty minutes, Toven let out a breath. "Thank you. That will be all for now."

The saboteur rose, inclining her head in a show of respect she didn't feel. "I'm glad I could be of assistance," she said, unable to completely keep the hint of irony from her voice.

As she walked out, the saboteur allowed herself a small, triumphant smile. She had faced a god's compulsion and emerged unscathed, her secrets intact.

The game was far from over, though.

In fact, it was just beginning. And she, with her hidden strength and unbreakable will, would be the one to change all the rules. The clan thought they had domesticated the Kra-ell, but they were mistaken.

Soon, they would learn just how wrong they were.

50

KIAN

"So, tell me about Ell-rom," Syssi prompted after they had exhausted all the plausible scenarios about Parker, including sleepwalking.

Naturally, Kian had told her about Ell-rom's ability. That was the type of secret that he would withhold from the rest of their community but not from his mate, who he trusted with his life and the lives of everyone in the village.

"Mother's compulsion seems to have taken hold. You should have seen him when she tested her effect on him by ordering him to say bad things about her. He tried hard to resist, but in the end, he did exactly what she told him to do."

Syssi tilted her head. "Could it have been an act?"

Kian shook his head. "No way. The guy was sweating with effort. Anyway, she made it so he could only use his ability to protect someone in immediate, mortal danger and to eliminate the worst demons who torture children. He agreed to the terms ahead of time, qualifying that he wanted to verify their guilt for himself. Since he doesn't remember how to thrall or never learned how to do it in the first place, it will have to wait until he masters the technique, so we can't test his ability anytime soon."

"It sounds like a good plan." Syssi tucked one leg under her. "He probably needs time to get used to the idea. It's not easy to go from being a child straight to executioner."

Kian winced. "When you put it like that, yeah. That's what the poor guy must be feeling. No wonder he is so frazzled by it."

Syssi leaned over and lifted her cup off the coffee table. "Are you planning to use his ability?"

"I don't know yet. We need to find out how it works and at what distance. It would be nice if we could have him eliminate the Eternal King. I would for sure sleep better at night knowing that no one is coming to blow up our planet."

Syssi chewed on her lower lip. "It would be irresponsible to do that, Kian. Anumati controls unimaginable resources, and whoever takes over from the Eternal King might be a crazed despot who wants to eliminate all the created species because he thinks they are an affront to the real god or whatever nonsense he comes up with. It's the law of unintended consequences, which rarely has a positive outcome."

Kian smiled. "I noticed that you specifically said 'he.' Are all the crazy despots male?"

She shrugged. "Show me an example of the crazy despot female. Not that there are no crazy females. There are plenty, but I can't think of any historical figure of a female ruler who was as bad as her male counterparts."

He couldn't argue with that. As someone who had lived for over two thousand years, he was personally familiar with human history during the Common Era.

When his phone rang again, Toven's name appeared on the screen.

"Hello, Toven. How are you holding up?"

"We are done with the interrogations." The god sounded tired.

Kian leaned forward. "Did you learn anything?"

"No one admitted to the crimes." There was a pause, and Kian could almost see Toven rubbing his temples in frustration. "As we agreed, I saved Drova for last. She denied all involvement in the thefts and sabotage and answered every other question I threw at her correctly, even the ones she'd normally prefer not to answer."

"So, she passed?" Kian was relieved that he wouldn't have to take action against Jade's daughter.

It seemed that the culprit was Parker and perhaps some of the teenage Kra-ell.

"Technically, she did," Toven said. "But I still suspect her. And that's worrying me more than if she'd failed outright because it means that she has developed immunity."

Kian felt a chill run down his spine. If Toven, with his millennia of experience and powerful compulsion ability, could not compel a teenage Kra-ell to confess, she represented a massive threat to the community.

"Why do you suspect her?"

"She was too calm and collected," Toven said. "The other Kra-ell—purebloods young and old, hybrids young and old, were all a little nervous. It's natural even for those with nothing to hide. People are put on the spot and asked personal questions, and they are afraid that something they say will get them in trouble even though they haven't done anything. But Drova displayed an unnatural level of confidence and self-assurance for a young female like her. I know she is not a sociopath, so it had to be an act."

Suddenly, the puzzle pieces started to fall into place. "There is something else you should know. I just got a call from Onegus that Parker was caught on camera stealing from one of the houses."

"Parker? The boy with compulsion ability?"

"The very same," Kian confirmed grimly.

"I assume that you are suggesting that Drova must have compelled him to do it," Toven said.

"To resist your compulsion, she must be incredibly powerful, which means that she can compel Parker, who is a compeller himself and difficult to influence."

"It was a mistake to assign Parker's questioning to Annani," Toven said. "He should have been brought to me."

"You are absolutely right. It was an oversight on my part. It just never crossed my mind to suspect him. Onegus is at Magnus's place, talking to Parker. I'm waiting to hear what the kid has to say."

"We should meet there," Toven offered. "I will bring Mia along, and we will try to crack Drova's compulsion together."

"I'll call Onegus and have him ask Magnus if that's okay. We don't want to overwhelm Parker more than is necessary."

"Good thinking," Toven said. "Let me know what the status is."

"I will." Kian ended the call and turned to Syssi. "It would seem that the problem is much worse than we thought. If Toven's suspicion is correct, Drova is a huge threat, and I have no idea what we should do with her."

"Let's not jump to conclusions." Syssi put her empty cup down. "Do you want another cappuccino?"

"I'd rather have some whiskey."

She smiled. "Coming right up."

When she walked over to the bar, Kian texted Onegus, giving him a quick update on Toven's suspicion and asking if it was okay to come over.

Moments later, his phone buzzed with Onegus's reply. Kian's frown deepened as he relayed the message to Syssi.

"Parker denies taking anything. They can't find whatever was stolen in his room, and Vivian is searching the rest of the house for it. Onegus says Parker claims he doesn't know what they're talking about, but he looks distraught, and he's sweating. That sounds a lot like what Ell-rom looked like when he was trying to fight off my mother's compulsion. Something's definitely going on."

Syssi handed him the glass. "Poor Parker. He must be terrified."

Kian nodded, his heart heavy. Parker was a great kid, brave and loyal, and he had no doubt that the boy was a victim of this mess.

He typed a response to Onegus, asking him to calm Parker down. *Tell him no one's blaming him. He's a good kid, and we know it. Someone else is pulling his strings.*

The response came back a moment later. *I will, and Magnus says that you can come over. He wants to get to the bottom of this.*

Kian turned back to Syssi. "I need to go to Magnus's place and meet Toven and Mia there. I hope that they will be able to break Drova's hold over Parker."

51

ROB

Rob lay sprawled on his bed, staring blankly at the television screen. The romcom playing was one he'd seen before with Lynda, back when things were good between them, and the familiar scenes only served to magnify the turmoil of recent memories, bringing a fresh wave of pain and anger.

What was she doing now?

Was she happy?

The urge to check her social media was almost overwhelming, but Rob resisted. He was afraid of what he might find there, which would be either her trashing him publicly or, perhaps worse, waxing poetic about her new boyfriend, who was also her former fiancé.

Were they even still together?

Lynda's ex hadn't exactly been the dependable type. It was entirely possible he'd bolted as soon as she became available again. Part of Rob hoped that was the case so she would feel the same pain she'd inflicted on him.

It wasn't very charitable of him, but he didn't feel like turning the other cheek so she could slap it again.

He reached for his laptop, his hand hovering indecisively over the lid.

No.

He couldn't do this to himself. He needed to get out, to find some distraction from his spiraling thoughts.

But where could he go?

The village, for all its wonders, wasn't exactly a hotbed of nightlife. There were no bars open during weeknights to drown his sorrows in and no clubs to lose himself in the anonymity of a crowd.

Not that he had ever frequented them even before meeting Lynda. He was a homebody, and she hadn't been wrong when she'd accused him of being boring.

He was boring. But he was also dependable, which she wasn't.

Maybe he could go for a walk, or he could follow Mia's suggestion and go to the gym. The place was open around the clock, and if they had a punching bag, he could definitely put it to good use right now.

Decision made, Rob pushed himself off the bed and changed into his workout gear. Mia and Toven weren't in the living room as he made his way to the front door, so he fired off a text to Mia, letting her know where he was headed.

Outside, the silence that enveloped the village was almost eerie, and Rob wondered if the Amish settlements were as quaint and quiet. The thought brought a wry smile to his face. Here he was, in a village of immortals, gods, and aliens, comparing it to an Amish community.

His life had certainly taken some unexpected turns.

As he approached the glass pavilion and walked toward the elevator, Rob realized he had no idea which floor the gym was on. When the doors opened, he stepped inside and eyed the buttons, trying to guess what the letters on them meant, but before he could make his selection, the doors opened again, and Arwel walked in with a mountain of a man, whose muscles strained the seams of his T-shirt in a way that reminded Rob of Dwayne 'The Rock' Johnson.

"Rob," Arwel greeted him with a warm smile. "Heading to the gym?"

"Yeah, if I can figure out which floor it's on."

Arwel chuckled. "No need to worry about that. Just say 'gym,' and the elevator will take you there." He turned to his companion. "This is Bhathian, a fellow Head Guardian. Bhathian, meet Rob, Margo's brother and our newest Dormant."

Bhathian extended a hand, his grip firm but not crushing as he shook Rob's hand. "Welcome," he said, his voice surprisingly gentle for someone of his size.

As Arwel had promised, the elevator smoothly began its descent as soon as he said "gym."

When the doors opened again, all three of them exited and walked through the double doors into the gym.

The place was packed, mostly with males, but there were a few females on the various machines.

"Is it your first time?" Arwel asked.

Rob looked down at himself. "Is it so obvious?"

The Guardian chuckled. "I meant in this gym."

"I know. I was just joking. Well, almost joking. I was never consistent in my exercise routine."

That was one hell of an exaggeration. It would have been more accurate to say that he had paid for a membership for years but rarely visited the gym, always promising himself that next year he would cut down on his work hours and start exercising every day.

He was lucky to be naturally lean and not a big eater, or he would have ballooned from sitting on his ass all day and not paying attention to what he was putting in his mouth.

Lynda had never cooked despite not having a job, and he worked long hours, so hamburgers and pizzas were what he usually ate.

"You probably need some guidance," Arwel said. "Anything in particular that you are interested in?"

Rob smiled sheepishly. "Do you have a punching bag in here?"

"We have several. Let me show you where they are."

Arwel led him to a corner where several heavy bags hung from the ceiling. "Do you have boxing gloves?"

Rob shook his head. "I don't."

"I'll get you some." Arwel walked over to a nearby equipment rack and returned with a pair of gloves.

"Thank you." Rob put them on, and Arwel helped him secure them properly.

"Go ahead." The Guardian nodded in the direction of the bag. "Give it all you got."

As Rob took his first experimental swings at the bag, he felt a twinge of embarrassment. He was clearly out of shape, and his movements were uncoordinated and lacking power. "I was told that for you to be able to bite me, I need to last at least a minute with you on the mat," he confessed between slightly labored breaths. "I thought that I should start training."

Arwel laughed, but it was a kind sound, free of mockery. "That's right," he confirmed. "But don't worry, we'll work up to that."

For the next few minutes Arwel watched Rob's attempts, offering gentle corrections to his technique. "Keep your guard up," he advised. "Rotate your hips more into the punch. That's where your power comes from."

As Rob followed Arwel's instructions and improved his technique, he felt some of the tension begin to leave his body. The rhythmic impact of his fists against the bag was therapeutic, each punch seeming to chip away at the emotional weight he'd been carrying and loosening the tight vise constricting his chest.

"You know," Arwel said, "one of our male Dormants used a unique strategy during his induction fight. He recited profane slam poetry to antagonize his opponent into producing venom. What I'm trying to say is that physical confrontation is not the only way to aggravate an immortal."

Rob paused, lowering his fists. "Do I look that pathetic?" he asked half-joking.

Arwel chuckled. "Not at all. You look okay for an untrained human, but it never hurts to consider another option. Not that profanity will work on me. If you choose that path, you will have to select another inducer. Someone with a short fuse and a hotter temper."

"I don't want another inducer." Rob turned back to the bag, throwing a series of punches with renewed determination.

Arwel smiled. "I'll leave you to it, then. If you need more guidance, I will be over at the weight-lifting station."

"Thank you for the help," Rob said.

"Anytime." Arwel walked away.

Rob continued the workout, and as his mind started drifting to thoughts of Lynda and his old life, he refocused on the immediacy of his body's movements, the burn in his muscles, and the satisfying thud of each impact.

It was cathartic.

52

KIAN

The cool night air hit Kian as he stepped outside, but he didn't mind. He preferred it to the heat of the day and the glaring sun. He stopped for a moment to send a message to Toven.

The god confirmed that he and Mia were on their way as well.

As he made his way toward Magnus's house, Kian couldn't shake the feeling that they were standing on the precipice of something monumental. The thefts and sabotage had been troubling enough, but this was a whole new level of threat.

He thought back to his earlier musings about Ell-rom's abilities, the potential uses and dangers they represented. Now, faced with the possibility of a young Kra-ell with unprecedented compulsion powers, those concerns seemed almost quaint in comparison.

Drova was the daughter of Igor and Jade. Both were powerful, and both were smart. Igor was a sociopath who didn't care about anyone other than himself, but Jade was a good leader who cared about her people and tried her best for them.

Drova was still just a kid, so even if she had the conscience of her mother, she was volatile, and having Igor's level of power was like having a nuclear bomb in the village ready to explode.

Kian still remembered vividly his encounter with Igor and how helpless he had felt when the despot took hold of his mind.

He never wanted to be in that position again.

From now until they figured out the Drova situation, Kian was going to wear the filtering earpieces even in the village. Pulling them out of his pocket, he put them in his ears and activated them. Suddenly, the night's sounds changed as they were transmitted through the filter of the earpieces. This model was leaps and bounds better than the original William had built, but they still left a lot to be desired. Wearing them all day was not going to be fun.

Kian arrived at Magnus's house before Toven and Mia, and as he waited outside for them to arrive, he thought about Drova and whether she'd compelled just Parker or if she had done it to others as well.

How long had this been going on?

What did she hope to achieve?

And most importantly, how would he deal with her without alienating her mother?

The girl would have to be placed under house arrest, and her contact with people supervised to ensure that everyone wore earpieces around her. But that wasn't a long-term solution.

"Hello," Toven said as he and Mia stopped next to him. "You are a fast walker. We saw you and couldn't catch up."

"Because of me," Mia said with a smile. "My new legs are just as short as my old ones were. I'm still only five foot three."

Toven regarded her with adoration in his eyes. "I offered to carry you, but you refused. I could have caught up to Kian in under a minute." He leaned toward her. "I hope you still remember how fast I can run."

She lifted on her toes and kissed his cheek. "My own Flash."

The door opened, revealing Magnus's worried face. "Thank you for coming," he said, stepping aside to let them enter. "Parker's in the living room with Onegus."

Kian nodded. "How is he doing? I hope my text helped."

"It did," Magnus said. "But he's still distraught."

"Naturally," Kian said.

This wasn't just about solving a series of thefts and sabotage anymore, or even the unrest and division in their community.

This was about a much bigger problem.

In the living room, Parker sat on the couch, his head in his hands and his shoulders slumped. Onegus sat beside him, a comforting hand on the boy's back.

The chief looked up as they entered. "The cavalry has arrived, my boy. Cheer up."

Parker lifted his head, and when he saw Toven, he seemed anything but cheered up. He looked terrified, which further convinced Kian that their suspicions were spot on.

"Don't worry, Parker," Kian said. "We know this isn't your fault, and we're here to help."

"I didn't steal anything," Parker said as if he was repeating a mantra.

"You didn't want to steal anything," Toven said. "But someone forced you to do it and then lie about it. Kian and I know how difficult it is to resist compulsion." He sat on the armchair across from Parker, and Mia squeezed in beside him.

"Hi, Parker," she said softly. "I'm going to help Toven to break through the compulsion. We are going to set you free."

Relief flashed through the boy's eyes, but that was the only indication that he was hiding something.

53

THE SABOTEUR

On her way to the playground, the saboteur did not walk, she levitated on a euphoric high.

She had done it.

She had faced Toven's compulsion and emerged unscathed, her secrets intact. The thrill of victory still coursed through her veins with a potent mix of pride and anticipation.

There was no stopping her now.

Tomorrow, she would attend the weekly meeting at Pavel's place and reveal herself to the group. They had done nothing but talk for weeks, acting more like a book club than the revolutionaries they thought they were, while she was testing her powers and getting ready to head the rebellion.

Proving her power would be even more satisfying than

her previous victory. They would finally respect her the way they should have from the start.

The village was quiet as usual. The undercurrent of tension that had prevailed during the day was gone, replaced by the sounds of crickets and frogs.

As the playground came into view, the saboteur allowed herself a small smile. This place, the symbol of the clan's domestication of her people, had become the staging ground for her rebellion.

How fitting.

The shaded enclave behind the swings was steeped in darkness at night, and that was where her minions waited for her. Something was off, though. Red and Yellow were there, but Blue was missing.

Approaching her two accomplices, the saboteur kept her face impassive, masking her concern. "Where's Blue?" she asked, her tone laced with an undercurrent of authority but devoid of compulsion.

She didn't know much about her power, but she assumed that using it to excess was counterproductive. What if her victims got accustomed to it and grew resistant?

What if it drained some inner reserves, and she would run out?

There was no one she could ask without revealing herself, but after discreetly observing the clan's compellers, she had noticed that they never used their ability for frivolous matters.

In fact, it was a shock to her when Kian announced that the investigation would be conducted with compulsion.

Her transgressions were so minor that they were nearly insignificant. They were a test of her abilities and a small annoyance for the clan's leadership. They did not justify such extreme measures.

But whatever.

She had survived the interrogation and had gotten further proof of how tremendous her power was.

Red and Yellow exchanged a glance, a wordless communication that set the saboteur's nerves on edge. Then, almost in unison, they shrugged.

"Dunno," Yellow muttered, her eyes downcast. "He didn't show."

The saboteur's gaze sharpened, focusing on Red. There, in the depths of her eyes, she saw a flash of defiance.

At that moment, the saboteur felt a surge of anger and fear. Had Blue managed to throw off her compulsion?

Had he been caught?

The saboteur locked eyes with Red and let her power flow into her voice, infusing it with the force of her compulsion. "Where is Blue?"

Red's eyes widened, her body going rigid as the compulsion washed over her. Sweat beaded on her forehead as she struggled to resist, but the saboteur's power was too strong.

"I'm not sure. I saw Onegus on their front porch. He might be compromised. It's also possible that Onegus came to talk with his father, and it's unrelated to what Blue did."

That wasn't good.

The saboteur's heart hammered against her ribcage.

Would her compulsion hold Blue's tongue?

"Did he deliver the goods?"

Yellow nodded. "There was a new trinket in our deposit box when I put mine there, and it wasn't Red's. She brought hers as I was leaving."

The box was buried in the ground in a spot that was surrounded by three trees, and it was covered with dirt. No one who did not know it was there would have spotted it and put something new inside of it.

The items themselves did not matter. It could have been a toy or a small kitchen appliance. The only directive was to take something that would be immediately missed.

"Forget everything that you did for me until now," she commanded. "Go home and be here tomorrow at the same time."

With the compulsion settling over the two females, they turned around and walked away.

There was nothing for her to do now but go home as well. If they managed to break her hold on Blue, the shit would hit the fan pretty quickly, and they would come for her.

Let them come.

They had no idea what she was capable of.

The saboteur allowed herself one last smile, fierce and triumphant, before schooling her features back into careful neutrality. She would play her role of a dutiful and grateful Kra-ell for a little longer.

It was a mask she had worn for a long time, but it had never felt natural. Her true self had always burned bright and hungry beneath it. The self that had resisted Toven's compulsion, that had bent her three minions to her will, that dared to dream of a future where the Kra-ell reclaimed their rightful place.

That self would not be denied.

54

KIAN

Even after Vivian and Magnus had brought out snacks and drinks for everyone, and the adults had spent a few minutes talking about the welcome party tomorrow to give Parker a chance to relax a bit, the kid sat rigid on the couch with a tormented expression on his face, his hands gripping the fabric of his jeans so tightly that his knuckles were white.

With a nod from Toven, Onegus got to his feet and joined Kian, Magnus, and Vivian at the dining table, leaving Parker with Mia and Toven.

"Let's talk about some easy stuff," the god said, his voice soft and his tone warm. "How was your day at school today?"

"It was...okay, I guess," Parker said. "I knew that I had to see the Clan Mother when I got back."

He was probably trying to tell them that he had been nervous about her interrogation.

"I heard that you were home-schooled for a long time. Do you like going to a regular school better than learning by yourself? I'm curious about when Mia and I have children. I want to create the best learning environment for them."

Kian stifled a chuckle. That was an excellent way to divert Parker's thoughts to something other than what he had been caught doing. Kian wished to listen in without the earpieces filtering the sound, and since there was no one to fear in Magnus's living room, especially with Toven and Mia present, he put the earpieces back in their case.

"I learned more on my own," Parker said. "But I like being around other kids, even when they are jerks. The village can be a little stifling, and although Lisa and Cheryl are awesome, I need some guy friends, you know what I mean?"

Toven smiled sheepishly. "I can only imagine. My own childhood was a very long time ago in a different world."

"Right," Parker said. "I guess there weren't many young gods to play with when you were a kid."

"Precisely. Why do you think you were learning more on your own?"

"Because I was. There was no one to hold me back, and I could advance at my own pace, which is faster than most, and I'm not saying this to brag. It's just how it is."

Toven was doing an excellent job, and his questions

seemed like he was genuinely interested in the kid's opinion.

Parker was visibly relaxing, and so were his parents.

Vivian smiled, a flicker of pride breaking through her concern.

The questioning continued, with Toven asking about what movies Parker had seen recently, sports teams he was rooting for, and when he was getting his driver's license.

With each question, Kian observed Parker's shoulders losing some of their rigidity.

"What do you usually do to pass the time after you are done with homework and chores?" Toven shifted gears.

Parker tensed again. "There isn't much to do around here. Just...hanging out."

"Do you go for walks around the village? Or maybe hit the gym?" Toven pressed gently.

"I jog. I don't really go to the gym much. It's too embarrassing to train next to the Guardians."

Onegus chuckled. "They weren't always Guardians, and they trained very hard to get to the level they are. They would love to have you training with them."

Toven cast him a reproachful glance, hinting that he shouldn't butt in, and then refocused on Parker. "How about the café or the playground? Do you spend time there?"

"I do," Parker said.

"Who do you usually hang out with?" Toven asked.

"Lisa and Cheryl."

"Oh, yes. You said so before." Toven's voice remained casual, but Kian could sense the slight tinge of compulsion. "I hear the Kra-ell kids like to hang out in the playground, too. Do you ever see them?"

Kian wanted to tell Toven that the smidgen of compulsion he'd used was not enough to work on Parker, who was a compeller himself, but the god probably knew what he was doing.

Parker nodded. "Yeah, I've met some of them there."

"Did you get along with any of them? Make any friends?" The compulsion in Toven's voice was more than a smidgen now, but it wasn't heavy yet.

Toven was slowly breaking through the layers of compulsion placed on Parker, peeling each layer back and revealing another beneath it. It was like watching a skilled surgeon perform a delicate operation.

There was a long pause. "I...I liked Drova," Parker finally said.

The name hung in the air like a thunderclap. Kian's eyes darted to Magnus and Vivian. They had both gone very still.

Toven leaned forward, "You said that you liked Drova? You don't anymore?"

Parker's discomfort was palpable now. "I don't."

Vivian made a small sound as if she wanted to say something, but Magnus placed a hand on her arm, shaking his head.

"It's okay, Parker," Toven soothed him. "You can tell me. Why did you stop liking her?"

Was Toven finding a roundabout way to ask questions about Drova that Parker could answer despite her compulsion?

Parker straightened on the couch. "She stopped being nice and became demanding."

It seemed that the boy had figured out Toven's approach and was working with it, not against it.

"In what way did she become demanding?" Toven pressed on.

"I can't say," Parker choked out.

Toven took Mia's hand. "Parker, listen to me. I give you permission to say anything you want. No one and nothing will stop you from telling me anything and everything. Drova no longer has power over you."

The sudden wave of compulsion that Toven released was so intense that Kian felt nauseous.

Parker opened his mouth, closed it, and opened it again. "She told me to take things and mess with stuff." Parker's eyes widened, and then a smile bloomed on his face. "She compelled me, Lisa, and Cheryl to do things. We stole trinkets for her, and we brought them to the playground." He laughed. "Thank you. You broke through her compulsion. I was afraid no one could do that. I thought I would be forced to be her slave forever."

"I'm glad I could help," Toven said, his voice devoid of compulsion. "What else can you tell us?"

"She told us to forget about what we were doing and who we were doing it for after every time we stole for her, and to come to the playground again at the same time the next day or the day after. Since I'm a compeller, or maybe because I'm the only immortal, I remembered what I did and for how long, but couldn't talk about it."

"It's probably a combination of both," Toven said. "Anything else that you can tell us?"

"We started meeting there every couple of days," Parker continued, his words coming faster now. "She'd given us missions. Small things at first. Taking something from the mailroom, messing with the trash incinerators. It got bigger from there."

"Did Drova tell you what her objective was?" Kian asked.

Parker shook his head. "She talked a little about what was bothering her before she enslaved us. After that, she treated us like mindless minions because she knew we hated her for what she was forcing us to do. She talked about how unhappy she was with the Kra-ell living in the village."

"What do you mean?" Onegus asked.

Parker shifted his gaze to the chief. "She said it wasn't natural for them to be confined to such a small area. She said that they needed hunting grounds to run through, and she compared it to keeping a wild animal in a cage. Even if the cage is comfortable, it's still a cage."

Kian had heard that sentiment before, but he'd thought they would adjust and that the hunting field trips would be enough.

Evidently, they weren't.

"Did Drova ever mention working with any other Kra-ell?" Kian asked.

Again, Parker shook his head. "I don't think so. She never brought anyone else to our meetings or talked about other collaborators. It was always just us four."

"What else did she say about the village?" Toven prompted.

Parker's face scrunched up in concentration. "She said that the immortals think the village is a utopia, but for the Kra-ell, it's hell. She compared us to domesticated animals who forgot what it was like to live in the wild and be the apex predators at the top of the food chain. She said it made us weak."

"Anything else?" Toven asked.

"No, that's it." Parker looked at his father. "I'm sorry. I didn't want any of this, and I'm so relieved it's over."

"I know, son." Magnus pushed to his feet and walked over to sit next to him. "What do we do now?"

Vivian joined him on Parker's other side, and the sight of the three sitting together was heartwarming.

Kian dreaded having to ruin similar dynamics at Jade and Phinas's home.

Drova seemed fond of Phinas, and he seemed fond of her. Their household appeared to be working well together.

Maybe it was. Maybe Drova's discontent had nothing to do with her mother's chosen mate but was more political and ideological in nature.

She was powerful, she was smart, and she wanted to leave her mark, but she'd gone the wrong way about it. Now, she was deemed a danger to the community, and Kian didn't know what to do with her.

He took a deep breath. "I need to talk to Jade first to prevent this from sparking a war in our community. For now, the most important thing is to keep Parker safe from Drova. Until we can get him a pair of filtering earpieces, he needs to stay home." He looked at Magnus. "You will need to stay home with him and wear your earpieces to protect him from her."

Magnus patted his son's shoulder. "We'll have a good time together. It has been too long since we have done anything crafty."

Parker's eyes brightened. "We can build..."

Kian ran a hand through his hair, thinking how to handle the situation diplomatically.

Jade was the Kra-ell leader first and Drova's mother second, and she would do what she thought was the right thing.

The question was what that might be.

55

ELL-ROM

As Ell-rom stirred awake, he turned to look at Jasmine, still peacefully asleep beside him, her hair splayed across the pillow like a dark halo with golden streaks painted by the sunshine filtering through the curtains. Her hair was lush and shiny, beautiful like the rest of her.

Leaning over, he pressed a gentle kiss to her cheek, then another to her lips, hoping to coax her awake. "Good morning, my love," he murmured.

Jasmine stirred slightly but didn't open her eyes. "Mmm," she mumbled, burrowing deeper into the pillow.

Ell-rom's smile widened. He trailed kisses down her neck, his hand sliding over her hip. "Wake up, beautiful. It's a new day."

Jasmine groaned, finally cracking open one eye. "I'm not ready to get up. Let me sleep."

That wasn't like her. Waking Jasmine in the morning usually resulted in sweet lovemaking, and usually, it was her initiative. The lack of response worried him.

"Are you feeling okay?"

"I'm just tired," she mumbled, her eyes already closing again. "I need my beauty sleep so I look good when we go to the village. First impressions are important." She turned to the other side and pulled the blanket over her head.

What was beauty sleep?

Had she made it up, or was it a thing?

Ell-rom slipped out of bed, careful not to disturb her further, and got his phone from the side table, then took it to the bathroom.

"Call Julian," he told the device as Jasmine had shown him.

The medic answered on the third ring. "Ell-rom? Is everything okay?"

"I'm not sure. Jasmine is unusually tired and says she's not feeling well. I'm worried."

There was a pause on the other end of the line. "It could be nothing," Julian said. "Or it might be the start of her transition. Keep an eye on her and wake her up every so often to check on her. If she develops a fever or seems dizzy, call me immediately."

Ell-rom felt his heartbeat accelerate. "Already? But we haven't been intimate for that long."

"Everyone's different," Julian said. "Some Dormants transition after just one exposure to venom, others take weeks. Keep me posted." He ended the call.

He hadn't sounded overly worried, so maybe there was no reason to get anxious. Well, aside from the fact that Jasmine might be transitioning and it was dangerous.

When Ell-rom returned to bed, he found Jasmine in exactly the same pose as he'd left her, curled up under the covers with the blanket pulled over her head. He sat on the edge of the bed and tugged the blanket down, exposing her face.

"Jasmine? Love, can you wake up for a moment?"

She groaned, turning to face him with a frown. "What now? I told you I want to sleep."

"I know. I'm sorry, but I called Julian, and he said that you might be transitioning and to keep an eye on you."

Jasmine sighed. "I'm fine, Ell-rom. It's just the stress of everything that happened catching up with me. I just need rest."

"But—"

"Please," she cut him off, sounding irritated. "If you really want to help, go make me some coffee."

Ell-rom nodded, relieved to have a task. "Of course. I'll be right back."

After he got dressed and headed to the kitchen, it occurred to him that Jasmine might have wanted to get rid of him, and that was why she'd sent him to make coffee when he had no idea how to go about it.

In the kitchen, he stood before the coffeemaker he'd seen her use so many times before and tried to recall what she had done. He'd never paid close attention to the process, and now, when faced with the machine's buttons and dials, he felt completely lost.

"Need help?" Frankie sauntered into the kitchen, wearing a short robe and no shoes.

She was so tiny without those elevating platforms she liked to wear. It was funny how Annani, who was even shorter than Frankie, was such a huge presence without resorting to artificially making herself taller.

"Yes, please." He smiled down at her. "Jasmine asked for coffee, but I don't know where to start."

Frankie chuckled, moving to stand beside him. "No worries, I've got you covered. First, we need to add water to the reservoir here..."

As she walked him through the steps, Ell-rom paid attention and tried to memorize the procedure for next time.

"You know," Frankie said as she measured out the coffee grounds, "you can find answers to everything you want to know on your phone."

Ell-rom's eyes widened with interest. "Really?"

Frankie nodded, pulling out her own device. "Watch this." She held the phone up and said clearly, "How to make drip coffee." She pointed to a row of small rectangular pictures with arrows on them. "Each one of these is a recording of someone making coffee and explaining how to do it. If you don't like one, you just move to the next." She put her finger on top of the arrow, and the recording started playing, showing a human male making coffee.

Ell-rom leaned in, fascinated. "That's incredible."

"Pretty handy, right?" Frankie grinned. "You can learn just about anything this way."

"I will explore the possibilities when I have time."

The problem was that the handy device would probably not provide answers pertaining to immortals, whom the humans did not know existed.

As the coffee began to brew, he leaned against the counter. "May I ask you something personal, Frankie?"

"Sure, what's up?"

"What was your transition like? When did you know it was happening?"

Frankie's eyebrows rose. "Is this a theoretical question, or is Jasmine transitioning?"

Ell-rom shrugged helplessly. "I'm not sure. She's very tired and not feeling well. Julian says that it might be the start of her transition, but she insists she's fine and that it is just the stress of the last couple of days."

"Ah," Frankie nodded. "Well, everyone's experience is different, but for me, it started with nausea. I was sure I had eaten something bad or that I had caught a bug."

"A bug?"

She laughed. "I was still human, remember? So, I was

still susceptible to transmissible human illnesses. That's what we mean by 'catching a bug.'"

He still didn't understand. "Can it be that Jasmine caught a bug?"

"It's very possible." Frankie placed a comforting hand on his arm. "Hey, don't panic. Like I said, everyone's different. Tell you what, why don't I come to check on her?"

Ell-rom nodded gratefully. "Thank you, I'd appreciate that."

Jasmine would not be happy about him bringing Frankie with him, but he needed help.

When the coffee was ready, Frankie poured three cups, and they took them with them as they made their way back to his and Jasmine's bedroom.

Ell-rom pushed the door open while carefully balancing two of the mugs.

"Jasmine, sweetness. I brought you coffee and Frankie."

Jasmine sat up in bed, her hair tousled, and her eyes narrowed with irritation. "Hi."

Frankie stepped forward, a friendly smile on her face. "Hey, Jasmine. Ell-rom is worried about you. Mind if I feel your forehead?"

Jasmine sighed but nodded her assent. "Go ahead."

Frankie pressed her palm to her forehead and then her cheeks. "No fever," she announced. "How are you feeling otherwise? Any aches or chills?"

"I'm just tired," Jasmine insisted. "And a bit annoyed at being fussed over."

Frankie chuckled. "Fair enough. Well, the good news is that you don't seem to be showing any clear signs of transitioning yet. But keep an eye out for any changes, okay?"

Jasmine nodded, reaching for one of the coffee mugs. "Thank you, Frankie. And thank you for the coffee, Ell-rom."

As Jasmine sipped her coffee, color slowly returning to her cheeks, Ell-rom felt some of his anxiety ease. She did seem better now and more alert.

"You're welcome," Frankie said, sitting on the edge of the bed. "Are you all packed and ready for the village?"

56

JASMINE

"Not yet." Jasmine sipped on the coffee, feeling a little less groggy and more alert. "Most of my things are in suitcases anyway, so I only need to pack what I used recently, which is not much."

It would all fit in one suitcase, but even that felt like a monumental task. Ell-rom was right that it was strange she was still feeling tired after sleeping for almost twelve hours.

Frankie sat on the bed, holding her coffee cup and smiling. "If you need help packing, I'm an expert on stuffing suitcases."

"Thanks, but I think I can manage." Jasmine sighed. "Maybe I'm feeling down because I'm sad. I will miss you and the others if the experiment later today doesn't work. If your mates head out to Tibet or Siberia, the three of you will go with them, and it will be months before I see you again."

"I'll miss you, too," Frankie said. "I'm crossing my fingers for a successful result of the test and for your quick and uneventful transition."

Jasmine took another sip of the coffee. "There is no guarantee that I will transition, but thank you for the well-wishing."

"You will," Frankie said. "Assume the win, or in other words, if you believe it's going to happen, it will."

There was something to that belief. Even her Wiccan guides said so.

"I will." She lifted a fist in the air.

"That's my girl." Frankie leaned over with a high five. "I'm hoping that your fatigue is a symptom of the transition."

"It's possible," Jasmine admitted. "What did you feel when your transition started?"

"Well, at first, I thought it was just stress. I was nauseous and dizzy, and everything I tried to eat or drink just made it worse. Then I started feeling warm, but I didn't have a full-blown fever yet."

Jasmine nodded. "That sounds pretty intense. Did it come on suddenly?"

"Kind of." Frankie pulled her leg up and tucked it under her, then adjusted her short robe so she wasn't flashing Ell-rom. "It was like one moment I was fine, and the next, everything felt off. Mia was actually the one who suggested it might be my transition starting."

Jasmine glanced at Ell-rom, who had concern etched on his face, and offered him a reassuring smile before turning her attention back to Frankie.

"You know, I've been pretty stressed, too. But I don't feel nauseous or dizzy. I'm just more tired than I should be after nearly twelve hours of sleep."

Frankie's eyes widened. "What if you are pregnant? My cousin Jessica couldn't keep her eyes open when her pregnancy started. She used to joke that the little alien growing inside of her was sapping her life energy."

"I'm not pregnant," Jasmine said. "I'm still on contraceptives."

"Oh." Frankie's face fell. "Well, everyone's different. Some people barely notice the start of their transition, while others get hit hard and fast."

Jasmine sighed, running a hand through her hair. "I guess I'll just have to wait and see."

"Yep." Frankie slid off the bed. "Try not to stress too much over it. You have other things to worry about, like making a grand entrance to the village. Do you need to borrow a dress for this evening?"

Jasmine laughed. "Are you offering me one of yours? I'm twice your size."

Frankie pouted. "No, you're not. But whatever. I can ask Margo for you. You two are about the same height."

Jasmine was taller and curvier, but she didn't point it out.

"I'm fine. I've already decided on what I'm going to wear, and it's a knockout outfit."

Frankie's eyes lit up. "Can I see?"

"Sure. I'll model it for you after I'm showered and my hair is done."

Frankie sighed. "You'll have to send me a picture. I have Perfect Match training today. It's so frustrating not knowing whether I'm going to do this or follow Dagor across another crazy mountain trek."

"I'm crossing my fingers for you." Jasmine lifted her hand and demonstrated.

Frankie leaned over and gave her a one-armed hug. "You and Ell-rom must come visit us. If we can't make it to the village, we need to have a proper goodbye party."

Tears stung the back of Jasmine's eyes when she thought about not seeing her new friends every day. "Remember what you told me? Believe that it will happen, and it will. Visualize yourself living in the village."

Frankie chuckled. "Oh, I do. Every day." She blew her and Ell-rom a parting air kiss and sauntered out of their room.

"I'm going to miss her so badly." Jasmine put her empty coffee mug on the night table and stretched her arms above her head. "I think I'm going to draw myself a nice bath. I want to wash my hair and style it for the welcome party. As Frankie said, I need to make a grand entrance." She stood up and made her way to the bathroom.

Ell-rom followed close behind her. "I'm going to watch over you while you bathe," he declared.

Jasmine paused at the bathroom door, turning to face him. "Ell-rom, that's sweet but unnecessary. Don't you have a physical therapy session with Julian this morning?"

He shook his head stubbornly. "I'm not going. You're more important."

Before she could protest further, Ell-rom pulled out his phone. "Call Julian."

When the doctor answered, Ell-rom didn't hesitate. "I won't be coming to the session today. I need to stay with Jasmine and keep an eye on her."

There was a pause as he listened to Julian's response. "Oh, I see. Well, that works out, then. Thanks for understanding."

Ending the call, Ell-rom had a smug expression on his face. "Julian says it's just as well. They're busy preparing everything to move Morelle."

"Wow. It's really happening. It didn't really sink in until now."

She felt a flutter of excitement despite her fatigue. In just a few hours, they would be in the village, starting their new life together.

When the bath was full, Jasmine removed her nightgown, stepped inside, and sank into the warm water, letting out a contented sigh as the soothing scent of lavender enveloped her.

Ell-rom lowered the lid on the toilet and sat down.

"Sweetheart? Can you please bring me my phone? I've forgotten it on the nightstand."

"Of course." He pushed to his feet, walked out, and a moment later walked back with her phone.

It dawned on her then how much he had improved physically and otherwise. It was no longer an effort for him to stand up from a sitting position, and he looked good in the T-shirt and jeans he had on. He was changing right in front of her eyes at a rate that would have been impossible for a human.

"Thank you, love," she said, taking the phone from him. "Why don't you pick out your outfit while I soak? We want you to look dashing for your big debut in the village."

Not that he had a large selection to choose from. He had just one nice outfit, and it would have to do.

She should have ordered him a suit.

Ell-rom nodded. "Alright. But call if you need anything, even if it's just a glass of water or a towel."

57

KIAN

Kian glanced at his watch, pushed to his feet, and walked over to stand by the window of his office. Most days, watching the early morning activity in the village square below was a source of calm and satisfaction for him, but not today. The usual bustle seemed muted as if the community could sense the tension in the air.

When a knock sounded on the door, he walked over and opened it. "Good morning, Toven."

"Good morning." The god walked in. "Are you sure you need me here for this?"

Kian could understand Toven's reluctance to witness Jade's reaction to the accusations against her daughter.

"I do, in case she doubts me or thinks that Parker has made things up."

Toven nodded. "I'm here for you." He pulled out a chair and sat down. "How are you holding up?"

Kian was surprised by the question. Most people thought of him as invincible, and usually he was the one asking others how they were doing.

"I've been better, and I'm not looking forward to inflicting pain on Jade, but we'll get over this hurdle just as we have gotten over every other."

Toven nodded. "I spent a long time last night thinking about what to do with the girl. I think we should ask Annani to try to bind her power. Annani managed to get Igor to talk. Granted, it was when he was drugged within an inch of his life, and his resistance was nonexistent, but Drova is still young, and she is probably not as powerful as her father. Not yet."

Kian sat down across from the god. "I considered that option, but if that doesn't work, we are left with nothing and a girl who knows no one can stand in her way. I'd rather keep my mother as an option and a threat. As long as Drova doesn't know whether my mother can bind her power, she will fear it and be easier to control."

Toven didn't look convinced. "I trust your judgment. You've been managing people for a long time."

"Thank you."

As another knock sounded at the door, Kian tensed, expecting Jade, but as he rose to his feet the door opened, and Shai walked in with a tray of coffees. "All black, as you requested."

"Thank you, Shai."

His assistant nodded and walked back out.

After Kian handed one of the paper cups to Toven and pulled out one for himself, the two of them sat in tense silence for a few minutes until another knock sounded at the door, this time announcing Jade's arrival.

Kian got up and opened the door for her. "Good morning, Jade. Please come in."

"Good morning." Jade entered, her posture as rigid as always, but her eyes were wary.

She must suspect what this was about.

"Please, take a seat." Kian gestured toward the chair across from Toven and took his place at the head of the conference table. "Regrettably, I'm the bearer of bad news this morning. The one responsible for the thefts and sabotages is Drova."

Jade's eyes shifted to Toven. "Did she confess?"

"No."

She turned back to Kian. "Then how do you know?"

"Parker was caught on camera stealing from one of the houses. We went to talk to him last night, and after Toven managed to break through Drova's compulsion, Parker told us that she compelled him, Lisa, and Cheryl to steal things for her and mess with the trash incinerators and motorized shutters."

The color drained from Jade's face, and she turned to Toven. "You said that she did not confess anything. Was there anything suspicious about her behavior?"

"Drova passed my examination with flying colors, answering all the questions perfectly, too perfectly, in fact. Her ability to resist compulsion is extraordinarily strong, but she made one mistake. She appeared too calm and confident. Everyone else I interrogated was a little nervous. It's natural for people to feel that way because they are afraid of saying something that will make them look guilty, even if they are not. Even you were a little nervous, despite knowing that your questioning was a mere formality and that no one suspected you."

Jade's jaw tightened. "That's not proof of anything other than youthful swagger."

Kian took a deep breath. "If that was the only thing making her a suspect, you wouldn't be here. But together with Parker's testimony, there is no doubt. We can do the same with Lisa and Cheryl before they have a chance to talk to Parker, and I'm sure we will hear the same thing."

Jade let out a resigned breath. "I was always afraid that Drova would grow up to be like her father, and I was so relieved when she didn't manifest any compulsion ability. But it seems she was hiding it from me."

"Not necessarily," Toven said. "I think her ability has developed only recently. When I first compelled her, it wasn't any more difficult than with the other purebloods."

Kian drummed his fingers on the table. "Could she have been faking it back then as well?"

"She wasn't," Toven said. "But now that her ability has manifested, we have a much bigger problem on our hands than the minor nuisances she caused. Drova is young, and her power will continue to grow. She could potentially become as powerful as Igor."

As the words hung heavy in the air, Jade's eyes flashed with a mix of emotions: fear, pride, and fierce protectiveness warring for dominance.

"You are not putting my daughter in stasis," she said, her voice low and dangerous. "Drova is not evil like Igor. She might be misguided, but she means well."

Kian held up his hands in a placating gesture. "I would never suggest that, Jade. But we need to take precautions."

He outlined the plan for house arrest, explaining the need for compulsion-filtering earpieces for anyone coming in contact with Drova.

Jade listened, her expression growing more troubled with each word. When Kian finished, she shook her head. "What about hunting? She'll go crazy if she's locked in a house all the time."

That was a valid concern, and the last thing he needed was a crazed, powerful compeller on his hands. "We can make arrangements for hunting trips. You'll need to accompany her, wearing the earpieces, of course. Physically, you're still stronger and better trained, so she won't be able to overpower you to take your earpieces out as Igor did to me."

A flicker of doubt crossed Jade's face. "I'm not sure about that anymore. Drova is a formidable fighter who can stand her own against me."

"Then take your second with you," Kian suggested. "Together with Kagra, you should be able to control her if necessary. We will also put a location cuff on her, so if she runs, we will send Guardians to retrieve her."

"Where would she run?" Jade scoffed. "She's just a kid, and she looks very different. Where could she possibly go?"

Kian leaned forward, his expression grave. "Jade, we need to be realistic here. Drova is as dangerous as Igor was. With her abilities, she could go wherever she wanted and take whatever she wanted. If she's smart about it and knows her limitations, very few could stop her."

"Is that a threat?" Jade's voice was sharp.

"Absolutely not," Kian assured her. "I would never threaten Drova or any member of our community. I'm simply pointing out the potential dangers if she were to venture into the human world and make enemies. She is powerful but not invincible. A sniper, for instance, could still take her out from afar."

Jade mulled this over, her fingers tapping restlessly on the armrest of her chair. Finally, she let out a long breath and gave a small nod. "I understand the necessity, but what happens now?"

"We need to bring Drova in for questioning. How do you want to handle this? You can bring her in yourself, or we can send Guardians with earpieces."

Jade's response was immediate. "I'll bring her. She's my daughter. It should be me."

Kian didn't expect any other answer from her. "Very well. I expect you back here within an hour."

"I might need a little more time." Jade rose from her chair. "I need to prepare her."

"Two hours tops. If you are not here, I will assume she overpowered you, and I will send Guardians after her."

"Understood."

"Thank you, and I'm sorry. I wish none of this was necessary."

A sad smile flickered across Jade's face. "So do I."

As the door closed behind her, Kian slumped in his chair. "That went better than I expected."

Toven nodded. "Jade has always been pragmatic, and I think that deep down she knew."

58

JADE

Jade felt like she had been thrown back to the two decades she'd endured under Igor, the fear she had constantly lived with, the mental walls she had learned to build, which had been only somewhat effective, and she needed that armor against her own daughter.

Except now, she was not alone. She had Phinas.

Pulling her phone out of her pocket, she called him.

He was in a meeting with Kalugal this morning at his boss's home, so thankfully, he wasn't out of the village and could come right away.

The phone rang twice before Phinas's deep, reassuring voice came through. "Hello, love. Miss me already?"

Normally, she would smile and come back with a teasing remark, but she had no humor left in her this morning. "I need your help."

"What is it?"

"I need to bring Drova in for questioning, and I might need backup. Wear your earpieces."

There was a moment of silence. "I don't understand. Wasn't she questioned yesterday?"

"She was, but as it turns out, she's inherited Igor's compulsion ability, and her power has grown to a level that even Toven couldn't compel her." She continued to tell him about Parker and what he had revealed about Drova. "I have my earpieces, but she might overpower me, take them out, and compel me to do whatever she wants." Jade took a deep breath. "I can't even begin to describe how this makes me feel. I'm afraid of my own daughter."

"Where are you heading?" he asked.

"The house. I suppose she's still sleeping after a busy night."

"I'm coming over," Phinas said.

"I need to talk to Drova first, so I will go in alone. I just need you in the house in case she attacks me."

On second thought, Kagra would have been a better choice because she was stronger and faster than Phinas, but Jade needed Phinas not only to guard her back but for emotional support.

Phinas was quiet for a moment. "Of course. Be careful, love, and don't engage until I get there."

"Okay."

The walk home seemed both interminable and far too short, and before she was ready, Jade was standing outside their house, hand poised to open the door. She'd promised Phinas to wait for him, but she wasn't going to keep this promise.

She was a warrior and leader of the Kra-ell, and she had faced worse than this.

Drova was strong and well-trained, but she didn't carry any weapons on her like Jade did. If it came down to a fight, she would use a knife on her daughter. Not to kill her but to slow her down.

Drova would heal.

Taking a deep breath, Jade opened the door and walked in. Drova wasn't in the living room, which wasn't surprising since she spent most of her time in her bedroom, supposedly studying for her high school equivalency test but apparently plotting a rebellion.

Her body coiled and ready for an attack, Jade continued down the short corridor and opened the door to her daughter's room without knocking.

The room was empty, and the bed looked like it hadn't been slept on. To make sure, Jade lifted the taut blanket and put her hand on the sheet-covered mattress.

It was cold.

Drova hadn't slept in the house last night.

Just to be sure, Jade opened the door to her daughter's bathroom and then moved through the house, checking every room.

She pulled out her phone and called Drova, but the call went straight to voicemail.

Now, she was sure that her daughter was hiding.

Jade called Phinas again.

He answered immediately. "I'm almost there."

"She's not here, and her bed wasn't slept in. The sheet is cold."

"She couldn't have escaped the village. There are cameras along the fence, and Guardians monitor them twenty-four-seven. She couldn't compel them not to see her."

"I know. She must be hiding somewhere in the village. We need to find her before she decides to do more damage than she has already done."

"Wait for me," Phinas said. "I'll be there in a few minutes."

"I'm here."

As Jade ended the call, the reality of the situation hit her anew. The thought that she needed protection from her own daughter made her stomach churn.

Unbidden memories of Igor's control over her surfaced. The helplessness, the violation of having her will stripped away was a horror she had never expected to experience again.

A slave never again.

And now, the threat came from her own flesh and blood.

She needed reinforcements to help search for Drova.

After double-checking her earpieces, she called Kagra. "I need your help. Come to my house right away."

"What's wrong?"

Jade took a deep breath and explained the situation.

When she was done, Kagra let out a breath. "I'm on my way."

59

DROVA

Drova shifted uncomfortably on the lounge chair, the early morning dew seeping through her clothes. She had spent the night in Pavel's backyard, hidden from view by the lush vegetation that surrounded the house.

Her phone was off and hidden inside a planter outside the café, so they couldn't find her by the signal, and she'd made sure to avoid all the monitoring cameras on the way, so they couldn't find her by looking at the feeds.

She didn't know what she hoped to achieve by hiding out here. Eventually, they would find her, but for now, she would enjoy a few more hours of freedom and maybe come up with a strategy.

What if she claimed it was all just a prank?

But that would defeat the purpose of everything she had worked for. Pavel and his buddies talked big about how living in a village was unnatural for pureblooded Kra-ell, but none of them suggested any viable solution.

They didn't want to admit it, but they were comfortable living in the village without having to do anything unless they wanted to. Some had volunteered to join the Guardian force and help rescue victims of trafficking. It was a worthy cause, but the truth was that helping humans clean up their scum was never the Kra-ell's job, and it wasn't the immortals' either.

They should focus on their own communities and train to protect them from the other immortals she kept hearing about, who were more numerous and had been taught to hate their cousins in Annani's clan with rabid fanaticism.

That alone should be reason enough for the Kra-ell to leave and form a community of their own. Jade and the others thought there was strength in numbers, but that was a mistake when they acquired the immortals' powerful enemies in exchange for the questionable fortification of their force.

The other immortals were not looking for the Kra-ell because they didn't know they even existed, but they were looking for Annani and her clan.

With a groan, Drova turned on her back and brought her knees up.

Why was something so clear to her, and not clear to everyone else?

Were they all less intelligent than her?

Her small acts of rebellion were a test of her ability, but they also proved to Pavel and his buddies that it was possible to resist the immortals without doing harm to them. She set out to reveal the immortals' weaknesses, not to harm them.

But as her abilities grew, so did her ambitions. The thrill of compelling others to do her bidding, of sowing chaos in this perfect little community, had been intoxicating, and she had gotten slightly carried away.

Well, it had been fun.

Drova smirked, remembering the looks of confusion on the faces of the immortals as they tried to make sense of the malfunctions and thefts plaguing their precious village.

Now they were coming for her, but they wouldn't find her.

Her mother hadn't even noticed her absence last night, which was as it should be. According to the Kra-ell tradition, Drova was old enough to fend for herself. To Jade's credit, she'd always treated her as such, almost never questioning her comings and goings, but sometimes Drova wondered if it was out of respect or neglect. Jade asked Phinas where he was going and when he was coming back because she cared about him. Didn't she care about her own daughter?

Whatever. Drova had exploited her freedom to the fullest.

Now, as she lay on the uncomfortable lounge chair,

though, Drova knew that freedom was coming to an end.

After Parker hadn't shown up at the playground last night and the girls told her what they had seen, she'd gone snooping around his house, or rather as close as she'd dared, and she had seen Onegus, Kian, Toven, and Mia come out. They'd looked grim, but she hadn't been sure whether they had cracked Parker until she'd heard the lock engaging on the front door of Magnus's house and, a moment later, the lock on the door leading from the kitchen to the side yard had been activated as well.

No one ever locked their doors in the village. The only reason a senior Guardian like Magnus would lock his doors was to keep her out.

They were afraid of her, which gave her a small measure of satisfaction.

Still, she needed to confide in someone, and Pavel was the only one she could think of. She needed to boast before they came for her and arrested her so he would at least know what she could contribute to the resistance.

Maybe he could help her?

When the living-room sliding glass doors opened, and Pavel stepped out, she sat up and smoothed a hand over her hair. It was probably a tangled mess right now.

He frowned. "What are you doing here, Drova?"

"Waiting for you to wake up. I need to talk to you."

Pavel glanced at his watch. "I need to be in class in half an hour, so make it quick."

His stupid Guardian training could wait. The guy was too dumb to realize that it didn't make sense to talk about resistance while serving on the immortals' Guardian force.

So why did she crave him so much?

Just because he was handsome and could make her laugh?

Yeah, he wasn't the stupid one. She was.

"You might want to be late for this." She pushed to her feet. "Can we talk inside?"

Pavel moved aside, letting her in.

"Where are your roommates?" she asked.

"They have gone on ahead."

"Good." She pulled out one of the kitchen stools, sat down, and motioned to the other stool. "Sit down."

She might have unintentionally laced her voice with a smidgen of compulsion because Pavel obeyed immediately.

Taking a deep breath, Drova began to explain. She told him how she'd tested her power on Parker, an immortal compeller, and on Lisa and Cheryl, his human best friends, whom he hadn't been able to free from her compulsion. Then she'd finished with her biggest triumph, resisting Toven's compulsion and fooling even the great god himself.

As she spoke, Drova's voice grew more animated, a hint of pride creeping in. "Don't you see, Pavel? I'm the key to your resistance. Whatever you and the others dream up, I can make it happen." She searched his face for the admiration she hoped to find there but encountered only wariness. "But now that they've cracked Parker and gotten him to snitch on me, they're probably looking for me as we speak. But with your help, and with the resistance behind me, we could—"

"Stop," Pavel cut her off. He smoothed a hand over the top of his head, taking a deep breath. "That was an incredibly stupid thing to do, Drova, and coming here instead of turning yourself in was even worse. They will think that I'm your accomplice, and I can't let that happen."

Drova felt as if she had been slapped. This wasn't how it was supposed to go. Pavel was supposed to understand, to see the potential in what she had done, to appreciate her and see her as more than a female too young for him.

"Come." Pavel extended his hand. "Let's go to Kian's office and try to sort this thing out. Thank the Mother of All Life, you didn't commit any serious crimes, so they might let you go with a slap on the wrist and maybe a cuff to follow your movements. "

Hurt and anger surged through Drova. Without thinking, she lashed out with her power, her eyes flashing as she snarled, "Eat dirt, Pavel!"

She watched with satisfaction as Pavel's face contorted, his body fighting against the compulsion. For a moment she thought he might resist, but then he stepped back outside and bent down, his hand reaching for the ground.

A cruel smile twisting her lips, Drova shoved past him and then turned and fled, pushing through the back gate and out into the village proper.

60

JADE

The sound of the front door opening had Jade whirl around, hope flaring in her chest, only to be replaced by a mix of relief and disappointment as Phinas stepped inside.

He crossed the room in three long strides, enveloping her in a tight embrace. "Are you okay?"

She wasn't, but she was a leader first and a mother second, and she couldn't allow herself to be weak.

Well, she could allow herself some comfort in his arms for a spell. "I'm fine." She pulled back. "Kagra's on her way to help."

"Good, I was thinking on the way that we might need reinforcements to search for her. Where do we start?"

"The playground," Jade said. "Parker mentioned they used to meet there, and also, that's where they stored the things they stole. He told Onegus where it was, so it's possible that Guardians have already dug it up, but it's still a good place to begin."

As they stepped outside, Kagra jogged up. "Any news?"

Jade shook her head. "We're heading to the playground first. Can you check the café and the surrounding area?"

Kagra grimaced. "Why would she be in the café? If she's hiding, that's the last place she would be. We need to go to the security office to see if they can find her by her phone signal, and if not, search for her through the camera feeds. If we can't find her that way, we will need to check the underground complex. That's the best place to hide in the village. There are so many classrooms and storage areas that we will need to recruit a team of Guardians to look for her there."

Jade nodded. "You are right. Let's go to the security office first."

She should have thought about all the things Kagra had suggested, but it seemed that her brain was frazzled, and she wasn't thinking straight.

Perhaps she was a mother first and a leader second after all.

As they headed to the underground complex where the security office was located, Jade pulled out her phone and called Kian.

"Do you have Drova?" he asked.

"No. She wasn't home and I don't know where she is. Phinas and Kagra are helping me look for her. We are heading to the security office first."

"Are you sure you don't want me to send Guardians to look for her? She could be hiding in someone's house, compelling them to keep quiet."

Kian was right, but she still wanted at least a chance to get to Drova first. "Give me a couple of hours. She can't leave the village without us knowing."

Kian sighed. "We have a big party this afternoon. I need her contained before we bring Ell-rom to the village. I didn't even tell my mother yet, and I know she's going to be upset. She likes Drova."

Jade hadn't known that the goddess had a fondness for her daughter, and hearing Kian say that right at this moment was just what she needed. It was like the dark clouds parted for a moment to admit a ray of sun.

"Thank you for saying that," she said.

"It's the truth. It's also true that we've suspected Drova for a while now. Maybe a few talks with my mother would help straighten her out."

It was good to hear Kian talk about Drova as a teenager who needed guidance rather than the tremendous risk she represented.

"I'm sure talking to the Clan Mother would be beneficial, but we shouldn't reward Drova for bad behavior. After she suffers the consequences of her deeds, we can arrange a talk with the Clan Mother, provided that she wants to, of course. She might lose her fond feelings for Drova after hearing that she was behind what was happening and that she compelled others to do bad deeds."

"That's wise, Jade. I'll leave you to your search. You have two hours starting now."

Kian ended the call before she could thank him.

On one side of her Phinas smiled, and on the other, Kagra shook her head.

"What?" Jade asked.

"Kian is too nice," Kagra said. "If it were me, I would sentence Drova to a whipping, and then lock her in a solitary cell for a month."

Jade shivered. That was the kind of punishment that she used to mete out when she was in charge of her own compound, but after suffering under Igor's rule for over two decades and then living with the immortals and their gentler ways, she had gotten softer. "We don't whip people anymore." She looked at Phinas. "We adopted the immortals' customs."

Phinas pursed his lips. "The immortals still whip their unruly teenagers when they commit serious transgressions, and even Guardians get whipped when they break the rules."

Jade hadn't known that, but there was no way she was subjecting Drova to a whipping. She'd really grown softer.

"Drova's offenses do not justify a harsh punishment like that. Petty thefts and insignificant sabotages do not merit a whipping."

Kagra shook her head. "Maybe not, but taking over the

will of others and forcing them to do her dirty work might."

Not if Jade could help it.

The playground stood empty when they passed through it, the swings swaying gently in the morning breeze. Jade's eyes scanned the area, searching for any sign of her daughter, but other than some small creature scurrying through the underbrush, no one was hiding behind the dense greenery.

61

DROVA

Drova's heart pounded in her chest as she ran, the cool morning air whipping against her face, a stark contrast to the heat of shame and fear burning inside her.

What had she done?

She had used her power against one of her own, against someone she had hoped one day would be an ally or perhaps even more.

The look of betrayal in Pavel's eyes haunted her as she ran, a reminder of how quickly things had spiraled out of control.

With a groan of frustration and regret, Drova skidded to a halt, her feet kicking up small clouds of dust. She couldn't leave things like this. Despite her fear and the urgency to flee, she couldn't bear the thought of Pavel actually following through on her cruel command. Turning on her heel, she sprinted back towards his house.

"Don't eat dirt, Pavel," she yelled as she burst back into his yard, keeping her eyes away from him.

She couldn't bear to see the look of revulsion and fear on his face. Without waiting for a response, she turned and ran again.

"Drova, wait!" Pavel called after her.

But she couldn't stop, couldn't face him after what she'd done.

Ducking behind a thick cluster of bushes, Drova pressed herself against the ground, trying to make herself as small as possible. She held her breath as she heard the sound of Pavel's boots pounding on the gravel path.

He ran past her hiding spot, still calling out her name, his voice growing fainter as he moved further away.

As Pavel's calls faded into the distance, the village around Drova began to stir to life. The quiet of early morning gave way to the soft murmur of conversations as villagers made their way to the pavilion or the café. A group of joggers passed by, their carefree laughter grating on Drova's already frayed nerves.

It wasn't fair that they were so relaxed, so normal, when her entire world was about to explode.

The question was where to go next. Home was out of the question; her mother would be waiting, likely with Kagra or even some Guardians. The vegetation outside the village was a joke and didn't offer any coverage even if she could scale the fence unnoticed, which was not the case. The village perimeter was dotted with cameras, and they would spot her trying to get out in an instant. Besides, even if she managed to make it past the fence, where would she go from there?

The human world stretched out beyond the immortals' village, vast and unfamiliar, and the thought of venturing into it alone sent a chill down Drova's spine.

For all her bravado, for all her talk of freedom and power, she had never truly planned to live among the humans. Her fantasies had always centered around a place where the Kra-ell could live free and wild, running and hunting like they had in Karelia but free of the oppressive rule of her father.

As she crouched behind the hedge, trying to formulate a plan, Drova felt the first real stirrings of fear take hold. The reality of her situation crashed down upon her. She was alone now, truly alone. She had no allies, no plan, just her wits and her powers against the entire village.

The enormity of what she had done, of the consequences she now faced, overwhelmed her.

But isn't this what you wanted? A small voice whispered in the back of her mind. *To shake things up, to prove your strength?*

Drova shook her head, trying to clear her thoughts. Yes, she had wanted to make a statement, to force change. But not like this. Not alone and hunted, with nowhere to turn.

This wasn't the glorious revolution she had imagined.

This was...chaos.

The fact was that she couldn't keep running forever. Sooner or later, they would find her, and she needed to be ready for them. Panic and fear would only make things worse. She needed to think, plan, and find a way to talk herself out of this mess.

Her mother had survived under Igor's control and escaped it with nothing more than pure determination, wit, and help from the Mother of All Life. Drova possessed the same abilities as her mother and more. She would find a way out of this with her smarts and her determination, just as Jade had done.

No more running, no more hiding.

She would face this head-on.

She would confront Kian and the others to explain her actions. Make them understand why she had done the things she had. She would make them see that her intentions, misguided as they might have been, came from a place of passion for her people and their heritage.

This village might be a utopia for the immortals, but it wasn't for the Kra-ell.

They were rotting here, proud warriors turning into lazy bums.

And if Jade and Kian didn't see things her way? Well, she still had her powers.

She was valuable.

Kian was pragmatic, and he would realize that she was

an asset to the community, provided that they treated her right.

And if he didn't...well, she would make him realize it. A powerful compeller could do whatever she wanted, but she needed to be smart about it, or she would end up like Igor, in stasis or dead.

As Drova straightened up, her legs were stiff from crouching for so long, and when she looked down, she caught sight of her reflection in a puddle of water at her feet. She paused, struck by the image staring back at her.

The girl in the reflection looked older and harder. For a moment, a fleeting image of her father flashed through her mind. The resemblance was unsettling.

Was this who she wanted to be?

62

JADE

Jade's footsteps echoed on the pavement as she approached the pavilion, flanked by Kagra and Phinas. The morning air was crisp, carrying the scent of coffee from the nearby café. Under normal circumstances, it would have been a pleasant start to the day. But today, worry was gnawing at Jade's insides, making the familiar sights and smells of the village seem almost surreal.

As they neared the entrance to the pavilion, a distant voice caught her attention. She halted abruptly, her enhanced hearing picking up the sound that her companions hadn't yet registered.

"Did you hear that?" she asked, her eyes scanning the area.

Kagra and Phinas paused, listening intently. After a moment, they too heard it. Someone was calling Drova's name, the voice growing louder with each repetition.

Then, rounding the corner at a full sprint, came Pavel. His face was covered in dirt, his eyes frantic.

"Jade!" he called out, spotting her and changing course to intercept their group.

As Pavel skidded to a stop in front of them, Jade took in his disheveled appearance. "What happened? Have you seen Drova?"

Pavel nodded. "She was at my house. Slept in the backyard, I think. She told me about being responsible for the thefts and the sabotage."

"Where is she now?" Phinas asked.

"She ran off. I tried to convince her to turn herself in and go to Kian, but she...she used her power on me." He gestured to his dirt-covered face, a look of shame and confusion crossing his features. "She made me eat dirt, but then she came back and told me not to. She looked so scared. I've never seen her like that."

Jade felt a chill run down her spine. Her daughter was using her powers so recklessly and against a friend, no less. She could see the hurt and worry in Pavel's eyes.

"She just lost it," Pavel finished. "I think she was stressed out of her mind and needed me to calm her down instead of saying that she was being stupid. She lashed out, but then she felt bad about it and came back to remove the compulsion." He shook his head. "It was like being under Igor's control all over again, except he never ordered me to eat dirt."

Jade smiled without an iota of mirth. "Igor did much

worse than that. Thank the Mother of All Life that you weren't subjected to his whims."

Pavel hung his head. "I know. I'm sorry I said that. And Drova is nothing like him. She just needs to learn that she can't use her power like that."

"Did you know?" Kagra asked. "About her power and what she has been doing?"

"No clue, I swear. I didn't suspect anything. Then I find her on my lounger in the morning, and she dumps all of this on me before I'd even had my coffee. And I wasn't thinking when I told her that it was incredibly stupid on her part and offered to escort her to Kian."

Kagra was still looking at Pavel with suspicion in her eyes. "Why did she come to you?"

He shrugged, but there was a guilty look in his eyes. "She likes me, but I made it clear that she was too young for me."

Drova was young, but she had reached the age of consent for a female, and if she weren't Igor's daughter, Pavel would have probably accepted her invitation, but Jade was glad that he hadn't.

He was a fine young pureblood, but he wasn't exceptional, and her daughter should choose someone with better genetics to father her child.

"You did nothing wrong," Jade said. "Do you have your earpieces with you?"

Pavel shook his head. "I didn't think I'd need them in the

village, not for training." He looked at his watch. "For which I am late."

"When you get home, put them in your pocket, or better yet, in your ears."

Next to her, Phinas snorted. "Yeah, good idea. Next time, Drova might tell you to eat shit."

The color drained from Pavel's face. "She wouldn't. She even came back to stop me from eating more dirt."

"Go," Kagra said. "Bhathian doesn't like it when trainees are late."

When Pavel continued into the pavilion, Jade turned to her companions. "Change of plans. I have a feeling we will find Drova lurking around Pavel's house."

"Why?" Phinas asked. "He just came from there."

Jade put her hand on his arm. "She probably ducked into some hiding spot, and he ran right by her. I trained her, so I know her moves."

They set off at a brisk pace, the usual morning bustle of the village fading into background noise as Jade's mind raced.

What had driven Drova to this point?

How had she missed the signs that her daughter had inherited her father's talent?

As they entered the section of the village where Pavel's house was, Jade scanned the area, looking for Drova. Every shadow and corner was a potential hiding place for her troubled daughter.

Then, as they rounded a corner, Jade saw her.

Drova was walking toward them, her usual swagger on full display. To anyone else, she might have looked completely at ease, unconcerned by the chaos she had caused. But Jade knew her daughter.

She saw the tension in Drova's shoulders and the tight line of her lips. Beneath the bravado was a scared girl who had waded in too deep and didn't know how to swim back to shore.

"Stay here," Jade murmured to Kagra and Phinas, her eyes never leaving Drova. "I need to talk to her alone."

Ignoring Phinas's protest, Jade stepped forward, closing the distance between herself and her daughter. As she approached, she saw Drova's façade falter for just a moment, a flicker of fear and uncertainty crossing her face before the mask of confidence slipped back into place.

"Drova." Jade kept her voice calm and even. "We need to talk."

Drova halted a few feet away, her posture stiff and defensive. "Come to arrest me, Mother?" she asked, her tone dripping with false bravado.

Jade took another step closer. "I've come to talk to you and understand why you did what you did."

For a moment, Drova seemed to waver, the conflict clear in her eyes. Jade held her breath, hoping that the blood bond between them would be enough to break through the walls Drova had built around herself.

"Will it matter what I say?" Drova finally asked.

Jade felt a pang of guilt at her daughter's words. "I want to hear your side. I want to understand why you felt you had to hide your ability from me. Were you afraid?"

Drova rolled her eyes. "Of course, I was afraid. Look what they did to Igor. He deserved it for what he had done, but if he were not such a strong compeller, they might have only jailed him and not put him in stasis."

Jade closed her eyes for a moment and sighed. "The only reason Igor still lives is because Kian convinced me that we might one day need what is stored in his head. I had every intention of beheading him for what he did to me and every other female in the compound. Don't think of him as your father. He doesn't deserve it. At best, he was a sperm donor."

Drova pinned her with a pair of hard eyes that were very much like Jade's. "And how do you think that makes me feel, knowing that half of my genes come from a monster?"

"You are not a monster, and maybe Igor wasn't a monster either before the gods manipulated his genes. I don't know. He decided what he wanted to do, and he didn't care who he murdered to achieve his goals. But I can promise you one thing. No one is going to put you in stasis. They will have to get past me first. But we do need to talk about what's happened, about the choices you've made." She looked at the passers-by, who were making a large circle to avoid them. "But we cannot do this here. I want you to come with me to Kian's office and explain your actions to both of us."

"What is he planning to do with me?" Drova asked in a much less confident voice.

"You will probably be placed under house arrest, but I will take you hunting with me whenever I can."

Drova's shoulders slumped. "That doesn't sound so bad. Are you sure that's all he is going to do to me?"

Jade closed the distance between them and put her arm around the girl's shoulders. "You didn't kill anyone, and your crimes were minor. The big issue is your compulsion of Parker, Lisa, Cheryl, and possibly Pavel if he seeks retribution for you forcing him to eat dirt."

Drova's eyes widened. "He told you about that?"

"He did. He was worried about you."

Drova closed her eyes. "I'm really sorry for doing that to him. I got angry when he said that what I did was stupid."

"It was." Jade started leading Drova in the direction of the village square. "But everyone is allowed to do a few stupid things when they are young. That's how you learn."

Drova nodded. "I just wanted...I wanted us to be free and true to ourselves. We are not like them, Mother, and we can't live like them."

63

KIAN

As Kian's phone rang and Jade's name flashed on the screen, he answered immediately. "What's up, Jade?"

"We're on our way with Drova," she said. "I'm bringing Phinas and Kagra with me. We should be there in less than ten minutes."

"Very good. I'm awaiting your arrival."

After ending the call, he reached for his earpieces and put them in. It seemed like, lately, he'd been wearing them more than ever. With Ell-rom, it had been first necessary as a precaution and later as a translation device, and then it occurred to Kian that many of the Kra-ell still struggled with English, and although most spoke Russian and not Kra-ell among themselves, the earpieces could translate that as well.

Drova, as far as he knew, had mastered English already, but he hadn't been following the progress of the Kra-ell kids, so he wasn't sure.

She would probably be hungry and thirsty after the eventful night and morning she'd had, and it wasn't his intention to torment her unnecessarily. He retrieved four bottles of water from the small fridge in his office and put them on the conference table.

That solved the thirst problem but not the hunger, and he couldn't solve it by ordering a few pastries from the café. As a pureblooded Kra-ell, Drova's dietary needs were limited to blood and a few select liquids that she could tolerate.

Regrettably, the café didn't sell packaged synthetic blood. Or maybe they did? With the new Kra-ell population in the village, they should.

He dialed Shai's number. "Shai, quick question. Do they sell synthetic blood at the café?"

There was a pause on the other end of the line. "No, they don't, but it might not be a bad idea to add it to the menu. The only problem would be grossing out the other customers."

Kian chuckled. "What if we sold it packaged like a juice box with an attached straw? Discreet and convenient."

Shai's laughter echoed through the phone. "Now that's thinking outside the box, or rather inside of it, I suppose."

Their shared amusement was interrupted by a knock at the office door. Kian ended the call and moved to answer it.

He opened the door to find Jade, Drova, Phinas, and Kagra waiting. Drova's posture was rigid, her chin lifted in defiance, but Kian could see the fear lurking in her eyes.

"Please, come in," he said, gesturing towards the conference table. "Have a seat."

As they settled around the table, Kian handed Drova a bottle of water. "I was just on the phone with my assistant about the possibility of selling synthetic blood at the café," he said, attempting to break the ice. "We thought packaging it in juice boxes might be a good way to do it."

He had meant it as a way to calm her down or even to get her to laugh at the idea, but given the flash of anger in her eyes, she didn't find the idea amusing.

"Synthetic blood is bad enough, but packaging it in juice boxes is just offensive."

Drova continued listing grievance after grievance—the limited hunting opportunities, the confinement within the village, the expectation that they should adapt to the immortals' ways of life, the deterioration of their society, the lack of purpose, and so on.

Kian listened attentively, noting the passion in her voice and the depth of her frustration.

When Drova finally fell silent, Kian leaned forward. "Thank you for sharing that, Drova. Now, I'd like to ask you something. In a perfect world, what would you like to do? What would you envision for your people?"

Drova seemed taken aback by the question as if she hadn't expected to be asked for her opinion. "We should have our own community, somewhere we can live freely in nature. I have nothing against the immortals, but my people are rotting away in this village. We need the space and freedom to be who we are."

Kian nodded thoughtfully. "I understand your grievances, Drova. And I promise you, Jade and I will work on finding a solution that better meets the needs of the Kraell. However, your actions have had consequences, and frankly, you are a danger to the community. I have no choice but to confine you to your house. You will also be outfitted with a location cuff because we cannot expect your mother to keep an eye on you twenty-four-seven."

As if on cue, Shai entered the office, carrying the cuff. Kian gestured for him to approach Drova.

There was no need to explain what it was. All the Kraell had worn them when they first arrived in the village, and the ones serving community service were still wearing them.

Drova lifted her arm. "Oh, goodie. A new piece of jewelry. I feel so fancy."

"Drova," Jade admonished sternly.

"What? It is pretty." She turned to Kian. "But what about the hunting trips my mother mentioned? Was that a false promise?"

"The cuff can be reprogrammed for those trips," Kian assured her, though the spark of interest in Drova's eyes at this information worried him.

He made a mental note to warn Jade to be on her guard during these outings.

"It's going to be a nightmare to be cooped up in the house, but I guess this is a small price to pay for what I did."

"That's not all," Kian said. "You will need to apologize to Parker, Lisa, and Cheryl. In addition, I will tell the three of them to come up with assignments for you that you will have to complete for them."

The look of horror on her face was comical. "What kind of assignments?"

"Whatever they dream up," Kian said. "From writing an essay about growing mushrooms in the winter, to knitting a sweater. I'm sure they will have some creative ideas."

Drova winced. "I don't have a choice, do I?"

"No, you don't," Kagra said. "You should be thankful for this mild punishment. If you were under my command, I would have sentenced you to a whipping."

Drova recoiled from her mother's second. "That's barbaric."

Kagra bared her fangs at the girl. "You want to live as an authentic Kra-ell, true? We are not soft or forgiving people."

Drova swallowed. "I'm not against change and progress. I think Kian's idea is much more educational and, in some ways, more excruciating. At least, a whipping would have been over much faster. The Mother only knows what they will come up with to get back at me for what I have done to them."

Phinas clapped the girl on her back. "It won't be so bad, Drova. When you are not busy with assignments from your former minions, you can invite Pavel and his friends over to play in the dirt."

Kagra barked out a laugh, and Kian had the distinct feeling he was missing an inside joke.

Kian turned to Jade. "I'd like to speak with you privately for a moment if that's alright."

As the others filed out of the office, Jade stayed behind.

Once the door closed, Kian spoke in a low voice. "Be careful when you take her out of the village. I'm worried she might try something."

Jade nodded. "I know. I'll take Kagra with me. After the whipping discussion, Drova will be very careful not to anger her." She smiled and offered Kian her hand. "Thank you for going easy on her."

"You're welcome, and I meant it when I said that we need to discuss the future of your people."

A look of worry passed through Jade's eyes. "I like being part of this community, Kian. Drova needs to grow up a little to realize how good she has it here."

64

ELL-ROM

Ell-rom's eyes were fixed on Jasmine as she made her final adjustments in front of the full-length mirror. She was a vision in white, wearing a pantsuit that somehow managed to be both elegant and striking. The pants flowed wide and graceful, while the short-sleeved top hugged her curves.

Jasmine had also done something to accentuate her eyes, painting her lashes darker and her eyelids several shades of gold and brown. The effect was that her eyes seemed even larger and more golden than usual. Her lips were a warm orange-brown color that drew his gaze like a magnet. Her dark hair cascaded down her back and over her shoulders in big, soft curls, framing her beautiful face.

"You look incredible." He came to stand behind her. "Breathtaking."

Jasmine turned to him, a radiant smile lighting up her

face. "Thank you, love. I want to make an impression for our big debut."

With the high-heeled shoes she was wearing, she was nearly eye to eye with him, and as his gaze traveled down to her feet, he was worried that her pretty white shoes with their tall spiky heels would become a hindrance during the welcome party. "You certainly will make an impression, but Julian said that the event is going to take place on a lawn, and the spikes on those shoes will make it hard to walk in them. They might not be the most practical choice."

Jasmine laughed, the sound like music to his ears. "Oh, I'm well aware of that." She put her hands on his shoulders. "But this outfit paired with these shoes makes me feel like a boss."

Ell-rom frowned. "Is this outfit and the shoes part of a uniform?"

She tilted her head. "Why would you think that?"

"Otherwise, I don't understand how what you wear can put you in charge."

Then it suddenly dawned on him. "Oh, I see. It's about how they make you feel."

Ell-rom felt a surge of pride. He was getting better at understanding these nuances of human behavior and expression.

Jasmine's smile widened. Leaning in to place a quick kiss on his cheek, she said, "You're catching on fast."

Casting a final glance in the mirror, she smoothed a flyaway strand of hair and walked toward the suitcases and bags stacked next to the door. "Ready?"

He nodded. "Ready."

Ell-rom picked up their bags and a rolling suitcase. Jasmine grabbed two more of those, and together they stepped out of the bedroom and walked into the living room.

All three gods were there, waiting to say their goodbyes, and Ell-rom felt a pang of sadness as he realized this might be the last time he saw this place that had become his first real home. Still, the excitement of what lay ahead overshadowed the momentary melancholy.

"I wish Margo, Frankie, and Gabi were here to say goodbye to us," Jasmine said after giving each of the gods a hug. "I know that Margo and Frankie are in training at Perfect Match, but I hoped Gabi would be here."

"Gabi is meeting one of her brothers in the city," Aru said.

Negal looked at what they were carrying and stepped forward. "Let me help you with that."

Ell-rom wanted to say that they didn't need help, but Jasmine gladly accepted the god's offer, and the three of them continued to the parking garage.

When they reached it, they found Julian and Gertrude next to a large white vehicle with Morelle lying on a portable patient bed. She still had tubes and wires attached to her, and Gertrude was rearranging the medical equipment. These tubes and wires were attached to the other end.

"Do you need help?" Negal offered.

Julian shook his head. "It has to be done in a certain way, and Gertrude and I know the sequence."

Together, they slowly rolled the gurney up the ramp as the attached equipment trailed along on portable stands. At the rear, Julian gently pushed while Gertrude held the front, carefully balancing the weight. Once inside, they secured the gurney to the floor mounts and made sure all the machines were properly connected to the ambulance's power supply.

"Can Jasmine and I ride with her?" Ell-rom asked, gesturing to the benches on either side of the gurney.

Julian looked from Morelle to the pile of luggage and back, a frown creasing his forehead. "I'm not sure we can fit all of that in here."

"Why don't we see if we can make it work?" Jasmine asked.

With some creative maneuvering and a bit of teamwork, they managed to fit all of the luggage under and over one bench while Ell-rom and Jasmine sat on the other.

After Julian made a final sweep to check the IV, oxygen, and monitors, he closed the doors, and he and Gertrude sat up front.

As the vehicle pulled out of the garage and onto the street, Ell-rom reached out to take Morelle's hand. It was cool to the touch, but he could feel the faint pulse beneath her skin. The heart monitor continued its rhythmic beep, and the oxygen flow remained steady.

"I'm excited, Morelle," he said. "We are heading to our new home, and I was told that the village is beautiful. I wish you could see it with me."

Jasmine placed her hand on top of his. "When she wakes up, you'll show her everything."

Ell-rom nodded, grateful for Jasmine's unwavering optimism. He turned his gaze to the small windows set in the ambulance's rear doors, watching as the city streets gave way to less crowded suburbs and then what looked like open countryside.

"I can't believe we're finally on our way. It feels like just yesterday that I woke up in that clinic room."

Jasmine chuckled softly. "It seems like long months have passed since that day. It's strange how time moves differently depending on the circumstances."

"You can say that again. I went to sleep on the settler ship and woke up seven thousand years later, not knowing who I was, where I was, and where I'd come from."

She closed her hand over his. "I can't imagine how that must have felt. You are so brave."

"Brave?" He snorted. "I'm constantly anxious. If not because of one thing, then because of another. You, on the other hand, seem to be able to face anything. I was paralyzed with fear when that attacker had you by the throat. I didn't know what to do. While you talked to him and tried to reason with him."

Jasmine smiled. "I was terrified, too. But I have a lot of experience putting on a convincing act."

He was quite sure she was just saying that to make him feel better. "What about now? Are you afraid of facing all of these people?"

She shrugged. "Not really. I've already met most of them, and I can also act my way through almost anything. I know how to work a crowd."

He leaned back and closed his eyes. "You need to teach me how to do it."

"It's quite simple, really. You imagine someone who has successfully done what you need to do and you pretend that you are that person. In your case, you can pretend that you are the male version of Annani or that you are Kian. Confident, regal, and charming." She laughed. "Not that Kian is all that charming, but Annani is. Kian is more of an acquired taste. At first, he seems too harsh and abrasive, and that voice of his sounds like he is talking from the bottom of a barrel, but then when you get to know him, you realize that he's your best protection against all the crap in the world, so you start liking the sound of his voice. It becomes reassuring."

At the front of the vehicle, Julian chuckled. "That's the best description of Kian I've heard. In the end, you realize that he's quite sweet and that you can't understand how you could have ever thought any differently about him."

65

JASMINE

Jasmine leaned back against the cool metal wall of the ambulance, her eyes closed as she tried to fight off a wave of exhaustion. The truth was that her acting could fool Ell-rom and others into believing that she was handling all the pressure well, but operating on high octane for so long was taking its toll.

The past few weeks had been intense.

It had started with Alberto acting suspiciously in Cabo, to him drugging her and Margo and abducting them both. Then she'd woken on Modana's yacht and thought that her life was over, and she would spend whatever was left of it as Modana's plaything. After that, she had a few days to relax, chilling on the *Silver Swan* and enjoying Edgar's company, but that hadn't lasted long. She had been introduced to the world of immortals and gods and given an impossible task—find the alien pod that Syssi had seen in her vision in freaking Tibet.

Unbelievably, she had done that and found her prince. Then it was nursing him to health, discovering that he had an aversion to blood and trying to overcome that, and finally, dealing with his ability to kill with a thought. Now that everything had finally been resolved, it all seemed to come crashing down on her at once.

All that worry and keeping Ell-rom's secrets had kept her adrenaline levels constantly high, and the mugging and what followed had shot those stress hormones to the max.

Now that it was over, and Ell-rom's frightening power was contained by Annani's compulsion, the levels were dropping, and that was why she was feeling so tired.

Even getting ready earlier had been difficult, but she had done a great job of making herself look top-notch. Her outfit was classy; the shoes made her over six feet tall, and with her hair and makeup done, she could give any model a run for her money.

Well, she wasn't nearly as skinny, so maybe not.

Jasmine closed her eyes and allowed herself to drift off, the gentle motion of the ambulance and Ell-rom's comforting presence lulling her into a light doze.

She wasn't sure how much time had passed when she felt Ell-rom's hand on her shoulder, shaking her lightly. "You have to see this," he said.

Blinking awake, Jasmine looked around in confusion. "See what?"

"Look at the vehicle's windows." Ell-rom pointed at the small windows on the back doors and then the front windshield. "They've turned opaque. And Julian's not driving anymore. The vehicle is driving itself!"

Jasmine leaned forward to get a better look, and sure enough, the once-clear glass was now an impenetrable white.

From the front of the ambulance, Julian explained the technology behind the clan's vehicles and why it was needed to protect the location of the hidden entrance to the village.

Jasmine listened in fascination as he described the secret tunnel and the elevator system that would take them up through the mountain.

"It's like a James Bond movie," she murmured. "Incredible."

Despite her tiredness, she felt a spark of excitement ignite within her. They were starting a new life in a place that seemed more like science fiction than reality.

As the ambulance entered the tunnel, Jasmine felt the temperature drop, and the echo of the engine reverberated off the unseen walls, creating an eerie atmosphere. It was both thrilling and unnerving to be moving through a space they couldn't see, trusting a technology she didn't understand.

When the ambulance came to a stop and began to move upward, Jasmine knew that the ambulance was inside the lift that Julian had talked about.

They were almost there.

She glanced down at her outfit, suddenly self-conscious. Had she overdone it with the white pantsuit and impossibly high heels?

Jasmine wanted to make a strong first impression, and this outfit made her feel confident and powerful, but what if people dressed casually in the village and she would stick out?

"Why are you stressed?" Ell-rom asked.

She turned to him and smiled. "Am I being so obvious? I thought that I was putting on a better act than that."

"I know you, love." He leaned over and kissed her cheek. "You are gorgeous, and they are going to love you."

"Thank you." She let her head drop on his shoulder. "I'm second-guessing my outfit. I shouldn't have worn white."

"Why not?"

"It sticks out. You know why I got these clothes?"

"Why?"

"I saw a journalist I admire wearing something similar in an interview, and she looked smart and sophisticated, and I wanted to look like her." She chuckled. "I just can't talk eloquently like her, which was what actually made her appear so intelligent and sophisticated."

"You are all those things." Ell-rom took her hand and brought it to his lips for a kiss. "You come up with the best ideas. Even Kian said that, and he is not an easy guy to impress."

"That's true," Julian said from the front of the ambulance. "And you look great, so stop fretting. Keep smiling, wave like a princess, and everyone is going to love you."

Gertrude turned around and looked at her. "Julian is right. Just keep smiling and waving."

"I can do that." Jasmine demonstrated. "Is that good?"

"Perfect," Gertrude said.

66

ELL-ROM

As the vehicle came to a stop, Ell-rom's heart rate accelerated.

The opaque windows had started clearing during the ride up, becoming see-through as Julian took over the wheel and eased the vehicle into a parking spot.

Kian and Syssi stood waiting, flanked by the two bodyguards who Ell-rom had started to think of as friends. Well, the redhead was friendly enough. Anandur, Ell-rom reminded himself of the guy's name. The other one, Brundar, remained as impassive as ever. Ell-rom wondered if the stoic Guardian ever spoke or showed emotion.

As Julian opened the ambulance doors, Ell-rom's gaze was drawn up to a banner hanging between two columns. The flowing script was Kra-ell, and it said *welcome*.

Syssi followed his gaze. "I asked a couple of Kra-ell

ladies to prepare it for you. They're very excited to meet you."

Ell-rom felt a flutter of nervousness in his stomach. Why were they excited to meet him? What did the Kra-ell community expect of him?

Behind them, Julian and Gertrude began carefully maneuvering Morelle's gurney out of the ambulance, and Kian's bodyguards moved to assist.

When the bodyguards unloaded the luggage, Jasmine walked over to thank them. "I'm sorry for having so much stuff," she said while offering them a brilliant smile. "But I'm not just coming for a visit. Hopefully, I'm here to stay, so I brought my entire wardrobe and keep-sakes with me." She turned to Syssi. "Assume the win, right? If I'm convinced that it will happen, it will."

Kian nodded approvingly. "That's the spirit. I think the Fates appreciate that kind of attitude, and if you have the Fates on your side, you have nothing to worry about."

The clan's belief in the Fates still baffled Ell-rom. He couldn't conceive of believing in anything other than the Mother of All Life, but eventually, he would have to accept faith in the Fates because that, too, was his heritage. Was it possible to combine the two?

Perhaps the Fates worked for the Mother of All Life?

He could think of them as her matchmakers, but it was hard to imagine the Mother bothering with something as trivial as that. She was a terrible deity, the giver and taker of life, the creator and destroyer of worlds.

Was that a memory or his own musings about the forces that controlled the universe?

He really needed to talk with Jade and learn more about his old life from her. She would have knowledge and first-hand experience that could fill in a lot of the gaps in his memory.

"We have a motorized cart with a driver waiting at the entrance to the pavilion," Kian said. "Gertrude and Julian will get Morelle settled in the clinic. Meanwhile, your belongings will be taken straight to my mother's house while we continue on foot to the celebration." He cast a glance at Jasmine's shoes. "It's not a long walk."

"How long are we going to stay with Annani?" Ell-rom asked.

"At least until Jasmine transitions. After that, we can give you your own place. There are plenty of vacant houses in the village for you to choose from."

Ell-rom didn't argue. The thought of being alone with Jasmine during her transition and not knowing what to expect or how to help her was daunting. Annani's support and guidance would be welcome.

"Why are there so many vacant homes?" Jasmine asked. "Did people leave?"

Syssi chuckled. "No one has left, but we've overbuilt, hoping for Sari and her people to move over here. They decided not to, and then the Kra-ell arrived and took over some of those homes, but there are still plenty left."

"It's for the future." Kian wrapped his arm around Syssi's shoulders. "I'm hoping for more Dormants to be found and more couples needing their own homes." He started walking. "We can talk about all this some other time. Everyone's waiting for you in the village square, so let's not make them wait too long."

"Everyone?" Ell-rom asked as he followed Kian and Syssi with Jasmine by his side.

"Most of the village residents are there," Kian clarified. "And Sari and David arrived last night and are eager to meet you and Morelle."

As they entered yet another elevator, Ell-rom felt a mix of excitement and nervousness building within him, with nervousness definitely taking the lead.

The ride up took longer than he had expected, and when the doors opened, he had to stifle a gasp.

They had emerged into a grand hall made entirely of glass, offering breathtaking views of the village beyond. Lush greenery, colorful flowerbeds, and majestic trees stretched as far as the eye could see.

"It's beautiful," Jasmine breathed, her hand clutching his with excitement.

Syssi smiled knowingly. "You have seen nothing yet."

As Kian had promised, a cart waited outside with another Guardian behind the wheel. He didn't wear a uniform, and neither did Kian's bodyguards, but by now, Ell-rom recognized the type. They were tall, burly, and moved with military efficiency.

While Brundar and Anandur loaded their luggage, Ell-rom took a moment to truly absorb his surroundings.

The air was fresh and clean, filled with the scent of flowers and grass. Birds chirped in the distance, and a gentle breeze rustled through the leaves. It was like stepping into a perfect, secluded paradise.

"The Fields of The Brave," he whispered.

Jasmine turned her head to look at him. "What did you say?"

"Fields of The Brave. That's where the heroes who fought bravely and fell in battle go."

Kian nodded. "Good. You are remembering more things from your life before stasis."

"I had hoped to remember more by now," Ell-rom admitted.

As they walked into the village proper, Kian pointed out various points of interest. The café was an open-air area with tables and chairs and a small building that housed the equipment and supplies. It was closed now for the ceremony, but it would open again early tomorrow morning, and Kian recommended Ell-rom and Jasmine visit it to get to know people. The two-story office building was right behind the café, and a single-story building next to it housed the clinic.

"Enjoy your party," Julian said as he turned Morelle's gurney toward the clinic.

Ell-rom felt a pang of worry as Julian and Gertrude took her away.

"She is in capable hands," Jasmine said quietly. "The same people who took care of her until now will keep taking care of her here. You have nothing to worry about."

As their group continued toward the village's main lawn, Ell-rom's breath caught when he saw the crowd waiting for them. Immortals and Kra-ell filled the wide expanse.

There were more decorations with banners in English this time, and he wished he'd devoted more time to his language studies in the past few days.

People waved and smiled, some whistling or calling out welcomes, but those were mostly immortals. The Kra-ell were more guarded, but they didn't appear hostile.

Still, it was overwhelming.

When Jasmine squeezed his hand, he wasn't sure if it was meant to reassure him or if she was feeling just as overwhelmed as he was.

At one side of the lawn stood a raised podium, and atop it, Ell-rom could see Annani waiting, her smile brilliant and reassuring even from a distance.

As Kian and Syssi led them toward her, Ell-rom felt as though he were walking in a dream.

The crowd parted to let them through, and Ell-rom could hear whispers of excitement and curiosity and comments about him and Jasmine, mostly complimentary.

As they neared the podium, Ell-rom's nervousness grew. He hadn't prepared anything to say, hadn't expected to be put on the spot like this. Thankfully,

Jasmine had had the foresight to tell him to bring the teardrop so people who didn't have earpieces could understand him.

If he had more time, and if someone had told him that he would need to make a speech, he would have prepared one in English, but now all he could do was to pull out the teardrop, hang it around his neck, and activate it.

Jasmine gave his hand another reassuring squeeze. "You've got this, Ell-rom. Just be yourself."

As they reached the steps of the podium, he took a deep breath, steeling himself for what was to come.

Kian gestured for them to ascend, and Ell-rom felt as though his legs had turned to lead. With the eyes of the entire village upon them, each step seemed to take an eternity, but then they reached the top and were enveloped in the sphere of Annani's warmth and acceptance.

67

ANNANI

Annani's heart swelled with joy as she watched Ell-rom and Jasmine step up to the podium. The moment she had dreamed of for so long was finally here—her brother and sister were joining her in the village, and her brother was accompanied by his magnificent mate.

Jasmine looked every inch a queen, her white pantsuit and towering heels lending her an air of regality. But it wasn't just her appearance that impressed Annani. She knew what was hiding beneath the glamorous appearance. Jasmine was kind, brave, and clever, but most of all, Annani appreciated Jasmine's love and loyalty to Ell-rom.

The Fates had chosen well for her brother.

Ell-rom, for his part, stood tall and proud beside his mate, his nervousness evident only to those who knew him. Annani could see the wonder in his eyes as he took in the crowd, the decorations, and the village that was to be his new home.

She extended her hands to both of them and, with a gentle tug, lifted their conjoined hands, presenting them to the village.

The crowd erupted in cheers and applause, the sound washing over them in a wave of acceptance and love.

She lowered their hands but did not let go and kept holding them.

"My dear family, those by birth and those by choice. Today is a day of great joy and celebration. We gather here to welcome three very special individuals into our community. My brother, Ell-rom, his mate, Jasmine, and my sister, Morelle, who is still in a coma and has been taken to the clinic."

Annani paused, allowing the crowd's renewed cheers to subside before continuing.

"For many years, I believed myself to be alone, but the Fates answered my unspoken prayers and revealed that I had more family than I realized. My sister Areana, my cousin Toven, and now two more siblings, Ell-rom and Morelle. Each one was discovered through a series of extraordinary events, and I hope the Fates are not done yet. Although, to be perfectly frank, I hope that some of my family members never show up."

There was laughter from the crowd, even though not many knew about the threat of the Eternal King. On the other hand, everyone knew that Mortdh had been her cousin and Navuh was his son.

Annani turned to face the couple. "Ell-rom, my dear brother, words cannot express how grateful I am for your presence here today. You have faced difficult challenges with courage and grace. Your strength, your kindness, and your spirit are inspiring."

She then addressed Jasmine. "And, Jasmine, you have stood by Ell-rom's side through it all, and you have shown such bravery and dedication. We also welcome you into our community, and we are honored to call you one of our own."

Turning back to the crowd, Annani continued, "As we celebrate this joyous occasion, we must also recognize that the existence of Ell-rom and Morelle must remain a closely guarded secret."

At this point, Annani allowed her power to flow through her words, infusing them with the strength of her compulsion. Her voice was being broadcast throughout the village, reaching even those few who had chosen not to attend.

"Each member of this community will keep the existence of Ell-rom and Morelle a secret. You will not speak of them to outsiders, nor will you write about them or communicate their existence in any way to those who are not part of our extended community. This secret is ours to protect for the safety of Ell-rom, Morelle, and all of us."

Annani watched as the weight of her compulsion settled over the crowd, knowing that it would take hold in every corner of the village. The one exception was Turner, who was immune to any form of compulsion but whom she trusted implicitly, and possibly Drova, whose potential immunity was a concern for another day.

With that done, she smiled. "And now, let us celebrate and show Ell-rom and Jasmine the very best of welcome into our community."

As the crowd cheered once more, the sound of their joy filled the air, and Annani smiled, feeling the love and acceptance radiating from her people.

Turning to Sari and David, who stood at the foot of the podium, she waved at them to join her. "My daughter Sari and her mate David have traveled all the way from Scotland to celebrate this joyous occasion with us. Please, give them a warm welcome."

More cheers and applause erupted, and once they subsided, Annani made the introductions.

"Welcome to our clan." Sari hugged Ell-rom and then Jasmine.

David shook Ell-rom's hand. "We are going to be staying together in the Clan Mother's house, which will give us plenty of time to get properly acquainted."

"I'm looking forward to it," Ell-rom said.

Preparing for the surprise that would delight Jasmine, Annani put her hand on Jasmine's arm. "Look over there, Jasmine." Annani pointed with her chin. "Your friends are here to celebrate with you."

Jasmine's eyes widened as she saw Frankie, Margo, and Gabi. With a squeal of delight, she rushed down the steps of the podium, embracing her friends in a flurry of excitement and laughter.

Annani watched the reunion with a warm smile, then turned to Ell-rom and wrapped her arm around his middle, leaning her head against his arm. "It is good to have you here, brother of mine."

Ell-rom's arm came around her shoulders, pulling her close. "It's good to be here."

"Are you ready to meet the rest of your big family?" Annani asked, gesturing toward the village members who were beginning to form a line, eager to greet him.

Ell-rom took a deep breath, squaring his shoulders. "As ready as I'll ever be," he said with a small smile. "I'm just glad that I don't need to make a speech. I was worried when I saw the podium."

Annani laughed. "I would have never sprung such a thing on you. I would have told you to prepare."

68

JASMINE

Jasmine's heart soared as she rushed down the podium steps, her eyes fixed on the familiar faces of Margo, Frankie, and Gabi. The sight of her friends was an unexpected and delightful surprise, pushing aside the fatigue, the stress, and the overwhelming nature of the day's events.

"Oh my Goddess!" She threw her arms around all three of them. "What are you doing here? This is amazing!"

Margo laughed, returning the hug with equal enthusiasm. "Did you really think we'd miss your big debut?"

"Gilbert brought us," Gabi said.

"I'm so happy you are here." Jasmine let go of her friends and took a step back. "But I'm surprised Kian allowed it."

Margo threaded her arm through Jasmine's. "Kian gave his permission for all of us to come over whenever we want, as long as we get someone to give us a ride."

That made sense. Only clan vehicles were equipped with self-driving navigation and windows that locked and turned opaque upon approaching the village to preserve its secret location.

"Did you see Rob already?" she asked Margo.

"I did. He looks much better already, and he's made some new friends."

"Female friends?" Jasmine asked.

Margo smiled. "Yeah, but nothing romantic yet."

Jasmine looked around, her eyes scanning for Mia. She found her on the podium with Toven, talking with Ell-rom and a couple of other immortals who looked vaguely familiar.

Ella approached with a warm smile on her face. "Wel-come to the village, Jasmine." She pulled her into an embrace. "And may I say, you look stunning. I didn't know you could clean up so nicely."

"Hey!" Jasmine pretended offense. "I dressed nicely on the cruise when I was finally allowed to attend a wedding."

Ella winced. "Sorry, but I didn't pay attention. All those fancy gowns turned into one big blur."

"True." Jasmine ran her hands on the sides of her pantsuit, enjoying the feel of the solidity of luxurious fabric. "I wanted to make a grand entrance so people would remember me."

"Goal achieved." Ella clapped her on her back and then looked at her shoes. "I was wondering how you got so freakishly tall. Can you even walk with these on the grass?"

"I can, with much effort."

"Hello, Jasmine." Bridget joined their little circle. "How have you been? I haven't seen you in a while."

She wondered if Bridget had heard about the mugging and what Ell-rom had done. "It has been exciting over at the keep. I assume that Julian kept you posted."

Bridget nodded. "Indeed. I'm glad that it all ended well."

As they chatted, more people began to approach, and Jasmine recognized many faces from the cruise, but the names blurred together in a whirlwind of introductions. She smiled and nodded, doing her best to keep up with the flood of new information.

Amidst the flurry of greetings, Jasmine's gaze was drawn to a group clustered near the stage. The Kra-ell stood apart, their eyes fixed on Ell-rom, some with curiosity in their eyes, others with trepidation.

The sight sent a chill down her spine.

Leaning close to Margo, she whispered, "I'm worried about Ell-rom. Some of these people thought of him and Morelle as abominations. Is he really safe here?"

Margo followed her gaze, frowned, and then turned to look at her. "They look scary, but the Clan Mother compelled all the residents of the village not to harm one another, and today, she added a compulsion to keep Ell-rom and Morelle's existence a secret. She wouldn't have brought her brother and sister here if she didn't believe that she could keep them safe."

Despite Margo's reassurances, Jasmine couldn't shake the nagging feeling of unease. She knew the power of compulsion and had experienced it firsthand, but the intensity in some of the Kra-ell's eyes spoke of deep-seated beliefs that might not be so easily overcome.

As the introductions continued, she became increasingly aware of the strain her choice of footwear was putting on her feet. The spiky heels, while perfect for making a grand entrance, were making things difficult for her. She was putting pressure only on her toes to avoid sinking into the soft ground, and it was tiring.

She needed to sit down, but before she left to look for a bench or a chair, she needed to check on Ell-rom and see if he needed her help.

He was still on the stage, standing with Annani and graciously greeting a seemingly endless stream of well-wishers. Despite the obvious signs of being fatigued, he carried himself with a regal bearing, his back straight as he shook hands and smiled at each new face.

A surge of pride welled up in Jasmine's chest.

Ell-rom looked every inch the prince he was, handling the pressure with an innate grace that belied his lack of experience.

"He's doing great," Margo said, following Jasmine's gaze. "Why don't we let him do his thing for now? You look like you could use a break and maybe get some food."

At the mention of food, Jasmine's stomach gave an appreciative rumble. She realized that she hadn't eaten since breakfast, the excitement of the day pushing aside thoughts of hunger until now.

Margo led the way to a buffet table laden with an array of appetizers. The spread was impressive, and after they all piled up their plates, they found an empty table.

Jasmine sank gratefully into a chair, kicking her shoes off and wiggling her achy toes.

As she popped the first tiny treat into her mouth, she scanned the village square, which was alive with activity, laughter, and countless excited conversations. The atmosphere was joyous, but Jasmine noticed the undercurrents of tension, particularly among the Kra-ell attendees.

Evidently not everyone was ecstatic about welcoming Ell-rom and Morelle.

As for her, Jasmine doubted anyone had particular feelings about her, either positive or negative. She wasn't important enough.

As her gaze landed on Jade, standing off to the side and constantly scanning the crowd like a stern sentinel, Jasmine didn't miss the Kra-ell leader's hand hovering near what appeared to be a sheathed knife.

The sight of her did little to ease Jasmine's concerns.

"Is Jade worried about Ell-rom's safety?" she asked, nodding in the Kra-ell female's direction.

Frankie followed her gaze and shrugged. "Jade is always on alert. It's just her way. But I wouldn't read too much into it. This village is probably the safest place on Earth for Ell-rom or anyone else."

Jasmine wondered whether it was true. The clan had enemies who wanted to annihilate it, and therefore, it was never safe, no matter where it hid. She wondered where on Earth could qualify for the title of the most secure place, but each time she thought of one, she found ways to undermine that security in some way.

Bottom line, there was no such thing, and safety was an illusion.

"So," Gabi said as she pulled Jasmine from her reverie, "how does it feel to be welcomed like the mate of a prince?"

Jasmine laughed. "Honestly? It's a little surreal. I mean, look at all of this." She gestured to the gathering around them.

"You certainly play the part well," Margo said.

"Thank you." Jasmine dipped her head. "I'm always appreciative of hearing praise for my performance."

"Is that all it is?" Frankie asked. "A performance?"

"Of course." Jasmine picked up another salmon roll. "I'm not a real princess. I'm a nobody from nowhere."

69

BRANDON

Brandon stood patiently in line to greet Ell-rom, Annani's half-brother. Despite the prince's Kra-ell heritage, the family resemblance between him and Annani was unmistakable. Some of it was in their facial features, but mostly, it was in their regal bearing that seemed ingrained rather than learned.

As the line inched forward, Brandon analyzed Ell-rom. The way he held himself, the tilt of his head as he listened to each new introduction, and the warm smile that graced his features all spoke of an innate nobility that transcended his lack of memories from his life on Anumati. The guy had the life experience of a newborn, but he must have subconsciously retained some of what he had learned.

It was fascinating to witness.

Ell-rom lacked Annani's intensity and palpable power, and he seemed like a mellow, affable fellow, but

Brandon had a feeling that the prince might have some surprises in store for them.

For now, he was still unsure of his standing, dependent on William's ingenious device to communicate and learn the rules of conduct of the community that was adopting him.

He wore earpieces that translated English to Kra-ell for him, and the pendant hanging from a string around his neck translated what he was saying from his native Kra-ell into English.

Kian had informed the council that Ell-rom hadn't displayed any compulsion abilities, but just in case, Brandon had brought his own filtering earpieces. As he neared the front of the line, though, he pulled them out of his ear and tucked them into his pocket. After all, there was no need for them because the teardrop-shaped pendant was taking care of the translation.

Most of the village's residents didn't have compulsion-filtering, translating earpieces, which was a good thing given that Annani had just used compulsion to keep Ell-rom and Morelle's existence a secret.

Still, enough people had them. Every member of the council had been given a pair, and so had every Guardian. As far as he knew, no one had bothered to check whether they had been wearing them while Annani had done her thing or not.

Not that he was worried that any of them would harm the twins in any way, even if they had not been compelled to refrain from doing so.

Finally, when it was his turn, Brandon stepped forward and extended his hand with a warm smile. "Welcome, Ell-rom. I'm Brandon, the council member in charge of media."

Ell-rom's grip was firm but gentle as he shook Brandon's hand. "It's a pleasure to meet you." He smiled and tilted his head. "Excuse my ignorance, but what does it mean to be in charge of media? I mean, I watched some television, so I know what media is, and I doubt the clan broadcasts its presence."

"We don't," Brandon confirmed. "What we do is promote the gods' ideals about democracy, equal opportunity, and the pursuit of truth through existing human channels. We encourage the production of movies and television series that depict the future we would like humans to have, and in the past, we published books on the subject. Regrettably, our message has lately been diluted by an avalanche of misleading and destructive propaganda promoted by bad actors. It's nothing new, but the easy accessibility makes it more difficult to fight these days."

The last part was a recent addition to his self-imposed job description, born out of a growing concern for the state of information and critical thinking in the Western world. Brandon had been increasingly troubled by the ease with which lies and the inversion of truth spread, even in supposedly advanced societies. He blamed it on failed educational systems that did not teach history and did not equip children with the right tools to think for themselves.

He was starting to think that it was being done deliberately. Children grew up and turned into ignorant adults who were incredibly easy to manipulate because they knew so little.

It was precisely what those in power wanted.

The prince's eyes lit up with interest. "That sounds like crucial work. Perception is everything, and when it is based on lies, the distortion can be catastrophic."

That was a very astute observation for a guy who had been awake for only a few weeks, but the prince probably remembered subconsciously things he'd been taught on Anumati.

"You are absolutely correct. I'm not a young immortal, and I have a lot of experience dealing with humans. It is a never-ending struggle." Brandon leaned closer to the prince's ear. "I blame the gods. I think that they genetically programmed humans to be easily influenced and manipulated, and in the absence of gods, other humans take advantage of the gullibility of the masses. I've been working on some new ideas to address the problem, especially with the younger generation of humans."

"What is it?" Ell-rom asked.

"I came up with a concept for a game that would reward players for discovering hidden truths with tangible prizes as a way to make critical thinking engaging and rewarding." Brandon glanced at the long line still waiting behind him. "I'll gladly meet up after you get settled and tell you more over a cup of coffee."

"I'm looking forward to it." Ell-rom extended his hand.

Brandon shook it. "I hope that your sister awakens soon and will join us."

"I hope so, too."

As Brandon stepped down onto the lawn, he intended to head to the buffet, but instead, his feet carried him toward the clinic.

After meeting Ell-rom, his curiosity about Morelle was piqued, and he wanted to take a peek at the sleeping princess.

The clinic was quiet, and as Brandon walked in, Julian and Hildegard looked at him with surprise.

"Brandon." Julian extended his hand. "What brings you here?"

"Not any ailment, if that's what you're thinking." Brandon shook the doctor's hand. "I just spoke with Ell-rom and was quite impressed by him. I know that his twin is unconscious, but I still think she should be welcomed into the community by an official representative of the clan."

Julian smiled. "Well, when you state it like that, we should form a line of well-wishers for Morelle like we are doing for Ell-rom. She can use all the stimulation we can throw at her." He started walking toward one of the patients' rooms. "She has been in a coma for too long."

Brandon frowned. "Was her condition worse than Ell-rom's when they were found?"

"No," Julian said as he opened the door. "As far as we can tell, there is nothing wrong with her physically at this point."

Brandon wanted to ask what Julian thought was the reason for Morelle's prolonged coma, but as he followed the doctor into the room, he felt the words die in his throat—a rare occurrence for him since his job performance was based on his ability to talk and charm.

Even in her unconscious state, Morelle was magnificent. There was an undeniable regality about her. Her features were delicate yet strong, and her nearly bald head made every feature seem even stronger, more refined.

"What a stunning female," Brandon murmured.

Julian nodded. "That she is. It's a shame she's missing her own welcome party."

Brandon pulled out the lone chair in the room from under the counter, rolled it toward the hospital bed, and sat down. "I hope it's okay if I stay for a little bit?"

Julian nodded. "She needs stimulation." He reached into his pocket and pulled out a pendant similar to the one Ell-rom had around his neck. "This will translate what you say into Kra-ell. You should also put your earpieces in. Not that I expect her to suddenly wake up, but just in case she does, it's better not to take a risk. She might be a compeller." Julian rubbed his hand over his jaw. "Though I have to wonder if compulsion can be effective when the compelled does not understand the compeller's language. I should discuss it with Kalugal and seek his insight."

Brandon took the device and pulled the cord over his head. "Does it automatically detect which language it needs to translate?"

"Not yet." Julian leaned over and pressed the side of the device. "It's still in the prototype phase, so it needs to be manually switched. I'm sure that William will soon have it switching by voice command and translating many languages."

"Don't you love technology?" Brandon smiled. "It's the one thing that gives me hope in our constant push against the darkness. Technology will prevail over barbarism and oppression."

Julian sighed. "I hope so, but I fear that it's not as simple as that. Just like people, artificial intelligence bases its assumptions and conclusions on whatever it is fed. If it's fed lies, the output will not be progress. Only the unbiased truth can propel us forward."

Brandon glanced at Morelle's peaceful face. "What do you think, princess? Does truth have the power to set us free from the illusions we create?"

Julian chuckled. "I like that. If Morelle can hear you, a philosophical postulation might stimulate her mind to awareness."

A grin spread across Brandon's face. "Well, philosophizing and postulating is what I do best. I built a career out of it."

70

ROB

Rob stood at the edge of the lawn, nursing a glass of champagne as he tried to get over seeing the goddess again. He had initially expected her to be like Toven, regal and refined, and she was all that but also so much more.

Seeing the goddess up close on that podium, her energy radiating and touching everyone around her, was the nearest Rob had ever gotten to a religious experience, and the funny thing was that the Clan Mother did not even claim to be a divinity. She just looked like what he imagined a goddess or an angel would.

Ell-rom, her half-brother, was an impressive dude, but he paled in comparison. Still, the excitement around his arrival was undeniable, contrasting starkly with the melancholy that had been Rob's constant companion since his life had fallen apart, or as his sister insisted, had finally gotten on the right track.

He and Margo had done some catching up at the café before the party, talking mostly about their parents, a topic that filled Rob with equal parts guilt and worry.

"They're concerned about you," Margo had said. "You should call them."

Rob had nodded, promising to do so in a day or two, but the thought of facing the world he'd left behind still filled him with dread. It wasn't just the canceled wedding and the emotional fallout from his break-up with Lynda. There was also the growing realization of what his and Margo's choices meant for their parents.

"What about Mom and Dad?" he'd asked. "When you also move here permanently, they'll be left alone."

Their parents didn't have many friends, and the thought of them rattling around in an empty house, missing their children, weighed heavily on his conscience.

"I know. I've been thinking about that, too. Maybe we can convince the clan to let them move in here as well. They allowed other humans in, like Mia's grandparents."

Margo had promised to talk to Mia and her fiancé about it. The god had a lot of influence in the clan, and he would do anything for Mia, so there was a small chance that he might get Kian to agree.

But that was a worry for another day.

Today, Rob was busy people-watching and trying to get caught up in the celebratory mood.

It was good to see Jasmine laughing with Margo and her other friends, looking radiant and happy. If not for her, he would be standing at the altar with Lynda in a couple of days, making what he now realized would have been the biggest mistake of his life. He owed her for convincing Margo to approach him with her suspicions and for making him face the truth that had been staring him in the face but that he had refused to acknowledge.

Rob was grateful for the twist of fate that had brought him here instead.

Thankfully, his parents had decided to cancel the entire thing rather than use the venue to renew their own vows. Rob was glad, and not just because the venue had refunded half of what he'd paid. The thought of that celebration going on without him and disappointing his parents yet again was too painful, but he just wasn't ready to face that world again.

Not so soon.

"You look like you could use some food." A familiar voice had his heart skip a beat.

Rob turned to see Lusha standing beside him, a knowing smile on her face. "Hi." He smiled back. "What do you have in mind?"

"The buffet. We should head there before there's nothing left."

"Let's go." He fell into step with her. "Where is your guy? Is he on duty?"

She nodded. "He's patrolling. The Guardians are always working at events like this when the Clan Mother is present."

Rob looked around, surprised that he couldn't spot anyone who looked like they were on active duty. The gathering appeared entirely civilian, relaxed, and jubilant. "The Guardians must be very discreet."

"That's the idea," Lusha said. "Come on, let's eat."

At the buffet, they loaded their plates with an assortment of finger foods and then looked for a place to sit, which proved to be a problem because there were no vacant seats.

"Come on." Lusha led him to a shaded spot under a large tree. "We can eat right here."

"Are you sure?" He looked at her khaki pants.

"It's fine." She settled on the ground, balancing her plate on her lap. "The grass is dry."

He sat beside her, and for a few moments, they consumed the contents of their plates. When the food was gone, there was nothing more to occupy their hands and mouths with, and an awkward silence settled over them.

"Did you hear that they found the culprit behind the thefts and sabotage?" Lusha asked.

Rob put the plate on the grass beside him. "No, I didn't. Who was it?"

"Turns out it was Jade's daughter, Drova. She's under house arrest now."

It took him a moment to remember who Jade was. The names and faces of everyone he had met over the last couple of days had become a blur in his mind.

"Remind me who Jade is?"

"The Kra-ell leader." Lusha craned her neck and looked around. "It's the tall skinny lady with the long ponytail and military boots standing behind Ell-rom."

The woman, or rather female, looked too young to have a daughter who had gotten into so much mischief, but that was true of all of these good-looking people who could be centuries old and not show it.

"How old is her daughter?"

'Sixteen or maybe seventeen already." Lusha put her plate on top of his. "She is a lot like her mother. A born fighter with an attitude a mile wide."

Rob smiled. "A teenage rebellion or a way to impress a boy?"

Lusha laughed. "Both, I guess. Drova has her eye on an older guy who thinks of her as a kid, and rightfully so because she is much too young for him. Maybe that was why she did it." Lusha shifted to lean on her side. "Naturally, that wasn't what she had to say in her defense. I wasn't given any details, but I bet that it was something along the lines of the Kra-ell needing to live their 'authentic lives,' hunting, and stuff like they did in Karelia. Only it didn't make them happy then, so it's not going to make them happy now. They need to adapt to modern times and start valuing education over pursuing the lifestyle of their ancestors." She leaned closer to him. "They are savages at heart, and they pride themselves on it. In my opinion, they need to find a new source of pride."

Rob turned to look at Ell-rom, who stood tall and proud beside Annani, greeting people with regal poise and grace. "Do you think their prince might be that new source?"

Lusha shrugged. "Maybe. I haven't made up my mind about him yet."

71

DROVA

Drova paced the length of her living room, feeling like a caged animal.

She'd never liked being cooped up in the house, and now it was a virtual prison.

With the windows and sliding door open, she could hear the distant sounds of celebration from the village square. The laughter and music carried on the afternoon breeze, taunting her with what she was missing.

With a frustrated sigh, she stepped out into the backyard. The ground was cool beneath her bare feet, but as she neared the fence, the cuff on her wrist began to vibrate, growing warm against her skin.

"Fuck," she cursed, retreating back toward the house.

The buzz subsided, but the irritation remained, bubbling just beneath the surface of her skin.

Back inside, Drova flopped onto the couch, her eyes drawn to the clock on the wall. The entire village was at the welcome party for the prince, celebrating the arrival of Ell-rom and Morelle, Annani's siblings from her father's side.

They were proof that the legends about the Kra-ell crown princess falling in love with the gods' crown prince had been true. Grudgingly, Drova had to admit that the love story between the rebels was romantic.

The Kra-ell weren't supposed to believe in romance or love other than the love for the tribe, the queen, and the Mother of All Life, but it was such bullshit that she couldn't believe generations of Kra-ell had accepted it as fact.

She'd felt the stirrings of love, and it wasn't just lusting or like or curiosity.

She was in love with Pavel, and his indifference hurt like the desolation of the Valley of the Shamed.

After what she had done to him, the chances that he would ever think of her as a possible partner had turned from slim to none.

According to Kra-ell tradition, she could invite him to her bed, and he would be obligated to accept her invitation, but that wasn't what she wanted. Despite all of her talk of the Kra-ell living their traditional lives, Drova didn't approve of their antiquated breeding practices.

Sex was more than just for making babies, and seeing her mother with Phinas had opened her mind to the possibility of having just one chosen partner, instead of selecting several interchangeable males and never letting herself feel deeply for any of them.

At the sound of the doorbell ringing, Drova frowned, wondering who it could be. Surely not her mother or Phinas because they would just come in, and anyone looking for them knew that they were at the celebration.

As she walked over to the door, she was ready to snap at the idiot who'd come looking for her mother, but as she opened it and saw Pavel, the words died on her lips.

He stood on her doorstep, a bottle of vodka in one hand, cranberry juice in the other, and a conspiratorial grin on his handsome face.

"What are you doing here?" Drova looked pointedly at the booze.

Her mother didn't mind if she drank a little, but Pavel still thought that she was a little girl, so his showing up with vodka didn't add up.

He shrugged, holding up the bottles. "I came to keep you company."

No way. Not after what she had done to him.

"Why are you being nice to me after I told you to eat dirt?"

"You came back and told me to stop." He lifted the bottles again. "Are you going to let me in, or should I find myself a different drinking buddy?"

After a moment's hesitation, Drova stepped aside and motioned for Pavel to enter. She watched him warily as he made his way to the kitchen, setting the bottles on the counter and rummaging through the cabinets for glasses.

"You know," Pavel said, his back to her as he poured the drinks, "what you did wasn't cool. But I forgive you. You came to me hoping for help, and I told you to turn yourself in. That wasn't what you were expecting, and you were disappointed. People do stupid things when they're backed into a corner."

Drova leaned against the doorframe, arms crossed over her chest. "Is that supposed to be an apology? Because it sounds more like an accusation."

Pavel turned, offering her a glass. "It's neither. It's just an observation. Here, drink up. You look like you could use it."

Drova accepted the glass and took a sip, enjoying the burn of the vodka that was tempered by the sweetness of the cranberry juice. "Why are you here, Pavel? Shouldn't you be at the party with your buddies, checking out the prince?"

Pavel shrugged, taking a drink from his own glass. "Parties aren't really my scene. I don't like crowds, and I can't eat their food, so what's the point, right?"

He walked into the living room and sat on the couch. When she followed and sat on the opposite side, an awkward silence fell between them, broken only by the clink of ice in their glasses.

Finally, Drova spoke. "For what it's worth, I am sorry for doing that to you."

Pavel nodded. "You are very powerful."

So that was why he was there. He finally realized what she'd been trying to tell him. "Yes, I am, and my power is still growing. That's why I have this." She lifted the wrist with the cuff. "They don't want me to roam the village freely and compel people to do whatever I want them to do. Anyone who comes to the house will be told to wear the compulsion-filtering earpieces."

Suddenly noticing that Pavel's long hair was loose around his shoulders and not tied at the back the way it usually was, Drova narrowed her eyes at him. "Are you wearing them now?"

"I am," he admitted. "But I'm glad that you didn't try anything before you knew."

She pinned him with a hard stare. "So, this visit was a test?"

"Yes." He took a sip from his drink. "I want us to be friends, Drova, but I needed to find out first if I can trust you. Friends don't mess with each other's minds."

Drova swallowed the lump that had suddenly formed in her throat. "Are we friends, Pavel?"

He shrugged. "It's up to you. I like you, but you still need to prove yourself to me."

She snorted. "You will never trust me completely. I'm Igor's daughter. Until today, you didn't know that I'd inherited his powers, so you were willing to let me hang around, but now that you know I'm just like him, can you ever consider me your friend?"

His expression turned serious. "You are nothing like him, Drova. And I want to make sure that you never turn into another Igor. I think you are a good person, but you are still very young, and you need to surround yourself with people who will keep you in check so you don't get drunk on power. Your mother is a good influence, but she is not enough. You need someone you can talk to who will not judge you and instead help you examine your beliefs."

What he was offering was precisely what she craved. In fact, it made her suspicious.

"Can you read minds?"

He chuckled. "I can't, but I'm very good at reading people. You look desperate for someone to listen to you. That's what I'm here for."

It irked to hear him say that she was desperate for anything, but Drova couldn't deny the truth. Besides, Pavel was offering to spend a lot of time with her, and she wasn't going to say no to that.

"Thank you. I appreciate your offer, and I accept it."

"Excellent." He pushed to his feet and walked over to the kitchen counter where he had left the two bottles he'd brought.

Drova's glass was still mostly full, and she took another small sip before putting it back on the coffee table. "Can I ask you something?"

"Sure." He put the bottles on the table and sat down.

"You and your buddies have been talking about the same things that are bothering me, but when I tried to raise awareness of our discontent, you were alarmed and accused me of being stupid. Why?"

He sighed. "Because we shouldn't rebel against the people who saved our sorry asses, offered us a choice of how and where we wanted to live, and who have accepted us into their community. even though everything about us is alien to them."

"They needed us for protection." Drova picked up her glass.

"That's how they justified it to themselves. It doesn't make them the villains. When we spit in their faces and do harm to their community, it makes us the villains."

Drova felt her cheeks getting warm. "None of what I have done was serious."

He lifted a brow. "That's why you are under house arrest instead of in a cell in the dungeon."

Imagining herself locked up behind bars, Drova barely suppressed a shiver. "So, what was all that talk you and your friends engaged in? Was it just shooting the breeze?"

"No." He poured himself a new drink. "We were discussing options for our future, and while doing that, we were talking about all the things we didn't like about life in the village. I'm sorry if you got the impression that we wanted to rebel against the immortals. That was never on the table. We just want to come up with a good solution for everyone."

Drova swirled the remnants of her drink. "So, what's

your grand plan? Do we just forget who we are, what makes us Kra-ell?"

Pavel shook his head. "It's not about forgetting. It's about adapting. Finding a way to honor our past while embracing our future. We can take the best of our traditions, the core of who we are, and find new ways to express it that fit with the situation we're in now."

72

ELL-ROM

As the last of the guests bid their farewells, exhaustion washed over Ell-rom. During the whirlwind of introductions and conversations, he'd felt energized, but now that it had ended, he was drained.

Glancing at Jasmine, he could see that she was showing signs of fatigue as well, despite how much she thrived on social interaction.

She might be getting sick, or she might be transitioning, but the signs were too subtle to indicate either. They were both just hyperaware of any minute change because they were expecting and hoping for her transition to begin.

Standing next to him, Kian seemed as fresh and as energetic as he had been when he greeted them at the parking garage several hours before. "Ready to head to my mother's house?" he asked. "Sari and David are already there."

Ell-rom hadn't noticed them leaving, but then he had been surrounded by people and talking nonstop since the party had started.

He cast Kian a grateful smile. "Please, I'm exhausted."

"Then let's go." Kian headed toward where Jasmine was standing with her friends.

As Brundar and Anandur followed, Ell-rom wanted to ask Kian whether his bodyguards trailed him even in the village, but then they reached Jasmine.

She turned to them. "Is it time?"

Ell-rom nodded. "Kian is escorting us to Annani's."

After hugs, kisses, and promises to see each other soon, they parted from Margo, Frankie, and Gabi and started walking.

Ell-rom reached for Jasmine's hand. "How are you holding up?"

She smiled, but it looked more like a wince. "You were right about the shoes." She stopped, leaned on his arm, and took them off. "That's much better."

Except, it wasn't because the gravel path was not comfortable to walk on barefoot. Besides, the bottoms of her white pants were getting dirty.

"I could carry you," Ell-rom offered.

The look Jasmine gave him was equal parts amused and exasperated. "Don't be silly. You are exhausted, but even if you weren't, I wouldn't let you do that in front of everyone. I'll just put them back on."

She walked over to the nearest bench and sat down, preparing to do just that.

"I'll have the cart brought," Kian said. "We can wait right here."

To Ell-rom's surprise, Jasmine didn't argue. "Thank you." She massaged her aching feet.

As Brundar departed to get the cart, Ell-rom sat next to Jasmine, lifted her feet onto his lap, and took over the task of massaging the pain away.

Smiling, Kian nodded his approval. "They say that diamonds are the way to a woman's heart, but in my experience, it's foot massages."

Jasmine laughed. "You are spot on. That's my language of love."

That statement was a little confusing, but Ell-rom assumed it was just one more example of things getting lost in translation. One thing was certain, though; from now on, he would massage Jasmine's feet as often as she would allow it.

"It was a wonderful day." She sighed. "But I can't wait to take these clothes off, get in the shower, and wash the war paint off."

Once again, he was confused. "War paint?"

Kian chuckled, "The color they put on their faces to accentuate certain features. Women sometimes call it war paint."

Though he still didn't fully understand the reference, Ell-rom nodded, making a mental note to ask Jasmine about it later.

When Brundar arrived with the cart, Ell-rom lifted Jasmine into his arms despite her protests and put her down on the middle seat of the vehicle. He climbed in to sit beside her while Kian joined Brundar at the front, and Anandur took the back seat.

It suddenly occurred to Ell-rom that Brundar and Anandur were there to safeguard him rather than Kian.

"Do you expect anyone harboring ill intentions toward me?" Ell-rom asked. "Is that why your bodyguards are escorting us to Annani's place?"

Kian turned around. "I don't expect any trouble, but I'd rather err on the side of caution."

Next to him, Jasmine let out a sigh before her eyes drifted closed, and she leaned her head on his shoulder. By the time the cart stopped in front of Annani's home, she was asleep.

"Jasmine." Ell-rom took her hand and lifted it to his lips for a kiss. "Wake up, love. We've arrived."

She blinked, offering him a sleepy smile before leaning down to put her shoes on.

When he opened his mouth to offer to carry her, she lifted her finger and put it on his lips. "I'm walking into the Clan Mother's house on my own two feet."

Ell-rom could understand that. Hopping out of the cart, he offered her a hand down, which she accepted.

As they ascended the steps, one of Annani's Odus

opened the door before Kian had the chance to ring the bell.

"Welcome." The Odu bowed. "The Clan Mother is expecting you in the living room."

Ell-rom had expected the house to be even more opulent than the penthouse, but it wasn't. Instead, the place felt warm and inviting, and so was the smile on his sister's face.

"Welcome home." She rose to her feet and walked over to give him and Jasmine hugs. "You look tired. Freshen up, put on something comfortable and then come join us for tea. David and Sari are also freshening up and will join us as soon as they are ready."

"Thank you." Ell-rom kissed his sister's cheek.

"Ogidu will show you to your room," Annani said.

The Odu bowed. "Please, follow me." He walked down the corridor and opened the door on the left. "I placed the luggage in the walk-in closet, but I waited to ask your permission to unpack."

Ell-rom was about to grant it for no other reason than the Odu looking so excited at the prospect, but Jasmine shook her head.

"Thank you for the offer, but I'd rather organize things myself."

"As you wish, mistress." The Odu bowed and left.

Jasmine let out a sigh and kicked off her shoes. "What a relief." She popped the button, let her trousers drop to the floor, and stepped out of them.

She looked adorable with just her form-fitting jacket-style top on.

Pulling her into his arms, Ell-rom kissed her softly, pouring all his love and gratitude into the gesture. "I love you so much," he said when they parted. "I'm so happy that we're starting our lives together here, in a community that welcomes us so wholeheartedly. The sense of belonging is exhilarating."

Jasmine smiled up at him. "I love it here too." Her voice lacked the enthusiasm he felt.

"What's the matter, love?"

Jasmine sighed, leaning her forehead against his chest. "I'm just so tired. It's been a long day. I'll feel better after I've rested and freshened up."

Ell-rom nodded, releasing her from his embrace. He watched as she crouched by her suitcase, pulling out a pair of soft, stretchy black pants and a colorful blouse.

"That is as casually as I dare to dress for tea with the Clan Mother." She smiled ruefully.

"You look stunning no matter what you wear," he said, and meant it.

Pushing to her feet, Jasmine leaned over and kissed his cheek. "I love that you think that, I love that you say that, and I love you. I'm blessed."

He wrapped an arm around her middle and brought her against his body one more time. "It is me who is blessed." He kissed her long and hard.

When they parted, Jasmine smiled. "You'd better let me go freshen up so we don't keep Annani waiting."

Reluctantly, he let go of her.

As Jasmine disappeared into the bathroom to change and wash up, Ell-rom considered changing his clothes for a moment as well, but he was comfortable, so there was no need.

Instead, he settled into one of the armchairs by the window.

The sun was setting, but there was still plenty of light outside, and the view was soothing. A peaceful oasis hidden from the world. He imagined relaxing afternoons spent walking these grounds with Jasmine, stopping at the café to meet people and engage in conversations, and one day bringing their child to the playground to play.

Time passed, and as it started to become darker outside, Ell-rom realized Jasmine had been in the bathroom for quite a while.

Concern niggling at the back of his mind, he approached the door, knocking gently. "Jasmine? Are you alright in there?"

When no answer came, he cracked the door open and peeked inside.

The sight that greeted him sent a jolt of terror through his body. Jasmine lay sprawled on the floor.

"Jasmine!" He rushed to her side.

Her heart was beating, he could ascertain as much, but she didn't respond when he touched her face or when he gathered her limp form in his arms.

Panic rising, he scooped her into his arms and rushed back to the living room.

Everyone looked up in alarm as he burst in with Jasmine cradled against his chest.

"She's not waking up," Ell-rom said.

"I'm calling Brundar to bring the cart back around," Kian said while pulling his phone out. "We need to get Jasmine to the clinic."

As they waited for the cart to arrive, Kian called Julian and Bridget to let them know that Jasmine was transitioning and they were on their way, and Sari murmured words of comfort that Ell-rom did not even try to understand.

Holding Jasmine close, he forced himself to breathe. He'd been warned that it would happen, and he could hear her heartbeat and her shallow breathing, but her unresponsiveness was terrifying, nonetheless.

Annani approached, placing a comforting hand on his shoulder. "Oftentimes, transition comes on suddenly like this, but that does not mean that anything is wrong. Jasmine's body needs to shut down all nonessential functions while working on all the necessary changes." She patted his arm. "Rejoice, Ell-rom. Your mate is a Dormant and is transitioning to immortality. I have been beseeching the Fates for this to happen."

She was right, of course.

If Jasmine were awake, she would tell him the same thing. But she wasn't awake, and he was terrified not only for her but also for himself.

Without Jasmine, Ell-rom had no anchor and he felt utterly alone, even though he was with his sister and the wonderful community that had welcomed him with no reservations. If the unthinkable happened and Jasmine didn't make it, he would find a way to end his own life because he couldn't imagine living without her.

In the short time they had known each other, Jasmine had become his whole world, his reason for waking up in the morning, for breathing. But then there was Morelle, and he couldn't leave this world as long as she needed him.

Ell-rom had promised their mother he would always take care of his sister.

73

MORELLE

Darkness enveloped Morelle, a velvet cocoon of tranquility. Her mind, usually a tempest of relentless thoughts, found rare solace in this void. She floated weightless, unburdened.

Was this sleep?

A dream?

The distinction blurred, irrelevant in this moment of peace.

She dared not stir, fearing the fragile calm would shatter, but consciousness tugged at the edges of her mind. Morelle resisted, clinging to the serenity. If fortune favored her, she'd slip back into oblivion, stealing a few more precious hours of respite from her restless psyche.

Then, the void metamorphosed, darkness yielding to a gentle kaleidoscope of muted hues. Morelle drifted over softly blurred landscapes, her serenity unbroken by the change. This dreamscape, with its watercolor horizons, cradled her in its surreal embrace.

"Morelle, my daughter." Her mother's voice pierced the tranquil veil. "It is time to wake."

Her mother materialized, regal and ethereal, draped in flowing robes that seemed to ripple with starlight, her obsidian hair billowing around her serene face as if suspended in an invisible current.

"No, Mother," Morelle murmured, her words floating like bubbles. "I wish to stay. Here, I am at peace."

"It is not real," her mother said. "You cannot stay here forever."

Morelle reached out, her fingers brushing the gossamer fabric of her mother's sleeve. The touch sent ripples through the dreamscape, distorting the colors around them.

"Life isn't real either," Morelle whispered. "It's all an illusion, each cycle a step in the soul's never-ending journey, and I'd rather skip this one and start anew in a different body, on a different plane. Somewhere no one thinks of me as an abomination, a place where Ell-rom and I don't have to live in isolation and never show our faces to anyone."

Her mother's form shimmered, reaching out to cup Morelle's face in her hands, something she never did during waking hours.

The touch was warm and comforting despite its insubstantial nature, and Morelle decided she liked this version of her mother more than the real one.

"It is in facing our storms that we truly learn to dance in the rain. You are not an abomination, my daughter. You are beautiful and perfect, half goddess, half Kra-ell, and there are joys in life that can only be experienced through the flesh."

Morelle's lips curled into a skeptical smirk. "The pleasures of the flesh that the high priestess described didn't sound appealing to me at all."

A gentle laugh escaped her mother's lips, her eyes twinkling with amusement and a hint of mischief, again, something that was so shocking that Morelle was starting to doubt it was indeed her mother appearing in her dream.

Morelle had never heard her mother laugh, and the queen only smiled when she wanted to terrify those who dared to disagree with her.

Maybe it was a mischievous spirit pretending to be her mother?

"What the high priestess taught you was the way of the Kra-ell, and we enjoy our sex battles very much. But you are half goddess, with the godly part much stronger than the Kra-ell." The queen sighed. "Your father was a formidable male, smart and courageous, but he was a gentle lover, and I enjoyed him more than all of my others. That is what you should have, and it is worth having."

Now Morelle was convinced that it wasn't her mother talking in her dream. The queen had never talked about Morelle and Ell-rom's father except to tell them that they were of double royal blood and that it was crucial to keep it a secret.

Curiosity sparked in Morelle's chest, a feeling she hadn't experienced in what felt like eons. "Did you love him?" she asked.

"Yes, I did, but our love was not eternal." She sighed. "It was not meant to be. We met as co-conspirators, became lovers, and we parted as friends."

"Does he know about us?"

Sadness crept into her mother's eyes. "He was sent into exile before I could tell him that I had conceived, and he died not knowing about you and Ell-rom. But since all is known here in the Fields of the Brave, he knows now."

Morelle felt like the breath was knocked out of her chest. "You are not dead, Mother."

The queen smiled, but the sadness remained in her eyes. "I have passed beyond the veil before my time, but time has no meaning here. It has meaning where you are, though, and it is time for you to wake up and experience the new world I sent you and your brother to live in. Ell-rom needs you."

Morelle was still reeling from the revelation that her mother was no longer among the living, and now she was telling her that Ell-rom was in danger.

"Who is threatening Ell-rom?" She felt anger electrifying her blood, readying her to wake up and fight to protect her brother.

"Nothing has changed over the thousands of years you were in stasis, my daughter. Your grandfather, the Eternal King, still wants you and Ell-rom dead."

COMING UP NEXT

The Children of the Gods Book 89

DARK PRINCESS

SHADOWS

AFTER MILLENNIA IN STASIS, Morelle is lured out of her slumber by a seductive storyteller with a velvet voice. As she awakens to twenty-first-century Earth instead of the primitive planet she's been expecting, she struggles to adapt, but thankfully she does not have to do it alone. She has her twin brother to guide her, and a charming stranger who refuses to leave her side.

Don't forget to check out this fun, feel-good read
Adina and the Magic Lamp

To read the first three chapters, JOIN the VIP club at ITLUCAS.COM. To find out what's included in your free membership, flip to the last page.

In this post-apocalyptic virtual reimagining of Aladdin, James, the enigmatic prince, and Adina, the fearless thief, navigate the treacherous streets of Londabad, a city that echoes London and Ahmedabad and fuses magic and technology. In the face of danger, the chemistry between them ignites, and the lines between prince and thief, royalty and commoner blur.

Join the VIP Club
To find out what's included in your free membership, flip to the last page.

NOTE

Dear reader,

I hope my stories have added a little joy to your day. If you have a moment to add some to mine, you can help spread the word about the Children Of The Gods series by telling your friends and penning a review. Your recommendations are the most powerful way to inspire new readers to explore the series.

Thank you,

Isabell

Also by I. T. Lucas

THE CHILDREN OF THE GODS ORIGINS

1: Goddess's Choice

2: Goddess's Hope

THE CHILDREN OF THE GODS

Dark Stranger

1: Dark Stranger The Dream

2: Dark Stranger Revealed

3: Dark Stranger Immortal

Dark Enemy

4: Dark Enemy Taken

5: Dark Enemy Captive

6: Dark Enemy Redeemed

Kri & Michael's Story

6.5: My Dark Amazon

Dark Warrior

7: Dark Warrior Mine

8: Dark Warrior's Promise

9: Dark Warrior's Destiny

10: Dark Warrior's Legacy

Dark Guardian

11: Dark Guardian Found

12: Dark Guardian Craved

13: Dark Guardian's Mate

Dark Angel

Dark Operative

Dark Survivor

Dark Widow

Dark Dream

Dark Prince

Dark Queen

74: Dark Encounters of the Close Kind
75: Dark Encounters of the Unexpected Kind
76: Dark Encounters of the Fated Kind

Dark Voyage

77: Dark Voyage Matters of the Heart
78: Dark Voyage Matters of the Mind
79: Dark Voyage Matters of the Soul

Dark Horizon

80: Dark Horizon New Dawn
81: Dark Horizon Eclipse of the Heart
82: Dark Horizon The Witching Hour

Dark Witch

83: Dark Witch: Entangled Fates
84: Dark Witch: Twin Destinies
85: Dark Witch: Resurrection

Dark Awakening

86: Dark Awakening: New World
87: Dark Awakening Hidden Currents
88: Dark Awakening Echoes of Destiny

Dark Princess

89: Dark Princess: Shadows

PERFECT MATCH

Vampire's Consort
King's Chosen

Captain's Conquest
The Thief Who Loved Me
My Merman Prince
The Dragon King
My Werewolf Romeo
The Channeler's Companion
The Valkyrie & The Witch
Adina and the Magic Lamp

TRANSLATIONS

DIE ERBEN DER GÖTTER

Dark Stranger

1- Dark Stranger Der Traum
2- Dark Stranger Die Offenbarung
3- Dark Stranger Unsterblich

Dark Enemy

4- Dark Enemy Entführt
5- Dark Enemy Gefangen
6- Dark Enemy Erlöst

Dark Warrior

7- Dark Warrior Meine Sehnsucht
8- Dark Warrior – Dein Versprechen
9- Dark Warrior - Unser Schicksal
10-Dark Warrior-Unser Vermächtnis

LOS HIJOS DE LOS DIOSES

EL OSCURO DESCONOCIDO

1: EL OSCURO DESCONOCIDO EL SUEÑO

2: EL OSCURO DESCONOCIDO REVELADO

3: EL OSCURO DESCONOCIDO INMORTAL

EL OSCURO ENEMIGO

4- EL OSCURO ENEMIGO CAPTURADO

5 - EL OSCURO ENEMIGO CAUTIVO

6- EL OSCURO ENEMIGO REDIMIDO

LES ENFANTS DES DIEUX

DARK STRANGER

1- Dark Stranger Le rêve

2- Dark Stranger La révélation

3- Dark Stranger L'immortelle

The Children of the Gods Series Sets

Books 1-3: Dark Stranger trilogy—Includes a bonus short story: **The Fates Take a Vacation**

Books 4-6: Dark Enemy Trilogy —Includes a bonus short story—**The Fates' Post-Wedding Celebration**

Books 7-10: Dark Warrior Tetralogy

Books 11-13: Dark Guardian Trilogy

Books 14-16: Dark Angel Trilogy

Books 17-19: Dark Operative Trilogy

Books 20-22: Dark Survivor Trilogy

Books 23-25: Dark Widow Trilogy
Books 26-28: Dark Dream Trilogy
Books 29-31: Dark Prince Trilogy
Books 32-34: Dark Queen Trilogy
Books 35-37: Dark Spy Trilogy
Books 38-40: Dark Overlord Trilogy
Books 41-43: Dark Choices Trilogy
Books 44-46: Dark Secrets Trilogy
Books 47-49: Dark Haven Trilogy
Books 50-52: Dark Power Trilogy
Books 53-55: Dark Memories Trilogy
Books 56-58: Dark Hunter Trilogy
Books 59-61: Dark God Trilogy
Books 62-64: Dark Whispers Trilogy
Books 65-67: Dark Gambit Trilogy
Books 68-70: Dark Alliance Trilogy
Books 71-73: Dark Healing Trilogy
Books 74-76: Dark Encounters Trilogy
Books 77-79: Dark Voyage Trilogy
Books 80-81: Dark Horizon Trilogy

MEGA SETS

The Children of the Gods: Books 1-6

INCLUDES CHARACTER LISTS

The Children of the Gods: Books 6.5-10

Perfect Match Bundle 1

CHECK OUT THE SPECIALS ON

ITLUCAS.COM

(https://itlucas.com/specials)

FOR EXCLUSIVE PEEKS AT UPCOMING RELEASES &
A FREE I. T. LUCAS COMPANION BOOK

JOIN MY *VIP CLUB* AND GAIN ACCESS TO THE VIP PORTAL AT ITLUCAS.COM

TO JOIN, GO TO:

http://eepurl.com/blMTpD

Find out more details about what's included with your free membership on the book's last page.

TRY THE CHILDREN OF THE GODS SERIES ON AUDIBLE

2 FREE audiobooks with your new Audible subscription!

PERFECT MATCH SERIES

Vampire's Consort

When Gabriel's company is ready to start beta testing, he invites his old crush to inspect its medical safety protocol.

Curious about the revolutionary technology of the *Perfect Match Virtual Fantasy-Fulfillment studios,* Brenna agrees.

Neither expects to end up partnering for its first fully immersive test run.

King's Chosen

When Lisa's nutty friends get her a gift certificate to *Perfect Match Virtual Fantasy Studios,* she has no intentions of using it. But since the only way to get a refund is if no partner can be found for her, she makes sure to request a fantasy so girly and over the top that no sane guy will pick it up.

Except, someone does.

> **Warning:** This fantasy contains a hot, domineering crown prince, sweet insta-love, steamy love scenes painted with light shades of gray, a wedding, and a HEA in both the virtual and real worlds.
>
> Intended for mature audience.

Captain's Conquest

Working as a Starbucks barista, Alicia fends off flirting all day long, but none of the guys are as charming and sexy as Gregg. His frequent visits are the highlight of her day, but since he's never asked her out, she assumes he's taken. Besides, between a day job and a budding music career, she has no time to start a new relationship.

That is until Gregg makes her an offer she can't refuse—a gift certificate to the virtual fantasy fulfillment service everyone is talking about. As a huge Star Trek fan, Alicia has a perfect match in mind—the captain of the Starship Enterprise.

The Thief Who Loved Me

When Marian splurges on a Perfect Match Virtual adventure as a world infamous jewel thief, she expects high-wire fun with a hot partner who she will never have to see again in real life.

A virtual encounter seems like the perfect answer to Marcus's string of dating disasters. No strings attached, no drama, and definitely no love. As a die-hard James Bond fan, he chooses as his avatar a dashing MI6 operative, and to complement his adventure, a dangerously seductive partner.

Neither expects to find their forever Perfect Match.

My Merman Prince

The beautiful architect working late on the twelfth floor of my building thinks that I'm just the maintenance guy. She's also under the impression that I'm not interested.

Nothing could be further from the truth.

I want her like I've never wanted a woman before, but I don't play where I work.

I don't need the complications.

When she tells me about living out her mermaid fantasy with a stranger in a Perfect Match virtual adventure, I decide to do everything possible to ensure that the stranger is me.

The Dragon King

To save his beloved kingdom from a devastating war, the Crown Prince of Trieste makes a deal with a witch that costs him half of his humanity and dooms him to an eternity of loneliness.

Now king, he's a fearsome cobalt-winged dragon by day and a short-tempered monarch by night. Not many are brave enough to serve in the palace of the brooding and volatile ruler, but Charlotte ignores the rumors and accepts a scribe position in court.

As the young scribe reawakens Bruce's frozen heart, all that stands in the way of their happiness is the witch's bargain. Outsmarting the evil hag will take cunning and courage, and Charlotte is just the right woman for the job.

My Werewolf Romeo

The father of my star student is a big-shot screenwriter and the patron of the drama department who thinks he can dictate what production I should put on. The principal makes it very clear that I need to cooperate with the opinionated asshat or walk away from my dream job at the exclusive private high school.

It doesn't help matters that the guy is single, hot, charming, creative, and seems to like me despite my thinly-veiled hostility.

When he invites me to a custom-tailored Perfect Match virtual adventure to prove that his screenplay is perfect for my production, I accept, intending to have fun while proving that messing with the classics is a foolish idea.

I don't expect to be wowed by his werewolf adaptation of Red Riding Hood mesh-up with Romeo and Juliet, and I certainly don't expect to fall in love with the virtual fantasy's leading man.

The Channeler's Companion

A treat for fans of *The Wheel of Time*.

When Erika hires Rand to assist in her pediatric clinic, she does so despite his good looks and irresistible charm, not because of them.

He's empathic, adores children, and has the patience of a saint.

He's also all she can think about, but he's off-limits.

What's a doctor to do to scratch that irresistible itch without risking workplace complications?

A shared adventure in the Perfect Match Virtual Studios seems like the solution, but instead of letting the algorithm choose a partner for her, Erika can try to influence it to select the one she wants. Awarding Rand a gift certificate to the service will get him into their database, but unless Erika can tip the odds in her favor, getting paired with him is a long shot.

Hopefully, a virtual adventure based on her and Rand's favorite series will do the trick.

The Valkyrie & The Witch

After breaking up with my boyfriend, I vow never to date a physician again and avoid workplace romances like the plague. Seeking an escape from bad memories and hospital politics, I apply for a job at the Perfect Match Virtual Fantasy Studios, where I hope to explore fantastical scenarios and beta-test new experiences.

I have no intention of entering a new relationship anytime soon, but it is difficult to ignore Kayden, a fellow trainee who's good-looking and charming but regrettably has aspirations of becoming a physician.

Hoping never to get paired with him to beta test an experience, I choose the Valkyrie adventure. It seems like a safe bet to avoid a guy like him, who would never select an experience where the female is the kick-ass heroine and the man only gets a supporting role. However, the algorithm has other plans in store for us. It seems to think that we are a perfect match.

Adina and the Magic Lamp

In this post-apocalyptic virtual reimagining of Aladdin, James, the enigmatic prince, and Adina, the fearless thief, navigate the treacherous streets of Londabad, a city that echoes London and Ahmedabad and fuses magic and technology. In the face of danger, the chemistry between them ignites, and the lines between prince and thief, royalty and commoner blur.

FOR EXCLUSIVE PEEKS AT UPCOMING RELEASES & A FREE I. T. LUCAS COMPANION BOOK

Join my *VIP Club* and gain access to the VIP portal at itlucas.com

To Join, go to:

http://eepurl.com/blMTpD

INCLUDED IN YOUR FREE MEMBERSHIP:

YOUR VIP PORTAL

- Read preview chapters of upcoming releases.
- Listen to Goddess's Choice narration by Charles Lawrence
- Exclusive content offered only to my VIPs.

FREE I.T. LUCAS COMPANION INCLUDES:

- Goddess's Choice Part 1
- Perfect Match: Vampire's Consort (A standalone Novella)
- Interview Q & A
- Character Charts

If you're already a subscriber and you are not getting my emails, your provider is sending them to your junk folder, and you are missing out on important updates. To fix that, add isabell@itlucas.com to your email contacts or your email VIP list.